Other books in this collection:

When Love Goes Bad
Falling In Love... Again
Forbidden Love

LOSING IT FOR LOVE

THE CINDERELLA EFFECT: MAKEOVERS, MIRACLES AND ROMANCE

The timeless love stories from
True Romance and True Love live on.

Edited by Barbara Weller,
Cynthia Cleveland and Nancy Cushing-Jones

A BROADLIT BOOK

BroadLit

July 2012

Published by

BroadLit ®
14011 Ventura Blvd.
Suite 206 E
Sherman Oaks, CA 91423

ISBN 978-0-9855404-7-0

Produced in the United States of America.

This collection is dedicated to all of you who are looking for true love or have already found it.

Losing It for Love

The Cinderella Effect: Makeovers, Miracles and Romance

Table Of Contents

INTRODUCTION....11

TRAILER TRASH....13
She treated me like dirt and ruined my life.

She Begged The Doctor:
"CHOP MY NOSE OFF!"....35
It's ruining my life!

WORKING ON A NEW ME....61
It's a lot of hard work, but the payoff is incredible.

THE DOG DAYS OF SUMMER....85
I learned that size doesn't always matter.

Sweet Romance!
BACK-TO-SCHOOL MAKEOVER....93
"Falling in love made me beautiful!"

NOTHING TO LOSE....117
Everything seemed to be my fault and I tried to eat my troubles away.

HE WANTED A SUPER MODEL....137
And I don't know how to be a blonde bimbo.

I FEEL LIKE A TEENAGE FREAKSHOW....157
My only wish in life is to be able to look in the mirror without wanting to die, and if extreme plastic surgery is my only chance at happiness . . . I'm more than willing to risk my life.

True Love Knows No Pounds. . . .
I'M LARGE AND IN CHARGE....171
So where's my lover boy?

I HAVE BECOME ONE OF THE BEAUTIFUL PEOPLE....184
I went from being the ugly girl to being one that turns heads.

NOWHERE TO HIDE....209
Sometime you just have to face the facts.

She Had To Learn The Hard Way:
"BEING SKINNY DOESN'T MEAN A THING"....227
Especially when your hot, MTV-ready body attracts the wrong kind of guys.

WEIGHT WOES....247
Seeing past the pounds.

LOOKS CAN BE DECEIVING....257

INTRODUCTION

All of us long for true love. Unfortunately, however, some of us despair of ever finding it.

Often it's because we live with a gripping sense of defeat brought on by some unwanted a feature. Usually our nemesis is our weight, although sometimes it's a particular part of our body, like a nose or a chin that is undeniably out of proportion to the rest of our face.

There are more than enough thoughtless or shallow people in the world who may insist upon defining us by our single most troubling physical feature. We're fat, we're ugly, we're not sexy. And even though we silently rage against this horrifically narrow assessment, we may eventually become complacent, figuring that this is the way it will always be for us – *because we don't think we can change ourselves.*

And so, to our emotional rescue, come the women in this collection of stories who are our inspirational champions. They decided to take charge and radically change the way they looked. In so doing, they triumphed over the formidable opponents we all face every day: bad habits, occasional self-pity and the pernicious devil inside of us that tells us we can't do it so why even try. In shedding pounds – lots of them – they also shed destructive self-perceptions.

Most of these women did not go eagerly down this road, however. They balked and resisted and rationalized and procrastinated just like the rest of us. But eventually something clicked in their head that led them out of the zone of wanting to change and into the determined mindset of actually doing it.

Perhaps they overheard a particularly biting observation from someone they respected – or even from someone they loathed. Or perhaps they wanted to look good at an upcoming family wedding or to catch the eye of a particular man. All of them, however, were tired of perpetually feeling bad about themselves.

Although their motives for changing the course of their lives were different, our heroines all learned the same lesson in the end: It's easier to find your true love when you start by genuinely loving yourself.

The things we do for love . . .

TRAILER TRASH:

Treated me like dirt and ruined my life.

My life was so bad I hated to wake up in the morning. The sight of the sun blazing through my windows filled me with despair. Time to go back to school for another day of hell.

But what could I do? At sixteen I hardly had any choice in the matter. School was mandatory—and I still had another two horrible years to go.

As I showered, tears rolled down my face. It was so hard for me to bear another day of being ridiculed, of people whispering and calling me "trailer trash" and saying things behind my back. This would be yet another day of feeling as though I didn't belong. Another day of wishing I could fade into the woodwork.

I didn't know how much longer I could endure school in my small town. It was unbearable. The only saving grace was the handful of new friends I'd made—that, and the fact that this was the last day of school before summer vacation. Somehow, I'd get through it.

School hadn't always been that way for me. When I was little, I loved school. I looked forward to it every day, bounding out of bed in the morning, eager to get to school, where I could learn something new and show off my knowledge. I was always the teacher's pet.

Then, one day in third grade, a new girl moved into our district. I can remember clearly the day she showed up, because life as I knew it was over. Her name was Stephanie Anderson, and she had golden blonde hair, big blue eyes, and beautiful, stylish clothes. Everything she wore was obviously brand new and expensive. Her hair was perfect, she smelled like flowers, and she had an amazing assortment of school supplies that I'd never seen before. She moved and behaved with the confidence of a miniature adult.

At first she was quiet. I could see her watching the class, sizing us up. It didn't take her long to see that I was Mrs. Leigh's pet and knew the answers to every question. That's when the trouble began.

It seemed as if at that moment, Stephanie decided my reign was over and she was going to be the new class star. Unfortunately, it didn't take her long to achieve that goal. The other kids were as impressed and awed with her as I was. The girls flocked around her at recess and the boys whispered amongst themselves from afar as they checked her out.

Stephanie told story after story about the big city where she'd lived previously. It turned out that her father was the new town doctor. Her family had moved into the biggest, fanciest house in town. The kids were all fascinated and hung onto her every word. She presented herself as an expert on every subject and was soon regarded that way by everyone else. After all, most of us had never been farther than the next town—and here was Stephanie, the big city girl. Surely, she must know what she was talking about.

When I approached the group of girls that had gathered around her that first day, Stephanie immediately stopped talking. She gazed at me as if I were something she'd found on the bottom of her shoe, then turned to my best friend, Megan, and whispered something to her. The two girls giggled and I knew they were laughing at me. Absolutely humiliated, I turned and walked away from them. It was the first time I'd ever spent recess alone, but it was a beginning of a pattern that would continue for years.

In just one day, Stephanie had completely changed my life for the worse. As time passed and she learned more and more about me, she found reasons to make fun of me and put me down. Her barbs went from sly whispered remarks to outright insults. The worst was the day she told me to stay away from her, that I was nothing but trailer trash.

I'd never even heard the phrase "trailer trash" before. Unfortunately, the ugly name stuck. Every time I saw her, she'd chant, "Ash, Ash, Trailer Trash" just loud enough for me and the other kids to hear, but never loud enough for the teachers to notice. She launched an attack on me that totally annihilated my self-confidence. All I knew was that somehow I'd ended up on the outside looking in.

Even the teachers seemed to dote on Stephanie. It was absolutely sickening the way they singled her out for special privileges, even creating awards for her to receive for things she'd done. They never saw the barracuda side of her, only the Stephanie that kissed up to them and brought them presents and displayed perfect manners—just as long as they were watching.

If I'd been older and more experienced, I might have been able to retaliate. But up until that point, my world had been safe and secure; I had no idea how to deal with someone as hateful and vindictive as Stephanie Anderson.

No one had ever made a big deal of my living in a trailer before. In fact, I lived in the nicest trailer in a large and beautiful trailer park that was immaculately kept up. The trailers were all new and beautifully furnished, and there were strict rules in place to keep the park looking lovely. All of the families that lived there were nice, and like one big extended family. I'd always loved the trailer park.

Stephanie also made fun of my appearance, making me feel ugly and ashamed. I'd always dressed nicely but never gave that much thought to my appearance. If I was clean and my clothes matched, that was good enough for me. My main interest had always been my schoolwork and my many friends.

The most upsetting thing was how everyone seemed to turn on me immediately, just because of Stephanie's disapproval. No one wanted to go against her, lest they should find themselves the next object of her scorn.

As the year progressed, my grades dropped slightly, as did my class participation. I was sick often and missed a lot of school. My parents and teachers were concerned about the change in me, but I never told any of them what was behind my misery. I just figured that Stephanie was so powerful, there was nothing they could do to change things, either.

All through elementary school she and I always seemed to end up in the same class. When we entered middle school and started changing classes, I was relieved that we were only in one together; but the damage was already done. The reputation she'd branded me with as "trailer trash" dogged me. Because of it, no one seemed to want anything to do with me, especially in the increasingly social world of middle school.

By high school, I'd completely given up on anything ever changing. I retreated into my shell. Over the years I'd put on a bit of weight, gotten glasses, and I'd completely quit paying attention to my personal appearance, except to make sure I was clean and my hair was brushed. I dressed in baggy clothes that completely hid my maturing figure, trying to fade into the woodwork. Life seemed easier that way.

Now it was the last day of tenth grade, and in spite of my earlier despair I found myself actually looking forward to it. Since we were in high school, I was more removed from Stephanie's sphere of power and had managed to make a few new friends. The last day of school always ended with an ice cream social where everyone passed their yearbooks around to have them signed, all of us rejoicing at the thought of a summer free from schoolwork and worries.

As I came into the common area of the courtyard that afternoon, I could see Stephanie holding court. The other popular girls buzzed around her like a swarm of bees. I held my head high as I passed her, headed for my new friends who were just a few yards away.

Stephanie locked her gaze on me. In her phony Southern accent she said loudly, "Well, well, girls, there goes the Trailer Trash Queen! You'd think she'd lose some weight and do something with that hair, wouldn't you? And those clothes, my God!"

The girls looked at me and burst into giggles. Even my new friends looked at me as if seeing me for the first time through Stephanie's eyes.

That was it. I'd had enough of that nonsense. I grabbed my yearbook and ran as fast as I could to get away from the sound of their laughter. As far as I was concerned, I was never going to school again. Perhaps Mom would home-school me the next year. All I knew was that my pride had been hurt one too many times, to the point that my self-esteem was nonexistent. All thanks to Stephanie.

As if she hadn't already done enough damage, she'd even managed to win Michael over to her side. In the third grade,

Michael and I were inseparable. Our moms had been friends for years, so we'd grown up together. He and I had done absolutely everything together. We shared a million interests at an age when boys and girls were not usually close.

However, when Stephanie started her onslaught of terror, I'd begun isolating myself. Even Michael's repeated attempts to remain my friend went ignored. I guess I'd finally snubbed him one too many times, because he finally quit coming around.

By high school, he was Stephanie's constant companion. I couldn't believe he was dating her, of all people. Of course, the small, scrawny, dark-haired boy had morphed into the most handsome boy and best athlete at our school. And Stephanie, who got everything she wanted, got him, too.

This final humiliation on the last day of school was just too much. I didn't even wait for the school bus to arrive. I simply took off walking toward home. Anything, just to get away from the taunts and laughter.

As I walked, I thought and thought. I was so angry that I was ready to explode. I wanted to kill Stephanie with my bare hands. It was the first time I'd ever gotten angry at her. Before that I'd just felt so intimidated and humiliated that I'd just slink away from everyone as quickly as possible.

As I thought back to all the events that had transpired between us, I began to see a pattern. Stephanie attacked; I ran. Why on earth hadn't it ever occurred to me to fight back? Why had I simply let her dish it out while I took it? Suddenly, it seemed like the craziest thing on earth. I had simply played the victim, never even considering the possibility that I had the power to fight Stephanie—and win.

Well, I thought, holding my head up high and walking more determinedly than I had in years, that bitch has another thought coming! Ashley Warner had taken her crap long enough, and she wasn't going to take anymore. It was time I took my life back . . . even if it was years later than I should have.

When I arrived home from school, a sense of relief swept over me. Three glorious months of freedom from taunts and teasing! Three months of freedom from teachers and books and homework. Three months to totally make myself over. That was exactly what I was going to do. Now I had a plan.

I sat down at the desk in my room, switched on the computer that my mom and dad had bought me when I started high school, and immediately began making a list. I wanted to change every aspect of my appearance and personality. Three months, I decided, should be just about enough time to accomplish that.

At the top of my list was losing weight. Although I wasn't horribly overweight, I had gained about twenty pounds that definitely needed to come off. I also planned to replace my glasses with contacts and get a totally new hairstyle.

Then there was my wardrobe to consider. That was in dire need of a makeover. Besides, once I'd lost the weight, new clothes would be in order. The more I worked on my list, the more excited I became. I was ready to fight fire with fire—and Stephanie was going to see that I couldn't be pushed around any longer.

I was up early the next morning and headed to town. I immediately went into the drug store and headed straight for the magazine rack. I bought every magazine that offered fashion and beauty tips.

"Planning on doing some reading, Ashley?" Mr. McGuire, the elderly store owner asked with a smile as he rang up one magazine after another.

"Actually, I'm doing some research for . . . a school project." I laughed, amused at my own spin on my new plan.

He shook his head and muttered something about how the schools pressured students nowadays by assigning them homework even on their summer vacation. I just laughed to myself and let him think whatever he wanted. This was one school project that was certainly worthwhile.

I pored over the magazines until a pattern started to emerge of the style that I liked. I read over makeup and skin care tips, as well as exercise and diet advice. I realized this project was going to require more than I'd realized. The time and determination were no problem—I had plenty of that. But clothes, makeup, and hair products were expensive, not to mention the cost of contacts.

I was sure that my parents would spring for a new school wardrobe. They always handed me a credit card, told me how much I could spend, and trusted me to do my shopping, though I doubted they'd be willing to finance my entire makeover. That meant I needed to get a summer job—and fast.

The next morning I headed back into town again to look for a job. My original plan was to ask around at all the stores and see if anyone needed summer help. But as soon as I rounded the first corner, I saw a *help wanted* sign in the beauty shop window. That was the job for me! I crossed my fingers that I was qualified for the vacant position and headed straight through the shop's door.

They were looking for a receptionist to answer the phone and schedule appointments. That would be perfect. I'd just spent the previous school year working one period per day in the school office where I answered phones, scheduled appointments, filed, and did a number of other tasks.

Miss Sylvia, the shop's owner, interviewed me and hired me

on the spot. Not only would I be making a decent hourly wage, but all of the services of the salon were offered to employees at a fifty percent discount! I felt that God was smiling on me that day. I ran home excitedly to tell Mom about my good fortune.

Mom was a bit surprised at my sudden enthusiasm and desire for a job, but I think she was just so happy to see me in good spirits that she didn't ask too many questions. She and Dad were both very happy for me. They told me to let them know if there was anything I needed.

I would work five mornings a week starting the very next day. In the mornings I'd work at the salon, then work on the rest of my project in the afternoons.

My first morning of work I got up early, dressed in my most attractive outfit, applied a small amount of makeup, and headed out the door well before I was due at work. It didn't take me long to pick up on the ins and outs of the salon, and pretty soon I had that very busy front desk under control.

While I worked I listened to the other employees and the customers talk about a variety of subjects. At the shop I got an education not only about beauty, but also about life. I heard stories of women and their cheating husbands, their wayward children, their financial difficulties, and the latest gossip about everyone in town.

I quickly settled into a routine. I was up early and out of the house to work each morning. Afternoons, I came home and worked out on the exercise equipment my parents kept in the spare bedroom. They both worked out daily and took good care of themselves. Now I was ready to follow their example.

I also worked hard at eating less. At first it was difficult to give up my favorite foods in the quantity I preferred. But after the first couple of pounds I was so encouraged that I managed to stick to my new way of eating without too much trouble. I was driven solely by the desire to show Stephanie Anderson that, contrary to what she thought, I was not to be messed with.

Time passed quickly. I was preoccupied with my job and with creating the new me. By the end of July I'd lost all the weight I needed to lose. I decided then that I'd approach Debbie, my favorite stylist at the salon, and ask her what she thought would be the most flattering style and color for my hair.

She was delighted to advise me. I showed her some photos of hairstyles I liked. Finally, we settled on platinum blonde highlights for my dishwater blonde hair—lots of them—and a Jennifer Anniston-style cut. I was so excited. Debbie told me to come back in on Saturday at about closing time, when she could do my hair without interruption. I could hardly wait.

On Saturday morning she did my highlights first—and the change was amazing. The color seemed to light up my face, bringing out my best features, especially my eyes. When Debbie was done, I hardly recognized myself. I'd been to the optometrist the previous day and picked up my new contact lenses, so I didn't have the clunky, old glasses to contend with. Between that and the new hairstyle, I could see the new me emerging.

Then Debbie and I started talking cosmetics. When I told her that I'd never really experimented with makeup she said, "Girl, you've got to be kidding me. Makeup is my life! Every woman can use a little help to emphasize what God gave her. You just sit back and let Aunt Debbie help you out!"

"You're the boss!" I said, laughing.

She was great, putting me totally at ease. Debbie taught me how to choose colors and apply makeup to my best advantage.

When we were done, she had me stand back and take in the full effect in the mirror. I was breathless; I never knew I could look like that. As Debbie said, I'd been hiding my light under a bushel.

While the cost for the cosmetics and hair and skin products was considerable, my employee discount helped. Besides, it was all worth it, since it was what I'd been working for all summer. I felt like a completely different person.

When I went home that afternoon, Mom looked at me, speechless. She had tears in her eyes as she said, "Honey, you look absolutely beautiful. What on earth have you done?"

For the first time in a long time, Mom and I sat down and had a heart-to-heart talk. All the years of frustration and unhappiness came pouring out as I told her how Stephanie had treated me, turning everyone against me—and worst of all, how I'd taken it laying down.

Mom was aghast. "Baby," she said hugging me close, "I had no idea what you were going through. Why on earth didn't you say anything? I've always wondered what brought about such a change in you. You used to love school. I thought you were just going through some kind of growing pains."

"I don't know, Mom. I guess I was just so ashamed, and Stephanie made me feel so ugly that I didn't even know how to tell the people I was close to about it."

"Well, Ash, I swear I could strangle that girl with my bare hands. But I'll leave the whole thing to you, because you seem to be on top of the situation. I want you to promise me, though, that you'll let me know if you need anything at all. It's just so good to see you happy again." She hugged me again.

"I've got it covered, Mom," I laughed, hugging her back and feeling freer and more lighthearted than I had in a very long time.

It had actually felt good to let my mother in on the pain I'd been experiencing for all of those years. I shuddered when I thought of how poorly I'd handled the situation—not fighting back, not confiding in Mom, and not doing anything to stop the pain that Stephanie was dishing out.

Now I was a new person, both inside and out. Just a few more finishing touches and I'd be ready for school to start again at the end of August. That gave me approximately one month to go.

The Saturday following my makeover I went into the shop and saw Penny, the nail technician. She applied acrylic nails for me and painted them beautifully. The nails made me feel elegant and sophisticated. Day by day, between the job and my new look, my confidence was growing.

I also started tanning every other day after work. I'd finish up my morning shift and then lock myself into the tiny tanning room for a dose of artificial rays. Within just a couple of weeks I had a nice golden tan. I even bought some dental bleach, applying it to my teeth nightly. Now I had a great smile and smiled a lot more.

Even the shop's customers noticed the new me. Several of the ladies complimented me on my new look. I have to admit, my confidence soared.

During August, I went shopping for my new wardrobe. Now that I'd let Mom in on my little project, she was eager to help me. We went into the city and made a day of shopping. She helped me choose outfits that were stylish and flattering, and she even added considerably to my school clothes budget. We had so many bags and boxes that it took us several trips from the car to bring them all in.

Then we went into my room, cleared out all my old clothes that were too big and unflattering, and replaced them with the new ones. When we were done, I breathed a sigh of relief. Only one more week to go before school started. I felt ready to handle Stephanie. Actually, I could hardly wait to see her face when she saw the new me.

Luckily, I hadn't run into her over the summer. Her family was touring Europe for the entire season. I wanted the element of complete surprise.

When the first day of school came I was excited but nervous. As I waited for the school bus at the corner, I wondered what kind of reaction I'd receive.

It didn't take long to find out. I was the last stop on the route, so the bus was full of kids I'd known my entire life. When I got on, all talking stopped. The bus was so silent, you could hear a pin drop.

Then Jeff, a boy I'd grown up with, whistled at me from the back of the bus. I blushed, but I was also very pleased. Obviously, my makeover had gone well.

"Hey, Ash!" he called out. "How about a date Saturday night?"

I just laughed and shook my head in amazement. Then I sat down in a seat where Megan, my old best friend—whom I'd hardly spoken to in years—was sitting.

We started talking and she said, "God, Ash. You look great! What have you done to yourself?"

"Well," I said modestly, "we're getting older now, and I just decided it was time for a new me. What do you think?"

"I think Stephanie is going to be green with envy, is what I think!" She laughed. "She's always been jealous of you, but this will just send her over the edge. You look great."

"Jealous?" I was incredulous. "Stephanie is jealous of me?"

"Of course she is. I can remember when she first came here in the third grade. You were the star of the class and she couldn't stand it. Why else would she have treated you that way? We all knew it—except for you. None of your friends were ever against you, you know. You just pulled away from us."

My head was reeling with this new revelation. How could I have been so stupid? I asked myself. Of course—Stephanie was jealous. Now that I looked back, with the benefit of years of distance from the original events, I could see it. Even though she'd had every advantage, Stephanie was very insecure; the only way she'd felt she could establish her place in school was to knock me down from mine . . . and I'd allowed her to do that.

"Megan, I'm really sorry I've acted so silly all these years," I told her sincerely. "The way Stephanie treated me was really hard to deal with. I guess I handled it very poorly. But I'm feeling like myself again, and I promise to make it up to all my old friends . . . if they'll just give me a chance."

"We sure will," she assured me, patting my hand. "Everyone has always hated how Stephanie treated you, but we were afraid to say anything. You just seemed to take it lying down, and we didn't want to risk speaking up and becoming her next victim. So . . . maybe we should be apologizing to you."

"Never mind that, Megan. What's past is past. I'm just looking forward to enjoying the last few years of high school."

The rest of the day went much like the bus ride to school. Old friends came up and complimented me on my new look. Everyone was amazed at how much I'd changed. Over and over again, Stephanie's name came up. I soon learned that everyone felt as Megan did.

It was amazing. For all those years I could have had the support of my friends, if I'd only chosen to stand up for myself—but I hadn't. None of them even liked Stephanie, but all were as intimidated by her as I was. Her opinion could make or break us. Well, now that I knew the truth, I vowed that her days of tyrannical power were over.

The only disappointing aspect of my first day of school was that Stephanie wasn't there. Her family had extended their European trip by a week, so she wouldn't be back until the following Monday. Her absence, however, gave me a great opportunity to renew ties with old friends. By the end of that first week, I couldn't believe how much my life had changed. I felt as if I belonged once again.

Even the teachers noticed the change in me and commented on how great I looked and how different I seemed. I decided that this was going to be my year to shine, not only socially, but academically. I set about to do my best in each class.

One afternoon after school, Mom and I were chatting at the kitchen table. I told her about how all the kids had welcomed me back into their group. I told her how everyone had been scared of Stephanie, and how they were saddened when I'd stopped having anything to do with them.

"Well, honey, I hate that you had so many miserable years," Mom said, "but you're on the right track now. I want you to enjoy the rest of your time in school. It won't be that much longer before you graduate and go out into the real world."

"Don't worry, Mom. I definitely plan to enjoy myself. Stephanie gets back on Monday, and seeing her face is going to be something else. And, Mom, thanks for all your help," I added with tears in my eyes.

"Anytime, honey, anytime. That's what I'm here for. It would have been good if you'd have realized it sooner."

"Well, you always said I had a head like a rock. I guess that's true, but now that I know how different things could have been, I think I've learned a lesson about letting people be there for me instead of pulling away. And now I have homework to do. I'm not going to get to be class valedictorian by just sitting around and socializing!"

Mom just laughed. "Now that's my old Ashley. Welcome back, hon."

I kept my job at the salon, though I had my hours changed to work after school and on Saturday mornings. Between work and homework, I stayed incredibly busy. I was so caught up in my renewed friendships and my happy new life that I hardly had time to think about Stephanie's return on Monday.

I'd noticed that Michael was also absent that first week of school. I'd heard through the grapevine that he'd be returning the same day as Stephanie. He'd been off working with Habitat for Humanity during the summer, and the school had given him special permission to finish the final house he was building before returning to school.

He'd have to make up the first week's work, but for Michael that wouldn't be a problem. We'd always had a friendly competition for first place in our class, and I think that was part of what drew us to each other as kids. I wondered how he would react to the new me. After all, he was Stephanie's boyfriend. Who would he be loyal to?

It didn't take me long to find out the answer to that question. The second week of school I was there early for a meeting of the French Club that was being held before classes began. When I emerged from the meeting, I saw Stephanie and Michael walking hand in hand down the hall.

There was a look of sheer horror on her face when she realized that the person in front of her was me. She just stood there, staring as if she'd been struck dumb, a look of pure hatred on her face.

Michael, on the other hand, reacted excitedly.

"Ash, you look terrific!" he exclaimed. "I guess you must have had a good summer!"

Then he held out his arms and pulled me into a great, big bear hug, just like he used to when we were kids. I reveled in the feel of his arms around me. When we stood back and looked at one another, I could only smile at him shyly.

"Yeah, I guess I did," I said. "I've been working at Miss Sylvia's. I guess some of their magic rubbed off on me!"

"Well, I think it's great. It's just like having the old Ashley back. I've missed you." When I looked into his warm brown eyes, it was just as if we were in third grade again—best friends with nothing standing between us.

The magic moment, however, was broken by the nasal whining of Stephanie's voice. "Michael," she said, trying to maintain her sweet image in his eyes but failing miserably, "we really need to get to class. And anyway, have you forgotten who she is? No matter what she looks like on the outside, she'll always be trailer trash."

"Stephanie, if I were you, I'd drop the 'trailer trash' thing right now," he scolded her firmly. "It's gone on long enough, and Ashley's had the good grace not to smack you good. You might live in the best house in town and have expensive clothes and a great car, but deep down, I think maybe you're the one who's trailer trash."

I'd never seen such a look of shock on anyone's face as I did on Stephanie's. I also saw pure hatred, and evil in it, too. Finally, she was revealing to everyone else what I'd known for years.

"If that's how you feel, Michael, then you're welcome to her!" she screeched at the top of her lungs. "I wouldn't spit on either of you if you were on fire."

Michael just laughed. "Grow up, Stephanie."

Then took my hand, pulling me down the hall and into a quiet alcove under the stairs. "Ashley, I want to apologize to you," he said then. "I should have stuck up for you years ago. I wanted to—but every time I tried to talk to you, you just shut me out."

I could see the hurt in his eyes. "Michael, please don't apologize. It was all my fault. I was just so embarrassed and ashamed when Stephanie made fun of me that I shut everyone out . . . even you, my best friend." I looked into his eyes. "I'm very, very sorry for doing that to you."

"Well, it did hurt to lose you as a friend, but don't worry about it now. I'm hoping we can pick up where we left off."

Suddenly, I felt shy again. "I'd like that, Michael. I really would."

Then we had to go to class. I had to keep reminding myself of my resolution to become class valedictorian. My mind was on Michael, and Michael alone.

The rest of the day, whenever I saw Stephanie, her eyes seemed to throw daggers at me. By lunchtime I noticed that none of her old friends were grouped around her in that adoring manner at lunchtime; instead, she was eating her lunch alone in a corner. It was the exact same corner where I'd eaten the previous year, when I'd been trying to hide from her abuse!

When I got home that day I told Mom all that had happened, especially the part about Michael. She was so happy, she couldn't stop grinning.

"Oh, honey," she said, "that was always the worst thing about the change in you—losing Michael. I'd never seen two kids as close as you two were. It broke my heart to turn that little boy away, day after day, when he came to see if you could play. I'm so happy for you both."

Just then, there was a knock at the door. I stayed at the table while Mom went to answer it. Then I heard a deep, masculine voice say, "Mrs. Warner, can Ashley come out to play?"

My heart skipped a beat. It was Michael!

"Of course she can, Michael!" Mom laughed, "Come on in."

There he was, standing in the doorway, looking better than ever and holding his hand out to me. "Wanna go for a walk, Ash?" he asked as he'd done so many times before, all those years ago.

"I'd love to," I said, taking his hand.

We spent that afternoon strolling down country lanes that we'd played in as children, exchanging stories about our summers.

I was so impressed with Michael and how he'd given his whole summer to go away and build houses for those who didn't have one. I was proud of him, too. He was the same old Michael, kind and willing to help others less fortunate. How could I have forgotten that?

He listened silently and soberly while I told him about my summer, pouring out to him all the years of hurt and anguish I'd suffered at Stephanie's hands, but also accepting my part in it by never standing up to her. He pulled me close and hugged me as if he wanted to protect me from all that had happened.

Then, before I knew it, he leaned down and kissed me tenderly on the lips.

"Ashley, I'm so sorry about all the years we've lost," he said in a husky whisper, "but I'm hoping, now that we've found our way back to each other, that we'll make up for lost time. What do you think?"

"Oh, Michael. That sounds so perfect to me. So, so perfect."

Michael and I were inseparable from that moment on. What had been a wonderfully close childhood friendship blossomed into true love for us.

One afternoon while I was at work at Miss Sylvia's, I overheard two of the ladies talking about Stephanie's parents.

"Well, he always ran around on her," Mrs. Wilkinson said, "so I'm not surprised to hear they're divorcing. And that poor little girl, Stephanie. Even though she had every material thing in the world, she always seemed like such a pathetic little creature, just doing anything for approval. She was always left in the care of nannies and such."

Debbie nodded in agreement. "Yes, it is sad. It just goes to show you that even the best families have their problems. I guess money doesn't solve everything."

I just sat there, amazed. So other people had seen through Stephanie, too! I felt badly for her, to think that she'd always been hiding her private pain behind a mask of confidence and self-assurance. I'd never known the true story of her life.

I never got the opportunity to speak to her, though, and tell her that I'd forgiven her for all the years of torment. I'd hoped we could put the past behind us and move on. I was even willing to reach out to her and try to be a friend in her time of need, but she wasn't in school that week. The following week, I heard that she and her mother had moved back to an apartment in the city.

Though I never saw Stephanie again, I certainly saw a lot of Michael. We dated our last two years of high school. When we graduated, we were co-valedictorians!

Now he's in college and I just got my cosmetology license. Miss Sylvia is retiring and selling her shop to me! I found my true calling in that salon: to help women feel good about themselves by improving their appearance. I know that beauty is only skin-deep, but looking good on the outside sure makes you feel a lot better on the inside. I'm living proof of that.

Michael and I are married now. We can afford to laugh about all those lost years. We actually have a mobile home in the same trailer park, very near my parents' place. When he comes home from school, he always yells at the top of his voice, "Hey! Where's my little trailer trash?"

Men! THE END

She Begged The Doctor:

"CHOP MY NOSE OFF!"

It's ruining my life!

I yanked on a pair of wrinkled slacks, a shapeless blouse that my mother had discarded, and an old jacket that I'd picked up at a garage sale. I barely glanced at myself in the mirror as I pulled a comb through my tangled hair. From past experience, I knew that if anyone looked at me, they would quickly glance away.

"I wish you wouldn't wear those old clothes! They look dirty!" Mom yelled when she saw me. "I've spent hours making nice clothes for you, Hannah, so there's just no excuse for you to go to school looking like a refugee from some third-world country!"

"I'm dressed fine," I said as I moved toward the door. "Mom, no one cares what I look like—least of all, me. And my clothes are clean, by the way."

"Well, I care what you look like. I know we don't have a lot of money, but I work hard trying to see that you get the things you need." My mother's voice sounded hurt rather than scolding.

"I know you do, Mom," I said. "You work harder than anyone I know. I'm sorry I'm such a disappointment to you."

"You're not, Hannah; I'm proud of your grades and you're a great help to me, but I'd like to see you take a little more interest in your appearance. I think that it's important, and I just wish that you tried to look a little nicer. If it's the homemade clothes you don't like, then we can probably afford a few things from the store."

"It isn't that, Mom. I'll try to look nicer, but I don't have time to change right now." I kissed her soft cheek and dashed out the door.

The high school, which I'd been attending for the last four years, was only five blocks away from my house. I thought I'd waited long enough that everyone would already be in the building, but I could see Lillian waiting for me on the steps.

"Hi, Hannah!" she said with a big smile. Lillian's smile beamed sunshine on anyone who looked at her. She was a beautiful girl, and for some reason, she was determined to be my best friend. I did nothing to encourage her. She just stuck to me like it was her duty.

"Hi, Lillian. Why aren't you already in class?" I asked.

"I was waiting for you, of course." She sighed as her eyes roamed over me. "I see you've dressed in your Sunday best again."

"Oh, well. You know it doesn't make any difference what I wear. Everyone looks at me just the same—or doesn't look at me just the same."

Lillian hooked her arm in mine and tugged me up the steps before she answered.

"You know how I feel about the way kids treat you. I think it's awful, but you shouldn't pay so much attention to them. If you didn't cover yourself up with such outlandish clothing and they got a better look at that figure of yours, they'd be nicer to you."

"Please—you know it wouldn't make a bit of difference to them. They only see what they want to see. They need someone to put down so they can feel superior. That person is me. Thank goodness it's my last year in this school."

"I think you're going to be the valedictorian. How can anyone feel superior to you? You've always been the smartest student in our class."

"Some people say it's because no boys will date me. All I do is study, according to them. Actually, I don't study all that much. I'm just lucky in that things seem to stick with me." My voice sounded dead and I shrugged. I didn't even care that I might be the valedictorian. In fact, it scared me, because the valedictorian had to make a short speech at graduation and preside over several other events.

On the way up the steps, Greg Makowski dashed by and bumped into me. He turned his head and grinned in a way that heated my body all the way to my toes. Oh, if I was beautiful and could attract a hot guy like Greg, I'd be in heaven.

"Excuse me. I'm late," Greg said.

I smiled. "It's okay."

We arrived at our first class before Lillian could answer my quip about being the valedictorian. I had a seat at the back of the room and I slipped in without being noticed. Lillian moved slowly up the aisle to the front of the room. She greeted everyone with that sunny smile of hers.

The kids were so friendly, that I felt jealous. I didn't want to have such feelings toward Lillian. She'd been my one true friend ever since she'd moved to Hopeville two years ago. She treated me just like she did the other kids, except that she went out of her way to be nice to me.

I didn't see Lillian for several hours after that. We both had different schedules. Lillian was in the chorus, and was also the star of her drama class. She also had the lead in the play, but after school, there she was—waiting for me on the steps outside.

"Hey, Hannah, why don't we go shopping and try on clothes for the Christmas dance?"

"Lillian, you know I can't go to the dance. I could never get a date."

"Come on, it'll be fun to try on some dresses, anyway. We could even look at some other things. It's Friday; I don't want to go straight home."

"Why not?"

"Because I'm tired of the routine. I want to do something a little different."

"Let me call my mom," I said. "I don't want her to worry if I don't come right home."

I called Mom, and she was pleased that I was hanging out with a friend. I knew that she would be. She often worried about my lack of a social life.

The first place we went to was a well-known department store. At first, we just browsed, but then Lillian saw a dress she simply had to try on.

My friend came out of the fitting room, and she totally looked like a princess. But that wasn't such an accomplishment for her. Lillian looked perfect in everything she wore.

A saleswoman came to me and asked if I'd like to try something on. I shook my head quickly, and she went away. A few minutes later, though, the woman returned with one of the most beautiful dresses I'd ever seen. It was a deep rose color, and she held it up against me. It set off the natural copper highlights in my red hair.

"Dear!" she said. "You simply must try this dress on! You have a great figure for it. You're very shapely and slender. You think those loose clothes you've got on hide your exquisite figure—but they don't."

I blushed with embarrassment, but I agreed to try the dress on.

It was perfect for me. It was cut a little low in the front and showed off just the right amount of cleavage. It clung to my tall figure until the middle of my thighs, and then it flared out. There was a row of very small appliqué rosebuds sewn around the neckline.

"Oh, Hannah," Lillian gushed. "You look absolutely wonderful in that! Why don't you put it on lay away for the Christmas dance?"

"Get this off of me this instant!" I told the clerk. I couldn't control the tears spilling out of my eyes. "I'm going home. I'm not going to buy a dress I'll never wear. I can't afford it, and my parents can't afford it. It would just make this ugly face look even uglier. Such a beautiful dress would only make me look pathetic."

I took the dress off and got into my old clothes as quickly as I could. The confused saleswoman picked up the dress and put it back on its hanger. "I'm sorry," I said. "It's a beautiful dress, but with this ugly face, no dress is going to do anything for me."

I rarely let the bitterness I felt show in my everyday life, but somehow, the dress caused me to be even more aware of my grotesque nose—a nose that looked like it had been created out of clay and clapped right onto the middle of my face. It even hooked down at the end, giving me the exact kind of nose that's drawn on Halloween witches.

I started for the escalator, but Lillian called to me and asked me to wait. I didn't want to wait, but I knew Lillian didn't deserve to be treated that way. I stopped at the top of the escalator.

"You know, you're exaggerating about how you look, Hannah," she said hotly. I was surprised, because it was rare for Lillian to use such a sharp tone of voice. "You need to think of someone besides yourself! You're so wrapped up in how you look that you won't let anyone get near you. If you were a little friendlier, then maybe people wouldn't notice how you look so much."

"That's easy for you to say; you've always looked like a prom queen."

"I know I've been lucky, but sometimes, being pretty isn't always wonderful. People expect you to be shallow, conceited, and dumb when you're pretty."

It hadn't occurred to me that Lillian could feel any other way about herself except wonderful. I thought of what she'd said about my being selfish. I hadn't ever thought about it that way, but I'd hated my appearance for so long that I couldn't remember thinking any differently.

We left without another word until we got outside.

"Would you like to get a soda, or something to eat, maybe?" Lillian asked. Her voice sounded kind, with just a trace of an apology. We went to the food court and sat down with our sodas.

"Hannah, I'm really sorry. I just didn't think it would bother you so much. I like you just the way you are, and I think a lot of your problems are only in your head."

"You just don't know what it's like to have this face. No one does. I know I have a decent figure, but no one ever looks at it . . . just my face. Do you know that when I was little, the other kids used to tease me and say I was a liar, and that's what caused my nose to grow?"

Lillian studied me intently for a few minutes. I sat drinking my soda and tried not to notice. Then, a sunny look passed over her face.

"You know, Hannah, you really have a pretty face—"

I snorted before she could get any further. "Lillian, I always thought you were an honest girl. You know very well what everyone calls me: 'Clown Nose,' 'Wicked Witch,'—and a million other things."

"But that's just it! You have a lovely complexion, your eyes are outstanding, and your mouth is beautiful. It's only your nose."

"Only my nose! Isn't that enough? No one in my family has this awful thing! None of the pictures of my relatives—past or present—show anyone with a grotesque bulb on the end of their nose!"

Lillian seemed to ignore my comments. "I'll bet if I apply makeup carefully, the nose won't show so much and people will get a chance to see you. I know they'd like you if you gave them a chance."

I guess I wanted to believe in miracles, because Sunday, Lillian stayed over my house so that she could help me get dressed and put on my makeup. She really was clever with cosmetics. She'd learned some great techniques from all of her theatre classes.

She applied foundation, and then added some translucent powder with a big, fluffy brush. Next, she shaded my eyebrows with a medium-brown color and applied mascara. Then, Lillian pulled out a little jar of stuff she'd brought with her. She carefully spread this over my nose, and that offensive protrusion just seemed to fade into the background!

Lillian insisted that I wear a pair of jeans and a fitted blouse, and she absolutely refused to let me wear the old jacket I'd come to consider as a necessary part of my wardrobe. Instead, she pulled out a new denim jacket that my mother had made. I did look better, but would it be enough?

Mom was happier with the way I looked as I waved good-bye to her the next morning.

"You look really nice, Hannah. More the way you should," she said. Mom turned to Lillian. "Thanks, Lillian. I'm glad you talked some sense into my daughter."

Lillian just smiled and said good-bye to my mother.

We arrived at school a few minutes early. Kids were hanging around the steps, talking to each other. A group of boys nearby called to us as we passed them.

"Who's the babe with Lillian?" one boy asked in a very loud voice.

My face turned red, but I kept on walking.

"Hey, hottie!" he yelled again in that same loud, obnoxious voice. "Are you gonna be a snob? We just want to talk to you!"

The comment made me turn to see who was being so rude. I looked straight at the entire group. They were speechless. They looked at me like I was some kind of being from outer space.

"Wow!" Loudmouth said, kind of under his breath. "Snobby is the word. It's Hannah! Whatcha done with yourself, Hannah? Where'd you get that figure?"

"Oh, she's been hiding that all along," said another boy. "I've seen her at the lake wearing a bathing suit. If it wasn't for that face, I'd ask her for a date, but who wants to look at that over a hamburger?"

"Why don't you creeps go do something constructive?" Lillian growled.

I'd never heard her talk to anyone that way . . . ever.

"Like maybe dunking your heads in a bucket of water and leaving them there for a while, huh?"

Lillian tugged at my arm and urged me away from them. I felt about five inches tall. I had been fairly sure that was what would happen, but I'd hoped against it. I did look a lot better. I liked the way I was dressed, and somehow, that helped me to not be quite so bothered by those rude boys.

I went to my classes and people were a little friendlier. At lunch, I was standing in line when this good-looking guy came up behind me. I placed my order and picked up my tray. I looked around for Lillian. She hadn't come in yet, but I knew she would be there in a few minutes. To my surprise and dismay, the guy followed me to a table and asked if he could sit with me!

"I guess so," I said. "I'm expecting a friend in a few minutes, but there's room for all of us."

"I'm Trevor Hampton," he said as he sat down.

"Hannah Pierce," I said. "I haven't seen you before. Are you new here?"

"Yeah, I've been going to school in Nevada, but Mom got a job here and wanted me to come with her."

"That's nice," I said. I was at a loss for words. Most boys didn't stay with me more than a few minutes. I expected Trevor to find some excuse to move to another table, but he didn't.

Lillian found me and I breathed a sigh of relief. I introduced them, and I could tell by the look on his face that Trevor thought she was hot. I felt better when I didn't have to try to make conversation. However, Lillian had to leave early to pick up a book report that she'd left in her locker.

"What classes are you taking?" I finally asked Trevor when I saw he wasn't going to leave.

Trevor named six classes and I was in two of them. We finished our lunches and he said he was glad to have met me. I knew he was just being polite, but it was nice to meet a sweet guy for a change.

I strolled to my next class daydreaming a little. It would be nice to have a boyfriend like Trevor, but I was sure it would never happen. I shook my head to clear it of such silly thoughts.

Another day came to an end in much the same fashion as the day before, except it was Monday and I had to get home to help Mom with the laundry. She was still a little old-fashioned, and, though we had a washing machine and she could do laundry anytime, she tried to do most of the wash on Monday.

By the time I'd arrived home, there were stacks of clean clothes all over the living room and it was my job to get them folded and into their proper places before supper. My younger sister, Dayna, usually helped me. Rather than be annoyed by having to do it, we enjoyed the time together.

We sat and folded clothes and talked about school, clothes, Mom and Dad, our twin brothers, and a little of everything else. Before we knew it, the clothes were all neatly folded. Each of us took armfuls of sweet-smelling towels and sheets to various places in the house.

The following morning, I started to put on the hideous old clothes that I usually wore, when I thought of Trevor. He had been very nice, and I hated for him to see me in those awful things.

So I dressed in a pair of jeans with a bright pink shell and the same denim jacket I'd worn the day before. I tried to put my makeup on like Lillian had, but I wasn't quite as successful. . . .

When I arrived at school, there was Lillian, waiting at the top of the steps, as usual, but Trevor was there, too. We all strolled into the building—passing the same group of rude boys that we'd passed the day before. They made some comments, but it didn't really bother us. We kept talking to each other and ignored them, knowing that that was the best way to keep them at bay.

As it happened, Trevor was in my first class. After class was over, Trevor waited for me at the door and we ambled to our next period together until we had to part ways and go to different classrooms.

"See you at lunch," he called as he turned to go into his classroom.

I waved, but didn't say anything in response. I really was

confused by his interest in me. Why was a guy being so nice to me? None of the others ever were . . . I just knew there would be some catch, and he would realize how unpopular I was and date some other girl.

At lunch, though, I saw him looking for me. Trevor filled his tray and made his way to my table, where I sat, waiting for Lillian to arrive.

"I hear you're tops in all the classes," he said as he sat down.

Now I knew why he was being so nice to me! He needed someone to help him with his studies! I should have guessed as much. I'd had that happen to me before. Some guy or girl would pretend to want to be my friend just to get me to help them with a difficult assignment or some class. I usually helped, pretending I didn't realize the reason why they were being so friendly.

"Yes, I guess I am," I answered. "Do you need some help with something? I suppose someone told you that good old Hannah is always there to help." I didn't even try to keep the bitterness out of my voice.

A puzzled look passed over his face, but he didn't say anything, because Lillian arrived with a cheerful greeting before he could answer my accusation.

"I see you guys are getting along great! I'm so glad; I just knew you guys would. Trevor had the highest grades in the school where he came from. Did you know that, Hannah?"

"No," I said, thoroughly ashamed that I'd accused him of wanting help with his schoolwork. It had happened to me so often in the past that I was always suspicious of people.

"Can you go to Tommy's Café after school? Maybe grab a bite?" Trevor asked. Tommy's was a popular hangout.

"I can't," I said quickly.

"Why can't you?" Lillian asked. "Today is Tuesday. You don't have to rush home on Tuesdays . . . do you?"

"Yes. Yes, I do," I lied. "I've got to help mom at home." I panicked. The place would be full of people who would just stare at me!

Trevor looked straight into my eyes and studied me as though he was going to sculpt me. He looked down—pensively—and then looked back up.

"I'm going to say something that may make you hate me forever, Hannah, but I just have to say it," he said, looking at me intently.

"I think you're a really attractive girl, except—"

"Except for this nose! It's huge and awful! I know! I've heard it all." I jumped up, grabbed my jacket, and turned to leave the cafeteria.

I felt strong arms grab me from behind. Trevor put a hand on each shoulder and pushed me back into my seat. I might have pushed any other guy away, but Trevor had always been nice to me.

It's just that I felt so hurt that he'd turned out to be like all the rest. He really had judged me by my looks.

I glared at him, and then at Lillian. She hadn't even made a move to stop Trevor from saying such mean things to me! Was she going to abandon me, too?

"Well, since you said it first," Trevor said. He didn't look away. He just kept staring at me like he could magically make my bulbous nose disappear.

"Look at me, Hannah," he said. "Look at me really close."

I did. All I could see was a handsome face with a light complexion, dark brown eyes, and hair almost the same color.

"Closer. . . ." he demanded.

"What kind of game are you playing?" I asked. I was puzzled.

He seemed to have a purpose to all of this, but I couldn't for the life of me figure out what it was.

"You're a handsome guy," I finally said. "What do you want me to say? You know you're attractive. Why do you want me to say it?"

"Look at my upper lip. Really look at it." He leaned his face in closer to mine. He wasn't more than a foot away from me.

"I see a tiny little scar. It looks like you had a small cut there once. That's all I can see."

"That's all there is to see. But do you have any idea of what made that little scar?"

"Of course not, and I'm getting tired of this silly game. I have a class in twenty minutes. I need to finish my lunch and go to the bathroom before I go back to class." I turned my attention to my lunch as though I had nothing else to think about.

"I had what is called a cleft palate—a harelip. I looked awful, Hannah. It interfered with my eating, and even my speech. Fortunately, my folks had it operated on while I was still a kid. In fact, it took several operations and I was nearly a teenager before it looked like this. I went through a lot of rough times until everything was corrected."

"What does that have to do with me?"

"For one thing, it lets you know that you're not the only person in the world who has a problem with the way they look, and it also lets you know that something can be done about it."

"I'm not stupid, Trevor. Remember? I'm the smartest kid in school? I figured out a long time ago that if I could afford cosmetic surgery, I could have this protuberance fixed, but my family doesn't have that kind of money." I got up and started to take my tray to the trash. "I don't want anything else to eat. I'm going to the bathroom. I'll see you in class."

"Wait a minute," Trevor said, laying his hand lightly on my arm. "We can do something about this, you know."

"We! Who is 'we?' " I demanded in a loud voice. People looked over at us and then looked away. I said more quietly, "Who is this 'we' you're talking about?"

"Why, Trevor and me, of course," Lillian put in.

"I guess you guys have been talking this over, haven't you? I hate for you to talk about me—I just hate it!"

"We didn't say anything about you that wasn't good. It's just awful to see you so miserable, Hannah. And we think there's a way for you to have cosmetic surgery, and we think you should consider doing it," Lillian said. "Trevor says we have one of the best cosmetic surgeons around right here in the city!"

"Who?"

Lillian told me the doctor's name, and I immediately recalled reading about her and how she helped people who were victims of domestic violence. Everything I'd read was positive, and I felt a little bit of hope rise up in me. However, I had never been abused. My folks were like the proverbial "salt of the earth." They were hardworking, down to earth, and basically wonderful parents. They just didn't have a lot of money, but we always seemed to have all of the necessities in life.

"My mother is the new head nurse at Mercy Hospital. I'll have her make some inquiries, if it's okay with you?" Trevor said.

"Let me talk to my parents first. I don't know how they'd feel about letting someone do something for us without us paying for it. They're awfully proud about anything like that. They feel that people should pay their own way."

"Okay. I'll see you soon, then, I guess," Trevor said.

Trevor started to walk away and then turned to me, sort of biting on his lip. Then: "Hannah, I don't think you look bad at all. I like you just the way you are, and I'd like to date you."

"You would? You do?"

"Yes—to both questions! I want you to come and have a burger with me. You're letting people who are just being mean control you. They're too shallow to notice anyone except the way they look on the outside."

"How'd you get so wise?" I asked. He sounded more like a grown man than an eighteen-year-old guy.

"Like I told you, I had people be rather nasty to me before I had my problem completely corrected, but there were always a few who were good friends to me, like Lillian is to you. Those are the people who matter."

He gathered up his things and took them to the trash. Then he turned and gave me a friendly salute as he walked away.

I felt better than I had in a long, long time. This wonderful guy liked me! He didn't appear to be just taking pity on me, either. I knew I owed a lot to Lillian for urging me to wear my hair different and use a little makeup. Also, I expect even Trevor would have turned away if I'd kept on wearing those ugly clothes.

That evening, after Dayna and I had finished the supper dishes and Mom had put the twins to bed, I went into the living room where Mom was reading and Dad was watching some show on television.

"Uh—can I talk to you guys for a minute?" I asked. I hated interrupting their quiet time, but I couldn't wait until morning. Mornings were too hectic in our household to talk about anything important.

"Why, sure, sweetie," Daddy said. "I thought you'd gone to your room to study. What's up?"

He looked at me with such love that I scolded myself for not being perfectly happy just being a part of this wonderful family. All of us kids knew that our parents loved us more than anything in the world. I realized that that is a very rare thing these days.

"I know you're going to think this is silly, but I hope you don't." I looked away a minute and then looked back. My parents looked puzzled.

"Yes, go on, honey," Mom said. "You hardly ever say or do anything silly, so I doubt we'll think that."

"You know how awful I've been dressing lately?"

Mom nodded. Daddy continued to look at me with that puzzled expression.

"Well . . . it's because I think if I dress that way, no one will notice me. I mean, notice how ugly I am."

"You're not ugly!" Daddy said indignantly.

"You love me; you don't really see me, Daddy. You don't see this awful face. It's just the face of your eldest daughter and you simply don't see how I look, but believe me, others do."

"Some people are fools," he said.

"I know. But, Dad, the truth is that it makes me feel awful. I can wear the nicest clothes, but when someone looks at me, they immediately look away. Some make fun, but most just seem embarrassed. I have a tough time dealing with that."

"I'm sure you do, honey," Mom said. "But you must be doing okay. I mean, you have wonderful grades and, lately, you've been going out with Lillian and that boy. I've heard you talking to Dayna about it."

"Sure, they're both my friends, but I still get these awful remarks from some kids—especially the boys."

"I'd like to horse whip those nasty kids," Dad said. His puzzled look had been replaced by a fierce frown.

"I doubt that would solve anything and just get you into

trouble," Mom said with a little laugh.

"I want a nose job," I blurted out. I was tired of skirting around the issue.

"You what?" Dad exclaimed.

"I want to have my nose worked on, and I'd like to have it done before the spring activities. It's too late for the Christmas dance, but I could look a lot better by spring. I'd look like a whole new person for the valedictory speech . . . that's presuming that I really do have the highest grades."

"But, Hannah, we can't afford such an operation. We have good insurance, but it doesn't cover cosmetic surgery," Dad said. "And I don't have enough saved to even begin to pay for that kind of operation."

"I know, I know!" I said. "But Trevor says there's a doctor in the city who will do operations for people who can't pay. He says she's helped to reconstruct some very battered women."

"You mean charity?" Mom asked. "You know we don't believe in taking something for nothing, Hannah. There's just too much of that going on nowadays."

"Maybe she would let me pay it off a little at a time, then. I could get a job and pay a little each month. Please—Mom, Dad—let me go see her and see what she says. I didn't want to go to her without your permission."

"I don't know—"

"Please, Dad. Just let me go see her. I'll try to make arrangements to make some small payments. Please, please! It's so important to me."

"I'll go with you," Mom said. "I doubt she'll make any arrangements without at least one of your parents present. After all, you are only seventeen."

"Then you mean I can do it? I can see if she'll help me? Thank you, thank you!"

Daddy had a mighty frown on his face, but he didn't say anything else. He usually went along with Mom's decisions about things like this, but I knew that if he really objected, he would say so. Really, I suspected they had both thought of cosmetic surgery long before I had, but knew how much it would cost, so they didn't want to get my hopes up. I also think they believed that if they acknowledged that my awful nose ruined my face, it would only upset me even more.

The next day, I dressed nicely and looked forward to meeting Lillian and Trevor on the school steps. It was easy to ignore the guys standing around making various comments as I went by. I had the feeling that I was going to be able to turn right around and let them look at me soon enough. Those creeps would be sorry they'd been so nasty to such a beautiful babe!

"Hi, you guys," I said to Lillian and Trevor. "Mom and Dad have said I can go see that doctor. Has your mom been able to talk to her, Trevor?"

"Not yet. She'll try to contact her today. They're both busy, so it might be a few days."

"Will you go to a show with me tonight?" Trevor asked. "Lillian has a date with Kevin and we thought it would be nice to all go together. Will you?"

"Yes, I will. I'd love to." I tried to sound casual about it, but it was the first real date I'd ever had—at seventeen years old! I sort of sucked in my breath and felt myself nearly panic.

I didn't need to be so worried, though. We went to a movie, and then walked to Tommy's Café. I thought I'd be uncomfortable, but with Lillian and her date and Trevor with me, I felt really bold.

When we went into the café, several kids stopped talking to each other and turned to stare at us. I was self-conscious, but

Trevor took my arm and steered me to a booth at about the middle part of the room.

We ordered hamburgers and soft drinks and sat and chatted for a while. Soon, a couple who were an item in school came over and asked if they could join us.

Soon, we were all having fun and chatting about the Christmas dance. I got very quiet when they started talking about the dance, because I was sure I couldn't go. However, I was in for a surprise.

We'd driven to the show in Trevor's ten-year-old car, and he took Lillian and Kevin home first. They lived in a small cull-de-sac in houses not far apart. They'd been best friends for most of their lives, and had only recently begun dating.

"That Christmas dance they were talking about," Trevor said. "I hadn't heard about any Christmas dance. When is it?"

"About the second week in December. I don't think they've set the date yet. The student council arranges it and I'm not on that."

"Why not?"

"I guess because I wasn't elected. I didn't run for election, but even if I had, I wouldn't have won."

"Now you're selling yourself short again, Hannah."

"No, I'm smart, remember? I'm just being realistic."

"Okay. Will you go to the dance with me?"

"Huh?"

"I said—will you go to the dance with me? I want to go, and I want you to go with me," he said matter-of-factly.

"I don't know how to dance. I've never gone to a dance before, Trevor."

"Well, I want you to go to this one with me. You can learn to dance. I'll teach you. Lillian and I can teach you, okay? It's time you had some fun."

By this point, we'd reached my home and he got out of the car to come around to open the door for me like a real gentleman, but I was out before he had a chance. He laughed and took my hand and escorted me up the steps. When we reached the top, he pulled me to him and I could feel his heart beating against my breasts.

A feeling came over me that I had never experienced before. A hot and quivery feeling disturbed my insides and my legs wanted to buckle under me. It felt wonderful and scary at the same time.

"Good night, Hannah." He bent and kissed me lightly on the lips.

I was so startled that I stepped back and looked at him like an idiot. He kissed me. I couldn't believe he'd kissed me! I'd finally been kissed—and by a very sweet, hot guy.

"Good night, Hannah," he repeated. "I'll talk to my mother and let you know what she says about the surgery."

"Okay."

I didn't hear anything about the doctor for several days. Then, Trevor met me one morning with a big grin on his face and told me that his mother had finally been able to speak to the cosmetic surgeon and get a phone number to call.

He handed me a card with Dr. Woetzel's name and phone number on it.

"Mom had to do quite a bit of coaxing to get her to see you. She said young girls often think there's something wrong with their appearance, but that it's usually something they're just being dramatic about. My mom told Dr. Woetzel that she thought she should look at you and then decide. Finally, she agreed to do it. Mom says she's about the friendliest doctor at the hospital."

"That's nice to know. Thank your mother for me, please. She

must be a very good person."

"She is. I want you to meet her soon."

"Okay. I'd like that."

I went home and told my parents and we made an appointment with Dr. Woetzel for Tuesday afternoon. I was so excited that I counted the days like a little kid. After all, I had more or less resigned myself to looking kind of weird for the rest of my life. After meeting Trevor, though, it didn't bother me quite as much as it had before. But I knew I'd be a much happier person if I looked normal. . . .

The doctor talked to me about my schoolwork and what I was planning to do when I graduated. This seemed strange to me. I couldn't see why my career plans were of any importance to the situation, but I soon found that she had a good reason. She was determining if I was stable enough to take the consequences of the operation and not let it determine my entire future.

"You do understand that we can't exactly perform miracles, correct?" Dr. Woetzel asked. "I'm glad you're planning for your future, regardless of whether you have surgery or not. You do appear to have a nose that is ill-proportioned to your face. However, I'm very hesitant to do surgery on young girls. I've had girls and boys come in with only a minor flaw, like a little bump or a nose they think is slightly too long. Generally, I won't operate on them until they're fully grown because sometimes, their faces begin to balance out as they grow older."

I felt my optimism plummet to the floor. I just knew she was going to decide against doing anything about my horrible nose—

But I was wrong.

"I do think the outcome, for you, will be quite beneficial, however. You have nice skin, a good figure, and your eyes are lovely. If we reshape your nose, it will improve your appearance quite a bit."

"W-we don't have much money," I stammered. "I'd like to get a job and pay you in installments, though. My parents can't afford to pay for my operation, but I can pay you a little at a time."

"I know that, Hannah. Mrs. Hampton explained the situation to me, and while you certainly don't have the same problem some of my other patients have had, I can see how the world can be very cruel to you. It's a pity that people can't look to the inner person, but in this day and age, appearances do count for so much. Now, when would you like to schedule your procedure?"

It was all so much simpler than I had ever anticipated. I arranged to have my operation at the beginning of the Christmas break, which was a week after the Christmas dance. That way, I could be partially healed before school started again.

It seemed as though my guardian angel had taken over my life, because it turned out that Dr. Woetzel needed a part-time office assistant to do filing and some typing. I'd been working with computers all through high school, so I was familiar with the office's system and knew that I was a real help to the staff.

Trevor and I went to the Christmas dance and had a wonderful time. My clever mother had gone to the store to see that rose-colored dress I'd adored so much. She made a little sketch, bought similar fabric, and made a dress just as beautiful for me. It cost less than two-thirds as much as the one at the store! I was so proud, and never hesitated to tell the other kids that my mom had made the beautiful dress for me . . . even though she'd asked me not to.

When school started again, I looked and felt like a new girl. My face was still a bit bruised, but by carefully applying cosmetics, I certainly didn't look any worse than I had before. In fact, I think

I looked better. However, Dr. Woetzel said it would be a few weeks before I would be able to see the full results.

I created something of a sensation, really. No one could believe how different I looked. For a while, I was a seven-day wonder. It wasn't long, though, before everyone's attention turned to other things, to my immense relief.

For our senior prom, I went as Trevor's date. Afterward, he whisked me away from the others and we drove to a little park not far from my house. It was a beautiful night. I never wanted it to end. We stopped under a big tree and sat on a tiny bench facing a lake.

"I don't want to lose you, Hannah," he said. "I want you in my life forever."

I looked at him. He was so serious that I nearly cried. I leaned over and kissed him on his cheek. But that wasn't enough for Trevor. He pulled me into his arms and kissed me in a way I had never been kissed before. I felt that warm stirring inside of my body again. . . .

"Oh, Trevor. I don't want to be away from you, either, but we're both going to college."

"I love you, I really love you. Let's get married. We can stay together forever then."

"I love you, too, but we're too young to get married. Can't we just continue the way we are for a while? It's so wonderful when you're near, but I'm afraid we'd be overwhelmed by marrying so young."

He studied my face as if he were trying to memorize it. "I'm afraid when you go away to college, you'll have so many guys after you that you'll forget about me."

"You should know me better than that—especially if you want to marry me! You know I'm not shallow like that, Trevor."

"But you're so beautiful now. I just know a lot of guys will be hitting on you."

"Trevor! That's such a sweet thing for you to say, but I learned a lot from you and Lillian before I had my surgery. I know what a person is inside is far more important than the way he or she looks on the outside. I won't ever live for just the way I look again. Never, never, never."

"Well, then, you aren't the valedictorian for nothing! You're a smart lady, Hannah Pierce."

"Thanks, but you'd have been in the running if you hadn't transferred here just last year."

"Well, maybe."

It turned out that Brian Rosen and I tied for the highest grades so we shared the spotlight for a while. That was fine with me, because, while I'm a lot more confident now about my appearance, I'm still a little shy about speaking in front of a crowd of people.

"I think you should become a model," Lillian said one day. We were sitting on the steps of the school, watching the kids go by. "You've always had a sensational figure, but now your face is just so pretty!"

"You're a wonderful friend, Lillian. I know how I look doesn't make any difference to you. I simply can't believe my good fortune in finding a friend as nice as you are, but I don't think I want to spend my life as a model—not that I think there's anything wrong with that. . . ." I laughed.

"Oh, well it's just an idea," she said. "You can do anything you want. As for me, I'm going to be a teacher. I've always wanted to be a teacher, and I can stay at home while I go to school."

"I think I'll study medicine," I said. "Maybe even become a surgeon like Dr. Woetzel. I've been seeing what wonders she accomplishes. I realize now that my problem was really not as serious as I was making it out to be. I mean, I see people come into her office who have been seriously deformed by accidents, severe burns, birth defects, and diseases. Some have been badly battered by someone, and Dr. Woetzel makes them as nearly whole as possible. I think I'd like to do something like that to help people."

Trevor and I are now attending the same college. He's interested in medicine, also, and plans on becoming a pediatrician.

I did meet and date other guys for a while, but I knew deep down that Trevor is the only man for me. In the second year of med school, we got married. It was a beautiful wedding. I walked down the aisle on my father's arm and was given over to the wonderful man I'm going to spend the rest of my life with. I can't imagine how I became so blessed. THE END

WORKING ON A NEW ME

It's a lot of hard work, but the payoff is incredible.

The alarm sounded for the third time that morning. As much as I wanted to, I couldn't hit the SNOOZE button again. I'd be late for work...again. I had already been warned by the perfect Miss Milly that my job was on the line if I continued in this vein. Groaning, I rolled over and sat on the edge of the bed. I'd slept nine hours and still had no energy. What the heck was wrong with me?

I pushed myself off the bed with a huff and dragged my body into the bathroom. As hard as I tried, I couldn't avoid the mirror. I leaned in close, only inches from my reflection, and poked a finger at my puffy cheeks. How in God's name had I let myself become so heavy? I didn't even recognize my own face. Behind me hung a full-length mirror. Despite my vow to get rid of it, a lack of energy on my part left it there mocking me, like a mortal enemy. I'd managed to hide the scale under the sink, but the mirror nailed to the wall was harder to ignore. It didn't matter. I deserved to see how I let myself go.

With a sigh, I closed my eyes and then stripped off my pajamas. I had to face the ugly truth: My once svelte body had exploded. Okay, if I was honest with myself I'd have to say that I'd never been skinny, but now I looked like a blimp. I studied myself from the front and the back and then my profile, where my body bulged in every direction. I didn't just look like a blob, I looked like a lump of wadded up and discarded bubble gum!

A tear slipped out of the corner of my eye and I washed it away when I stepped into the shower. "Kristen, get a grip. You're not that bad," I told myself out loud. "You can start a diet the second you step out of this shower."

I strengthened my resolve to become fit and start eating right as I finished washing my hair. I had to try on three different outfits before I found one that didn't cut off my circulation and actually allowed me to breathe. It was only last month when the other outfits had only been snug, but I could at least get into them. What had happened?

A quick glance at the clock showed me that I was going to be horribly late if I didn't leave that very second. Though I wouldn't have time for a decent breakfast at home, I'd just hit the drive-through on the way to work. Eggs on a biscuit with a little bit of ham couldn't be too bad for me, could it? Since I planned to start working out today I knew I'd work it off, so it didn't matter if it had a little more fat content than I wanted.

Feeling better because of my fitness plan, I headed out the door, stopped at a fast-food restaurant, and wolfed down my breakfast sandwich. I pulled into the parking lot at work, brushed the crumbs off my chest, and climbed out of the car huffing and puffing. This would be the last day that would happen, since I was going to get in shape starting right after work. I walked the short distance across the parking lot, surprised that I had to stop and catch my breath when I reached the front doors.

My heart lurched in my chest when I saw my boss, the perfect Miss Milly, waiting for me like a pit bull waiting to chew on someone's leg. I nervously glanced at the clock on the wall. Only ten minutes late. That wasn't too bad. Lord knows I'd been a lot later than that before, no thanks to the infernal snooze button. The damn thing should be outlawed.

"There you are, Kristen. I was starting to think you weren't coming in today."

I wanted to wipe that smug smile off her face. "No, no. I'm sorry I'm late, Milly. The alarm didn't go off."

Okay, it went off four times—but who was counting?

I could see her looking me up and down, a blatant look of distaste on her face. I squared my shoulders and raised my chin. I may not have been a size four like her, but most people weren't. I had nothing to be ashamed of. I tugged the hem of my shirt over my stomach and she moved her gaze back to my face.

"Don't worry about it. We're stacked up with work today. I'm just glad to see you. We might need you to put in some overtime. Can you handle that?" She gave me this look like she'd eaten too many prunes. I'd bet my last dollar that at fiftysomething, she was still a virgin.

"Of course I can. Whatever you need. I'm only too happy to help out." I may have been a little overweight, but I was a productive employee and dedicated to the company. Despite how many times I'd been late, they couldn't overlook that simple fact.

"You're probably going to have to take a working lunch and maybe work a couple of extra hours at the end of the day."

"No problem." I shoved my purse in my top desk drawer and turned on my computer.

"Here's all the data you need to input for now. I'll give you the rest as I get the numbers. We're really counting on you, Kristen. This job needs to be done by tomorrow morning."

"No problem. It'll get done."

For three hours I didn't move from my desk. I finally took a quick bathroom break, then went right back to work. Around twelve-thirty, Milly's secretary poked her head into my cubicle.

"Kristen, Bill is going to make a lunch run. Do you want something to eat? It's on the company since you're taking a working lunch."

My stomach growled, letting me know I hadn't eaten for quite a while. "That would be great. I'm famished. A bacon cheeseburger, fries, and a Coke works for me."

"Do you want giant-sized?"

"We're going to be here a while, aren't we?"

"Probably."

"Then by all means, giant-sized it is." I thought of my planned diet. Tomorrow. I'd get back to my eating properly tomorrow.

How bad could a couple of extra fries be anyway? They were just potatoes, after all. The numbers on my computer screen begged for my attention and I quickly forgot about that four-letter word, d-i-e-t. I barely even remembered eating my lunch as I only took bites between keystrokes.

At eight o'clock I finally finished. I sent the file via e-mail to Milly, who'd gone home hours ago, then shut off my computer and stretched my arms. God, I was tired. All I wanted to do was go home and soak in a tub filled with bubble bath and the scent of lavender.

Knowing I would be way too tired to cook an evening meal, I picked up some fried chicken on the way home. After my bath, which felt incredibly relaxing, I pulled on an old T-shirt and parked myself in front of the television with some ice cream. I consoled myself with the fact that if I was going to start my diet tomorrow, I needed to get rid of all the "good" food still in my apartment. No sense having it around if I was starting a fitness plan bright and early in the morning.

I curled up on the sofa with a quilt and some Death By Chocolate. Next thing I knew I was waking up to bright sunlight. What was I doing on the sofa? What time was it? Was this Saturday? Slowly my sleep-fogged mind cleared. My eyes raced to the clock. Nine. Oh, no—I was supposed to be at work a half hour ago! Oh, I'd really done it now!

I pushed myself off the sofa and raced for the bedroom. I didn't even have time for a shower. I pulled on the first blouse I tugged out of the closet. The buttons wouldn't even meet. Tears pricked at my eyes, but I blinked them away. I didn't have time for tears right now. I had to get to work immediately. I grabbed another shirt, praying it would fit. It was snug, but snug would have to do.

I ran a toothbrush over my teeth, grabbed my purse and raced out the door. The phone rang just as the door closed, but I didn't have time to go back in and answer it.

What about my good breakfast? I was supposed to start my diet today. A coffee and a croissant would have to do. I pulled into the drive-through of the closest coffee joint, got my order, then raced to work as fast as I could.

Milly was perched on the corner of my desk when I got there, with one leg swinging in obvious agitation. I couldn't say that I blamed her, but it still irked me to no end.

"We had revisions on the reports, Kristen."

"Oh, well, give them to me and I'd be glad to tackle them right away."

"The report had to be finished by nine sharp." She glanced pointedly at the clock hanging on the wall.

I swallowed nervously. "I'm really sorry I'm late. The alarm cl—"

"I really don't want to hear it again, Kristen. You've used that alarm clock excuse one too many times. Anyone in his or her right mind would have purchased a new alarm clock by now. Since you haven't, one has to assume the alarm clock isn't the problem."

Her gaze strolled up and down my body in obvious disdain. God, how I wanted to hit her!

"Your appearance of late has been sloppy, not that we can fire you for that, but I did warn you about your excessive tardiness."

Yep, she certainly had warned me. Some part of me hadn't taken her seriously, though. Maybe I should have. My heart skipped and my stomach churned with the hastily eaten cheese and blueberry croissant that was now sitting there like a lead balloon.

"But, Milly, I'm really sorry. It won't happen again. I swear—"

"I know it won't happen again. I won't allow it. You're a good worker, Kristen, but you've become undependable. It's to the point where you're sluggish. It takes you twice as long to do the work you used to do. One has to wonder if your excessive weight gain over the past six months is the key to all your troubles."

Excessive weight gain? Okay, I'd gained a few pounds, but this woman was practically calling me obese! How dare she?

"You can't fire me because of my weight. That's harassment."

"I'm not firing you because of your weight. I would never do that. I'm just telling you that if you want to find a new job somewhere, I'd think about getting into a really good fitness plan if I were you. It really might make you more suitable for the next company for which you choose to work."

She let that comment sink in for a moment—a moment where I'm sure my face turned about a hundred shades of red in utter humiliation. What did she know about weight loss? Milly was positively anexoric-looking, nothing but a bag of bones. A virgin bag of old hag bones, at that.

"I'm firing you, Kristen, because you almost lost us an account. I can't afford to go through this every time we have a deadline. Deadlines are nerve-wracking enough."

How would she know? I was the one who did all the work. I was the one who stayed until eight o'clock the night before while she'd waltzed out the door at five o'clock on the dot.

"I need you to clean out your desk. My secretary will bring you your final paycheck shortly."

My final paycheck. The words sounded so damn . . . final. I sat down at my desk and ran a hand over my keyboard. My keyboard.

Not anymore.

Someone else would sit at that desk where I'd sat at for six years. Six years that now amounted to absolutely nothing. I shoved what few belongings I had in a box conveniently sitting on the floor for my use. They'd thought of everything, hadn't they? Everything but how bad they'd made me feel.

Just then Milly's secretary, Beth, hesitantly approached my cubicle. She nervously clutched what I assumed was my paycheck in her shaking fingers.

"Is that for me?" I asked when she just stood there seemingly at a loss for words.

"Oh . . . yes." She handed it to me.

I shoved it into my purse without looking. I knew they'd have severance pay in there, too. The company was nothing if not generous.

"Are you done packing?"

"I think so."

Beth licked her lips. "I'm sorry, but I need to escort you out."

And here I'd thought the scene with Milly had been

embarrassing. Her hired hand escorting me out left me feeling downright criminal.

The words rushed out of my mouth before I could stop them. "I'm just fat and lazy—not a thief."

Obviously at a loss for words, Beth's mouth opened and closed like a fish left flopping on shore.

"I'm sorry, you didn't deserve that. Please, show me the way out. I'm ready."

The stares on my death march were the worst. I didn't see them, but I sure felt my former coworkers watching me as I walked out. Their gazes burned through my back like laser beams. I could hear their whispers, obese . . . slacker . . . lazy. That I didn't care how I looked.

I cared. I cared a hell of a lot, but I had always put the job first. That had been my first mistake. They would never find anyone as dedicated as me. I dared them to try.

On the way home I stopped to console myself with a real breakfast: pancakes, syrup, whipped cream, strawberries, the works. That day had been bad enough and it wasn't even noon. I didn't need to add dieting on top of it. If I couldn't find a job in this tight economy, paying my rent would come before buying groceries. Dieting would be only a piece of proverbial cake—no pun intended.

I decided to stop at my mom's house and tell her what had happened. I had unbuttoned my pants to make it easier to sit in the car. That breakfast had really filled me up. I deserved it, though, since I'd been thoroughly screwed. I guess Milly wasn't a virgin after all.

I quickly buttoned my pants, then ambled up the driveway to the front door. Mom was waiting with the door wide open, concern on her face.

"What are you doing here at this time of day? And why are you so winded? You sound like you just ran a marathon."

"I've had a very bad day, Mother. I guess it's left me breathless."

"Oh, my goodness. Well, come in, sit down, tell me all about it." She ushered me inside. I was more than winded, I realized after taking a couple of deep breaths to try and fill my starving lungs. It was all because of my job. They'd taken everything from me and left me nothing put a pink slip.

"Okay, honey, now tell me—what's wrong?"

"I got fired today, Mom." It sounded weird actually saying the words aloud. I didn't have a job. I was unemployed. How was I going to pay my rent? I had friends who had been out of work for months. The economy was terrible. What hopes did I have of ever finding work again?

"They fired you? Why? You always work so hard for them. I don't understand."

"I know. That's what I said, too. It seems I was late a few times."

"Late? You? Why, Kristen, I've never known you to be late for anything."

I sighed. "Some mornings it just seems hard to get out of bed, you know. And Milly, my boss, kind of hinted that she didn't like the clothes I've been wearing . . . among other things."

I sat helplessly as my mother look me up and down. Heat burned my cheeks.

"You do seem to have put on an few pounds lately. Actually, a little bit more than a few pounds. Your clothes are incredibly tight. Isn't that the shirt I gave you for your birthday last year? It used to swim on you."

"Maybe I have a thyroid problem." I would have gotten up and walked away from her and this conversation, but my legs felt too tired to move. All I knew was that it wasn't my fault. It had to be a thyroid problem.

She raised an eyebrow. Mothers. They always let you know exactly what they are thinking, without even uttering a word. "That could very well be. I believe your Aunt Joan had a thyroid problem. Let me call my doctor right now and see if they can squeeze you in."

"I don't have insurance, Mom. I lost my job. Remember?"

She patted my hand. "That's all right, dear. I'll take care of it for you. You don't need to worry about anything."

She left the room and two minutes later came back with a smile on her face. They'll see you this afternoon."

"Thanks, Mom. Now what am I going to do about rent? I don't have that much money saved up. They gave me some severance, but I'm really scared."

"Something will come up. You'll only make your situation worse by worrying."

Mom insisted on driving me to the doctor's office, telling me my mental condition prohibited me from getting behind the wheel.

"I haven't had lunch yet, Mom, have you? We've got a few minutes. Why don't we pull into a drive-through and get something quick?"

"Oh, that's a good idea. I am a tad hungry." Mom took a sharp right and we waited in line.

"Just get me a burger, large fries, and a soft drink."

"Diet?"

"No. Those taste funny to me. Just a regular."

"Funny taste or not, maybe you need to start drinking fruit juices." In a way only a mother can, she looked pointedly at my stomach, which was hanging over my pants in an unbecoming manner.

I tugged on the bottom of my shirt. "Mom, don't start on me today, okay? I've had a harsh enough time of it already. Besides, a little hamburger and fries and one drink isn't going to hurt me."

"All right, I'll lay off today—but depending on what the doctor says, I want you to start dieting as soon as possible. What happened to my skinny little girl?"

"I've never been skinny, Mom." Maybe I really did have a thyroid problem. It would answer a lot of questions in my mind. I envisioned getting the right kind of medicine and having the pounds melt right off me like nobody's business.

A smile tugged at my lips as I bit into my hamburger. Yes, tomorrow was going to be another day full of wonderful promises.

The doctor examined me from head to toe, concluding with the words, "That should do it for now. I really couldn't find anything seriously wrong. Your blood pressure is a little high, but that's probably due to your obesity. We'll wait until the test results are back so we can rule everything out."

At that point I couldn't hear a word he'd said. I know he kept talking, but my mind had fixated on one word.

Obesity.

The word reverberated around in my head until I felt like I was going to pass out. I was actually obese? Fat? I looked down at my gut and my thighs. My clothes that didn't fit. I was a cow—a fat slob of a cow. How had this happened? When had this happened? I used to be skinny, but now I was obese.

"How did it go, honey?" Mom asked the second she saw me.

I looked into her eyes, my vision blurring.

"Kristen, what's wrong? Are you sick?"

"Much worse, Mom." I heaved a sigh and looked at the floor. "I'm obese."

"Oh, what a relief. I thought you had cancer or something! You can go on a diet and get rid of weight. You can't get rid of a terminal illness."

"It might as well be a terminal illness. I'm not cut out for carrot sticks and lettuce. I'll probably be fat forever."

Mom opened the car door for me and helped me inside. "Sensible eating doesn't always mean starving yourself. It just means cutting back. Fast food is extremely fattening and you seem to eat a lot of it."

"Be serious, Mom. Fast food is convenient. It's not that bad for you. How could it be?" I tuned out any answers she gave me. No wonder I couldn't get up in the mornings; I had no energy and all that crap. I was carrying around all this excess weight. I realized at that moment that depression can weigh heavier than anything. I convinced my mother I'd be able to drive myself home. She looked concerned, but I did it anyway with the agreement that I'd call her the second I walked into my apartment.

After hanging up the phone, I looked around at the four walls I called "home". I had made it so very cozy, so utterly mine, full of antiques and bright colors. It always welcomed me with open arms whenever I walked through the door. How could I give it up when I couldn't pay the rent? Would I have to move in with my mother? I was going to turn into a fat version of Miss Perfect Milly. I'd be Miss Unperfect Kristen. Unlike Milly, at least I'd experienced sex.

Determined not to let that happen, I decided to go to an employment agency first thing in the morning. No sense letting moss grow under my feet. I was damn good at my job. I prayed they'd be able to find me something fast.

The next morning I was blown away at how crowded the employment agency was. I grabbed a magazine and sat down with a mocha latte and obviously a lot of time to spare, judging by the large number of people milling about.

"Isn't this crazy?"

I glanced toward the tiny woman in the form-fitting red suit next to me. I used to look like that. Okay, maybe not exactly like that, but pretty darn close. "Are all these people out of work?"

"Unfortunately."

"How are we ever going to find jobs?"

"A lot of people take temp work while they're looking. I think that's what I'm going to do. I'm Ginny, by the way."

"Hi, Ginny. I'm Kristen." I was surprised that such a skinny woman was talking to me. Not that I thought I wasn't worth talking to, but a lot of people ignored heavy people. However, looking around me I noticed all types of body shapes. Where did I fit in anymore? In the past I could get all kinds of men to look at me. Now I couldn't even look at myself in the mirror.

Nothing I could do about it right now. Once I got a new job I could afford a membership at a gym. I took a sip of my latte and cracked open the magazine. About halfway through, when they still weren't even anywhere close to calling me, I came upon an article that captivated my interest.

It compared the calories, fat content, and nutritional value of all the fast food restaurants. I was floored by the findings. I had assumed that fast food was reasonably good for you, so I was shocked to discover the incredibly high fat content in the burgers and fries I'd been consuming, often on a three-times-daily basis.

No wonder the scale had been creeping steadily upward! With

these facts in front of me, I understood where all the weight had come from.

When they finally called me, I was utterly devastated to find out that the computer industry was in even worse shape than my body. Things were beyond sluggish right now and the employment agency would look around for me, seeing as I was highly qualified, but they couldn't make any guarantees.

That night I sat in the dark, mindlessly watching television. A commercial came on for some ambulance-chasing lawyer. Call Bulldog Morgan for your case. He's on your side. He'll get you results!

I sat up straight, dropping the lap quilt on the floor. That was exactly what I needed: someone on my side. It wasn't my fault that I was obese—it was the fast food industry's fault! Why hadn't they put information about their food where the public could see it? If I had known that visiting the drive-through would make me gain fifty pounds of ugly fat, I wouldn't have done it. I would have brought healthy meals to work and saved my job and not put my life in jeopardy.

Regardless of the hour, I picked up the phone and dialed Mr. Bulldog Morgan. If I sued fast food restaurants for all the misery they'd caused me I wouldn't have to worry about losing my apartment. I wouldn't have to worry about anything; I'd be set for life. Fast food chains had mighty deep pockets.

To my surprise, even though I hadn't expected it at that late hour, a woman answered the phone. I scheduled an appointment for the next day, my heart lighter than it had been in quite some time.

Bulldog Morgan was a short, stout man with a spare tire around his stomach and a cigar hanging from the corner of his mouth. He tugged on his belt around his gut like I always tugged on the hem of my shirts. If anyone would be sympathetic to my plight, I knew it would be him.

After hearing my story he remained silent for a while, staring at the ceiling and chewing on the end of that cigar. Then he pounded on the desk, making me jump.

"By golly, I'll do it! We can make this a class action suit. There are thousands of people in your same predicament. All due to fast food, I can guaran-damn-tee it!" He looked satisfied with himself and my case. "This is going to be the opportunity of a lifetime—for both of us!"

I walked out of his office feeling much better about myself. The next morning I couldn't handle sitting around waiting for the phone to ring another minute. The employment agency might not call for days, even weeks. Why should I sit around waiting for them? I drove over to my mother's to tell her the good news in person.

"Mom," I said as soon as I walked in the door, "you'll never guess what I'm doing. My money problems are all solved."

"That's wonderful, Kristen. Did you find a job already? In this economy? I can't believe your good luck!"

"Nope. No job. Something even better." I couldn't keep the smile off my face.

"You met a wealthy man and he asked you to marry him?" she asked with a teasing lilt to her voice. "You sure work fast."

"Nope. No wealthy man. Don't need one. But I am going to be wealthy."

"Did you win the lottery?" She looked confused.

"Okay, I might as well tell you because you're never going to guess in a million years."

She refilled her coffee cup and sat down at the island in the middle of her spacious kitchen. "I'm all ears, honey."

"I met with a lawyer yesterday. He seems to think I have an excellent case."

"Against whom? Your former employer?"

"No, they actually had a documented case against me since I'd been late a couple times. I'm actually suing a bunch of companies that make millions. Everything is their fault, Mom. Everything. My weight, the fact that I lost my job, the decline of my health. They did it to me."

"You'll have to tell me who 'they' are, Kristen."

"Fast food restaurants."

"Fast food restaurants?"

"Yep. I never knew the drive-through lane would make me obese."

"I use the drive-through lane occasionally and I'm not obese. It's called moderation, Kristen."

I didn't like whatever Mom was implying right then.

"They don't post the fat content or calories or anything at their restaurants," I said evenly. "How was I to know it could possibly give me heart disease and make my weight skyrocket? Mom, I thought you'd be happy for me."

"Happy that you're not taking responsibility for your own actions?" She stared into her coffee cup like all the answers were there.

"Kristen, I brought you up to be responsible. I'm going to tell it to you like it is. You made yourself gain weight, not the fast food industry. You eat there sometimes three times a day. If you would just take a moment and be honest with yourself you'd realize the truth. Even if they had posted fat and calorie content on the door when you walk in, would you have stopped to read it?"

I refused to answer that question. "Oh, I don't have to stay and listen to this."

"No, you don't."

I grabbed my purse and stalked out the door as well as an obese person can stalk. "I'll talk to you later," I threw over my shoulder, not bothering to wait for her response.

That night I tossed and turned, my head filled with all the words Mom had said. By dawn I came up with one conclusion: She was wrong and Bulldog Morgan was right. It was his job to know what cases would win and which ones wouldn't. He'd had definite stars in his eyes with this one. I knew we'd win.

Deciding to take action with my life, if nothing more than to prove to my mother that I wasn't a lazy, good-for-nothing, I called the employment agency. They immediately found me a temporary position while I waited for a permanent job to open up. It was minimal pay, but I decided it was better than nothing at that point.

When I got there I discovered the woman I'd met in the waiting room the other day working there also.

"Hi, Ginny," I said tentatively. I didn't know if she'd remember me, and I didn't know if she'd treat me the same way the woman at the front desk had. She'd barely spared me a glance. She'd acted like I wasn't even human, and I knew it was because I was fat. Funny how the bigger one became, the more invisible they became to others.

"Kristen, how wonderful to see you again. I'm so glad we'll be working together." Ginny really looked like she'd meant what she said. Her eyes lit up when she saw me, like she was greeting an old friend. I liked her instantly.

The day passed quickly as we both input data into the computer and chatted idly about everything under the sun. At lunchtime we went to the office cafeteria. No way was I going to go to a fast food restaurant. That wasn't a great idea when I had every intent to sue them.

Since Ginny had brought her lunch, she saved us a table while I waited in line. In an attempt to be good for a change, I got a turkey sandwich, but I opted for white bread. I just couldn't stomach wheat, an apple, and a pasta salad. This had to be much better than my normal diet of cheeseburgers and fries.

I saw Ginny looking at my plate with a slight frown, but she didn't comment. The rest of the day flew by just as quickly as the morning had. That night I went straight from work to the lawyer's office so we could get started on paperwork. When I walked into the office the receptionist was in Bulldog's office with the door open. I couldn't help but listen in on their conversation.

"If you take this case, Mr. Morgan, I'm afraid I'm going to have to resign."

"What are you talking about, Patsy?" Bulldog barked out in his gruff voice.

"You've taken a lot of bogus cases that I frowned upon, but this one is a new low even for you. This one tops all the rest of the lowdown, shifty lawyers. This one takes the cake."

I loved juicy gossip as much as I loved a juicy cheeseburger. I wondered who they were talking about and who's case was involved.

"How can you even believe that an eating establishment is responsible for someone getting fat? Where is the accountability? No one held a gun to this woman's head and told her to eat there. No one told her to supersize all her meals. She's putting the blame on a corporation that is blameless, when she should be looking in the mirror."

I felt the blood drain from my face. I'd heard enough. I was mortified. I couldn't let this Patsy woman know I had heard every word she'd said. Quietly I walked out of the office, then came back in, quickly asking if anyone was there at the same time I slammed the door, leaving no room for doubt that someone had just entered.

Patsy came out of Mr. Morgan's office, her cheeks slightly pink. "Kristen, how wonderful to see you again. Mr. Morgan will see you now. Go right on in."

Yeah, I'll bet you're just loving the fact that I walked into the office right now! I thought to myself. I'd show her. Both she and my mother were wrong and I was going to laugh all the way to the bank. Me and Mr. Bulldog Morgan!

Mr. Morgan was still hot about this case. He raved about how we were going to make tons of money and retire in comfort. The more he carried on, the more I thought he sounded like an ambulance-chaser. Shifty. No good.

That's when the first niggling doubts set in. I looked at the contract he had ready for me to sign, but I couldn't bring myself to sign on the dotted line. Something held me back. Was it my conscience?

That night I tossed and turned again, mulling over what I was about to do. All I had wanted all those times was a quick, decent meal. How was I to know it wasn't healthy for me? In reality I had to have known—greasy fries, greasy burgers, sugar-laden soda pop. I was responsible. Dammit, I had opted to eat those things, day-in and day-out.

Patsy was right. My mom was right. No one had held a gun to my head.

I couldn't go through with the lawsuit. I just couldn't. I felt ashamed of myself for even considering the notion for as long as I had. I immediately called Bulldog and told him I refused to go through with it. He was beyond upset, but I was finally proud of myself for the first time in a very long time.

I thought about my new friend, Ginny. She was slender and

toned. Judging by her figure and what she'd eaten for lunch, she didn't get that way by frequenting the drive-throughs one too many times.

The next day I tried several times to bring up the subject of my weight . . . and her lack of it. At lunchtime, watching her eat a chicken breast, a salad, and a peach, I couldn't hesitate another minute. "Ginny, what's the secret to your success? How do you stay so thin? I'm guessing you don't eat greasy burgers and fries, do you?"

She smiled sweetly at me. She really was becoming a dear friend in such a short time. "I'm glad you asked, Kristen. I don't push my lifestyle on anyone, but if they ask about it, I'm more than happy to share. It's a lot of hard work, but the payoff is incredible. Would you believe that nine months ago I probably weighed more than you do right now?"

"Get out of here! That's impossible." I put down my sandwich, more interested in this conversation than stuffing my face. That was a first.

"I'm serious. I was the queen of fast food. The faster, the better. The greasier it was, the more I liked it. Then one night I thought I was having a heart attack. It turned out to be nothing more than indigestion, but it sure scared me—and it saved my life."

"Wow. That is scary."

"It changed my life. The doctor in the emergency room told me about this book that's all about eating right and exercise. It combines weight training and cardio workouts. It turned around my entire life. I'm finally happy for the first time ever."

"Great. I'd never be able to do anything like that."

I felt miserable. Ginny got fat and decided to start a fitness plan. Me? I call the first lawyer I stumble upon and sue an entire industry.

"You'll never know until you try, Kristen. I thought the exact same thing, but look at me now." She pointed to her own body. "And with this comes good health."

I looked at her toned muscles and sleek form with envy. She didn't have an ounce of fat on her. "Do you really think so?"

"I know so. Here's the name of the book." She grabbed a pen out of her purse and scribbled on a napkin.

I pulled it toward me. Body For Life. I was still convinced I'd be Fat For Life. Nonetheless, I went straight to the bookstore after work and picked up a copy. That night I read it from cover to cover, astounded by how easy it sounded.

Was it too good to be true? Ginny was my living proof that it worked, but she might have had more willpower in her little finger than I'd ever possess in my entire body.

Skeptical, I decided to give it one week to see what would happen. Ginny offered to let me use her guest membership at the gym to try it out. Dragging my butt out of bed at five o'clock A.M. so I could workout before going to work was by far the hardest thing I've ever done in my life. I walked into the gym filled with trim men and women feeling self-conscious and inferior in my sweats and a baggy T-shirt. No one seemed to notice me, though—that is, until I attempted to do a bicep curl. A good-looking buffed man walked over to me.

"Do you mind?" he said. Grabbing my arms, he showed me the correct way to lift.

"I think you'll be happier with the results if you can concentrate on good form."

"I doubt that. I'm only lifting five lousy pounds."

"It really doesn't matter how much you lift. Form is much more important. My name is Jim, by the way. Hope to see you around more often. If you need help or have questions, don't hesitate to ask."

"Do you work here, Jim?" That had to be the reason he wanted to help me. It was his job.

"Nope. But I'm here all the time. Only too happy to help out a pretty girl." He winked, then walked away.

Jim was just the incentive I needed to get my butt to the gym everyday that week, even if my muscles were so sore I could barely crawl out of bed.

By the end of the week I almost felt like I had some energy. Me—Little Miss Obese was totally digging getting up and exercising! I actually looked forward to it. How cool was that? Jim always smiled and waved when he saw me, which made me blush like a kid with a first crush.

I promised myself I wouldn't get on a scale until I'd completed the first week. When Sunday finally came around, I went into the bathroom with trepidation. What if it didn't work for me like it worked for Ginny? What if I was destined to remain fat forever? Maybe I should have followed through on the lawsuit just to get money, despite the fact that it made me feel dirty.

I forced myself to step on the scale. I stared at the result, stepped off and then stepped right back on again. The number couldn't be correct. Was the darn thing broken? Despite my disbelief, it read the exact same number again. Eight pounds lost? In one week?

I danced around the bathroom, then ran for the phone and called Ginny. "I lost eight pounds!" I practically screamed as soon as she said hello.

"You didn't 'lose' them, Kristen. That implies you'll find them again. You got rid of them. I'm so proud of you. I told you it would work if you just put some effort into it."

"Ginny, I can't thank you enough for telling me about this fitness program. You saved my life."

"You did all the hard work. I just got you started."

Six months have passed and I'm still working out. I don't look like Ginny yet, but I'm well on my way. It's not always easy, but I'm determined to meet my goals and lose all my excess weight. The slimmer I get, the more Jim's gaze follows me around the gym.

Yes, I'm a member now. The company that had employed us for temporary work was so impressed with the output that Ginny and I managed on a daily basis that they hired us after one month. We've become best friends and help each other through the program when we lose our motivation and times get rough.

I can't believe that I ever thought about suing a corporation because I had let myself go. Sometimes I'm embarrassed just thinking about it, but then I remember that I never signed on the dotted line—even though Bulldog Morgan called me every night for three weeks. I just couldn't do it. My mother had been right. Who would have ever thought?

I was responsible for my own actions. I caused myself to become obese. Now I was causing myself to lose that weight.

I'm prouder and happier than I've ever been in my life. Besides the cosmetic benefits, my doctor recently gave me the good report that my blood pressure is under control and I'm in very good health. I won't be eating myself into an early grave. I've learned so much about myself in the past six months. I've proved that there is nothing I can't tackle if I want it badly enough.

And on that note I have only one thing to say: Look out Jim! THE END

THE DOG DAYS OF SUMMER

I learned that size doesn't always matter.

Although I had been quite an athlete in school, I had let years sweep by without much exercise at all. One day, when trying to fit into some of my favorite slacks, I realized I had gained too much weight to even zip them up.

Devastated, I was determined to get control of my weight before it became too much of an issue. I wanted to join one of the local weight loss programs in town, but I couldn't afford it, nor could I afford to join one of the exercise clubs. So, I decided I would start walking every day.

My first thought was to get a partner, but then I decided that wouldn't allow me enough flexibility, so I set out on my own with my funny mutt of a dog, Squeak. It was hot our first day out, and we didn't get very far, but I did get in the required twenty minutes. After that, every day after work, Squeak and I hit the pavement, and I was truly feeling and looking a lot better. Even Squeak was showing signs of improvement.

Gradually, we added more minutes, distance, and speed. Soon I realized I had become bored with walking around my neighborhood. Although Squeak and I were never attacked by any of the numerous dogs, they barked at us incessantly and we always had to watch out for cars.

The most logical place for us to walk would be at the city trail.

It had been built a few years before and was quite a popular place. It would be a bit inconvenient because I'd have to drive to the park, but I felt that the positives would outweigh the one negative.

The trail was beautiful. Paved paths meandered through dense trees and occasionally crossed a babbling brook. Although it was a popular place, there were times I felt uneasy being alone in the woods with just Squeak. She hardly weighed ten pounds soaking wet, and her bark was not even a yelp; it was more of what her name implied—a squeak.

I tried to convince myself I was just being silly. We had very little crime in our town and what were the odds that I'd ever become a victim?

One day, on our way to the park, I stopped by my mom's house for a brief visit.

"You look wonderful," she exclaimed. I was glad I'd stopped by. Getting confirmation on my improving figure was uplifting.

"You think so?" I asked, fishing for more compliments.

"I know so," she assured me. "But I don't like you walking out there all by yourself. I'd feel better if you had someone with you."

"Oh, Mom! There are people everywhere—families, couples, and little kids. There's nothing to worry about," I protested.

"I'm sure you know best, but at least keep Squeak with you."

"Oh, absolutely," I laughed, and I held Squeak close to Mom's face for a kiss. "She'll protect me."

Mom giggled as Squeak licked her.

I felt good about Mom's compliments and I had been getting them at work too. They made it easier for me to talk myself into taking the long path through the park in order to get the best possible workout. There were evenings when I hit the trail late, but I still chose the long path. Sometimes I returned to my car just as the sun set. This day, because I had visited Mom, was going to be one of those days. I was late for sure, but if we walked fast, and if I carried Squeak some of the way, we'd get back to the parking lot before complete darkness set in.

Squeak and I were just about to cross one of the little bridges when I heard footsteps running up behind me. My heart started pounding. Mom's fears of my being out there alone flooded my mind. Squeak stopped dead in her tracks and turned to see who or what was approaching. I jerked at her leash to make her walk. My heart beat harder and harder as the steps got closer and closer. Finally, the person was at my side, and I was on the verge of screaming when a polite voice said, "Good evening," and a nice looking man passed on by.

The relief was overwhelming. I chided myself for being such a sissy. The rest of the walk was totally uneventful. The lights in the parking lot had already begun to flicker on and few cars were in sight. I made a mental note not to start out so late in the evening, and if I had to, I needed to take one of the shorter trails.

Unfortunately, my schedule at work changed, and we were forced to go to the park later. I was confident, however, that we were perfectly safe since there had never been an incident. Evening after evening we made our way around the trails, often returning to the car just before dark.

One evening, a terrible storm blew up from nowhere, and Squeak and I were on the backside of the longest trail. The daylight turned to darkness with only the piercing lightening to sporadically illuminate the path. I knew there was a pavilion close by, if only I could find it in the dark. Just then, my foot slipped off the pavement and my ankle twisted with a snap. The pain was so intense I actually saw stars, something I'd never believed really happened to people.

I had dropped Squeak's leash, assuming she would stay beside me. She licked the rain and tears from my face, but with the next clash of thunder, she scampered away. My heart broke. I knew she couldn't possibly make it on her own; she'd get lost in the woods or make it to the highway and get run over.

"Squeak," I yelled. "Squeak, come back, please."

I had never been in a situation like this. There was no one on the trail, the rain was pounding, and the lightening was too close for comfort. I was sitting in mud, holding an increasingly painful ankle, and my best friend was off somewhere in the dark probably scared to death.

As much as I wanted to find the pavilion, the pain was too intense to stand up, much less walk. I began to cry harder because of Squeak and because of the pain, and I began to shake from fear. I was under tall trees and the lightening was low in the sky. It looked like I was stuck here for the night, and if the storm didn't let up, no one would be on the trail the next day. I knew Squeak didn't stand a chance.

After screaming and yelling in vain, I lay down in the mud and simply gave in to whatever would be. The next thing I knew, Squeak was licking my face and squeaking with excitement.

"Squeak! You're okay!" I gathered her up in my arms and squeezed her. Suddenly, things seemed a lot better.

"Hello? Hello? Miss? Can you hear me?" I heard a voice calling.

"Yes, oh yes. I'm over here," I cried.

Of course, whoever was calling me couldn't see me, but I could hear his footsteps getting closer. Finally, he was kneeling at my side.

"Are you alright?" he asked with concern.

"Not really," I admitted.

"Can you walk?

"No, I think I broke my ankle."

"Okay then, hold on," he instructed, and he swept me up in his arms. "There's a pavilion just up the path. We'll go there."

The next thing I knew, I was in some stranger's arms being jostled up and down in the pitch black as rain pelted my face. Soon, I felt cold concrete on my back as the man set me down on what I presumed to be a picnic table.

"Thank you, thank you," I said. "But where's my dog?" I cried.

"Here," the man answered. "She's tiny and she fit in the pocket of my slicker." He handed her to me. "She may be tiny, but she's awfully smart. She led me right to you."

"You've got to be kidding," I said. "Squeak led you? I honestly didn't think she could do that. Oh, I love her to pieces, but I look after her, not the other way around, or so I thought."

"Well give her credit, because she certainly helped me find you."

"Pavilion G," he said.

"I beg your pardon?" I couldn't see he had spoken into a radio.

I was to learn that this man whom I could barely see was an off-duty policeman. He often jogged the trail himself and had seen Squeak and me on several occasions. When the storm began brewing, he had wisely cut his jogging short and gone back to his car, but he had waited for all the other people to leave, just to make sure everyone was okay. He became worried when my car was left in the lot. Soon he saw Squeak running out of the woods. She stood there in the rain, at the edge of the trees, making the most unusual noise he's ever heard any dog make.

"Like a squeak?" I asked.

"Yes, a squeak. Like a little stuffed animal, but she was very, very animated," he chuckled and then continued, "I knew when I didn't see you with her that something was wrong. I radioed the station; help is on the way."

"Oh, I am so embarrassed." I shook my head in disbelief at the predicament I had gotten myself into.

"Don't be! I've been trying to think of a way to meet you," he admitted. "So now, I've gotten the chance."

An SUV pulled up to the pavilion. I was carried to it and given a rather comfortable ride back to the parking lot. I prayed there wouldn't be an ambulance waiting. Thankfully, there wasn't. Under the lights I could see my rescuer—he was the jogger that had scared me that one evening.

"Oh, I know you! Well, I don't know your name, but I've seen you," I said with a huge smile as he lifted me into the backseat of my car. "Where are we going?" I continued.

"I'm taking you to the emergency room. And for the record, my name is Les. What's yours?"

I had to laugh. "Leslie," I told him.

In the hospital, Les took care of Squeak while the doctor set my foot. Then Les drove me home. It was almost daylight by the time I plopped down on my comfortable sofa.

"What a nightmare!" I exclaimed.

"Oh, I wouldn't look at it that way. I'm sorry you broke your ankle, but at least I got my chance to meet you. I never dreamed I'd get to spend the night with you!" he laughed.

"I wish I could say I had enjoyed it, but I cannot tell a lie. However, you'll never know how grateful I am."

He smiled. " As much as I'd like to stay and get to know you better, I'm sure you need some rest. Can I help you to your room?" he asked.

"No, you've carried me around enough for one day. You better be glad I've lost weight from all my walking or I could have broken your back."

"I don't think so," he said with certainty.

For the next few days, Les came to check on me. One day he called to tell me he had nominated Squeak for a Hero's Award and she had won! The newspaper would be out to take a picture of us that same afternoon. I was so excited. When I dressed for the picture, I wanted to wear my favorite slacks—now they fit like a dream—but I certainly didn't want to cut the leg out to accommodate my cast, so I settled for a slim-fitting skirt.

When the article ran in the paper, it read, "Squeaking Dog Saves Master." Everybody got a laugh out of that, but it was the truth. Les and I began dating immediately, and he became my walking partner—and more—as soon as the cast came off my leg. I had never felt safer or been happier in my life.

How fortunate I was to get caught under those dark clouds with my squeaking little companion. On that dark and stormy night, I met the love of my life. THE END

Sweet Romance!

BACK-TO-SCHOOL MAKEOVER

"Falling in love made me beautiful!"

Matt Jones was the heartthrob of Lincoln High. He fit the expression, "tall, dark, and handsome" to a tee. Every day, the Lincoln girls thanked the good Lord above for His wondrous creation. Every night, they dreamed sweet dreams about their dashing hero.

You'd think that all that adoration he got from the girls would make the guys hate Matt, but they didn't. Instead, they jockeyed for position as his best friend—currying favor, running errands, and catering to his every whim. Matt definitely had the "magic touch." Girls swooned, guys schmoozed—all in all, it was pretty disgusting.

Not that I was totally impervious to his charms. I am human, after all.

I confess that I, too, melted a little whenever he happened to look my way, and I'll admit that I often lingered by the water fountain a little longer than necessary just to watch him strut by with his entourage on the way to his locker. And, yes, I confess that I had a dream or two that starred Matt Jones. So what? A girl can dream, can't she?

I knew that it would never come true. I was a geek from Geeksville, and as such, I knew that there was no way on the face of the earth that I'd ever have a chance with a guy like him. And that was fine with me. I had my science projects and my photography club, the Shutterbugs. I was the secretary/treasurer of the Eco-Green Society. I even got one of the main parts in the all-school drama production of The Effect of Gamma Rays on

Man-in-the-Moon Marigolds. Of course, I suspected that I got the part not so much due to my great acting ability, but because the character, Tillie, was so much like me—a misfit interested in science. Still, everyone congratulated me on how well I did, and we placed first in the contest. All in all, I was a happy camper.

It's true the boys weren't exactly beating down my door. I'd never even had a date. I didn't belong to the popular crowd, and I didn't socialize with prom queens or cheerleaders. That would break some people's hearts, but I'm a practical sort, and I knew that I'd never fit in with those kids, anyway. So, why should I worry about it? I was satisfied with my station in life. I had my own little circle of friends. Maybe we were all freaks and geeks, but that was okay. We were true blue friends to the end—all for one and one for all.

Life had its moments of glory, too, like the time Charlie Bell shot milk out of his nose in the school cafeteria. That gave us fodder for conversation for a whole week.

My senior year at Lincoln High was going okay. It was no great shakes in the love department, but what else was new? When I woke up that fateful Monday morning, I had no idea how much my life was about to change.

The day started out pretty much like always, with Mom hollering at me to get out of bed. I quickly ate a bowl of oatmeal, gulped down a glass of orange juice, and ran out the door.

That Monday progressed uneventfully, save for a pop quiz in history class and a terrible moment when the power went out while I was typing my sixteen-page term paper in the computer lab. That day I finally understood why Mrs. Hicks was always admonishing us, "Don't forget to back up!" I had to type the paper all over again from scratch. Luckily, I had my notes to work from.

I was feeling stressed out from the pop quiz and the blackout incident, so I was glad that no other catastrophes struck me before it was time to go home. I rummaged through my locker trying to gather the books that I'd need that night. As an honor student, I always had tons of homework. I never could understand why honor students always have so much more homework than everyone else. Is it some kind of punishment from the gods because we have more brainpower than the other kids? I was pondering this very question when I shut my locker and discovered the hunk-of-all-time standing right in front of me.

I gasped. I thought it must be my imagination, so I rubbed my eyes and looked again. Much to my amazement, he was still there.

Matt, the prince of Lincoln High, had never given the slightest indication that he even knew that I existed. What in the world was he doing standing at my locker?

He flashed a bright smile. "Hi, you're Chandra Washington, aren't you?"

For a crazy moment, I couldn't remember what my name was. "Yes," I finally managed to utter weakly.

"I was wondering if you could help me."

"Help you?" My knees were about to buckle underneath me. I was painfully aware of what a mess I must've looked like. I'd just gotten out of phys ed, and we'd played a particularly vicious game of hockey.

"I'm having some trouble with algebra," he continued. "I wondered if you could tutor me."

"Tutor you?" I echoed like a dummy.

"Yes. I've heard about you."

"Heard about me?" I've got to stop this echoing business, I

thought. I'm not the Grand Canyon.

"Everyone knows that you're the smartest kid at Lincoln," he praised.

I blushed. What kind of planet was I on where Matt Jones not only knew that I existed, but also knew my name, and was complimenting me all over the place? Had I died and gone to heaven?

"Oh, I don't know if I'm the smartest," I replied modestly, although I knew that he was right. I had the grade point average to prove it. If there had been an Eggheads Club at Lincoln High, I would've been a shoe-in for president.

"I'm a willing pupil," he teased.

I blushed again.

"So, how about it, Chandra? My parents will pay you. Please?"

"I'm a little rusty in algebra."

"I'll bring you up to speed." He smiled.

"I don't know."

"Pretty please, with sugar on top?" His voice could melt butter.

"Well, maybe I could review the textbook before our first lesson," I conceded.

"Great!" he exclaimed. "How soon can we get started?"

"I'll need some time to prepare. Would next week be soon enough?"

"Hmm. I was really hoping that we could start sooner than that."

"How much sooner?"

"Well, I was really hoping tomorrow."

"Tomorrow?" I asked doubtfully, but then I looked into his beseeching, velvety brown eyes. "Tomorrow it is," I acquiesced.

"Is five-thirty in the library okay?"

"Great!" He dug his algebra book out of his book bag and handed it to me. "We're on chapter five, page three hundred and seventy-six," he said, consulting the page that he'd flagged.

"I'll need to find a copy machine," I said, looking around. "I think there's one in the office."

"Not necessary. Take it."

"Won't you need your book before tomorrow?"

"Naw."

"What about your homework?"

"I won't understand it, anyway." He shrugged. He turned to go, then turned back around. "I won't forget this, Chandra," he said, flashing that blinding smile again. "You're a lifesaver."

I watched as he sauntered off down the hall, his entourage joining him.

"Was that Matt Jones?" my best friend, Jasmine, gasped, clutching my arm.

"Yes," I answered, my voice full of wonder. I still couldn't believe what had just happened.

"Spill, girl!" Jasmine ordered. "What did he want?"

"He wants me to tutor him."

"Get out!"

"No, really. He wants me to tutor him in algebra, starting tomorrow."

"Way to go, girlfriend!" Jasmine high-fived me. "I knew that brain of yours would come in handy one day."

"Oh, and I guess it didn't come in handy during the last five minutes of the Quiz Bowl, when we were tied with Lakewood and I answered the question—"

"Yeah, yeah," Jasmine said impatiently. "How many times are you going to relive that moment? It was a fine accomplishment,

I'll admit, but this is really important. This is real life, not just some crazy bowl that doesn't amount to a hill of beans."

"Thanks a lot."

"You know what I mean. This is the big time. This is Matt Jones we're talking about, for heaven's sake."

"So? He's just a guy."

Jasmine stared at me, open-mouthed. "Just a guy? Bite your tongue, woman!"

"He is kind of cute," I admitted.

"What are you talking about, girlfriend?" Jasmine cried. "Kind of cute, shoot!" she scoffed. "That man is the bomb. Look out, Hiroshima!"

I laughed. Jasmine had a unique way of looking at things.

"Come on, Chandra, admit it," Jasmine continued. "You've got the hots for him just like the rest of us do."

"Well, maybe I do," I agreed, "But it won't do me a bit of good if I don't get cracking on this algebra. I don't know how in the world I'll be ready to tutor him by tomorrow."

"You can do it, girlfriend. They don't call you The Brain for nothing."

I had a lot of homework myself that night, but I put it aside to tackle chapter five in Matt's algebra book. I'd aced algebra my freshman year, so it didn't take long to refresh my memory. Chapter five was on quadratic equations. Piece of cake. After an hour or so of review, I was ready to impress Matt with my tutoring ability and transform him into a mathematical genius.

And I would have, too, if I could've located him. Tuesday afternoon at five-fifteen I was waiting eagerly in the library with sharpened pencils and sample problems—the whole works. At five-thirty sharp I turned toward the door, anxiously awaiting Matt's arrival. By six, my "willing pupil" still hadn't made an appearance. I was starting to get hungry, so I dug out a roll of Necco Wafers from my purse.

I'd told Mom that I'd be late for supper because I had to go to the library, and that I'd just pop something in the microwave when I got home. Now, I thought longingly of the lasagna that I was missing.

At six-thirty I packed up my gear and headed out the door. I was walking down the stairs when I saw Matt racing up them.

"I'm so sorry I'm late," he apologized breathlessly. "Coach just let us out of practice."

"You could've called," I pointed out.

"No phones on the football field," Matt answered lightly.

"You're lucky I'm still here."

"Very lucky," he agreed. "Say, I'll bet you're mighty hungry by now.

"No." I lied because I was still a little miffed.

"Come on, let me take you out for a bite. It's the least I can do. What do you like—Chinese? Italian? We could always hop on over to The Pit for the best ribs this side of heaven. What do you say?"

"No, that's all right."

"Come on," he cajoled. "Give me a chance to make it up to you."

Truthfully, I was awfully hungry, and those ribs sounded tempting. But Matt was the most difficult to resist.

"Okay, but first I have to call my mom and tell her where I'm going."

"Sure." Matt smiled.

He waited while I made the call. I told Mom that I was going out to eat with a friend. I didn't specify which friend, and I didn't tell her that he was a male. I just didn't feel like going into a long explanation. It was no big deal, I told myself. Still, I couldn't quiet the butterflies in my stomach, and I hoped that Matt couldn't hear my knees knocking.

Just wait till I tell Jasmine, I thought. She'll have a cow.

"The Pit?" Matt asked, linking his arm through mine.

"The Pit," I agreed, unable to suppress a smile. I'd been irritated at being stood up, but I quickly learned that you couldn't stay mad at Matt for long.

"I've never been here before," I said as we paused in front of a squat brick building with smoky glass windows.

"You're in for a treat," he said, holding the door open for me. He may be a slacker, I thought, but at least he's a gentleman.

We slid into a booth in the corner. I would've liked to have been more visible—after all, it's not every day that you go out to eat with Matt Jones—but all the other booths were taken.

I looked around. There were a few teenagers, but unfortunately, no one I recognized. The mahogany booths had high backs and there were red, checkered tablecloths covering the tables. Each table had a white vase with a plastic flower in it. Ours was pink.

"Why, hello there, sweetie," the waitress said, flicking her pencil out of her beehive hairdo so she could write on a pad. She had long red fingernails, and all two hundred-plus pounds of her was squeezed into a turquoise jumpsuit. "What can I get for you today? The usual?"

"Hello there yourself, Gail," Matt said. "The usual sounds good. You're looking fine as always."

Gail giggled. "Get along with you, sweet-talker," she said, obviously pleased. "Look me up when you turn legal."

"What about your old man, Harley?"

"That old crow?" she scoffed. "When you come calling, I'll just kick his skinny butt out the door."

Matt laughed.

Gail turned to me. "Don't mind us," she said. "We're buddies from way back. I remember when he was in diapers and I was fifty pounds thinner. What can I get for you today, hon?"

"What exactly is the usual?" I asked.

"Big old slabs of ribs dripping with sauce that will set your tongue on fire. They come with big, fat potato wedges and a nice tall glass of ice-cold lemonade.

"Sounds good."

"You want that without the hot sauce, though," Gail said.

"Hot sauce is fine."

"I've got to warn you, hon, that sauce has brought grown men to their knees."

"I've eaten some pretty hot stuff before. Mom says I have a cast-iron stomach. I'll be fine."

"Are you sure?" Matt asked. "When they say hot, they mean hot!"

"I'm sure," I said, an edge creeping into my voice. "I figure I can handle a little hot sauce." What was this, the Spanish Inquisition?

Matt and Gail exchanged looks. Matt shrugged. "The lady wants it hot."

"Then hot it'll be," Gail affirmed. She winked at Matt. "I'll bring some extra lemonade."

"This place is too quiet. We need some tunes," Matt said, strolling over to the jukebox. He selected the latest Hoobastank song.

"Ah, that's more like it," he said, settling back into his seat.

Matt silently regarded me with his amazing brown eyes. A slight smile played around his lips, and I began to shift uncomfortably beneath his gaze.

Finally, he spoke. "So, Miss Chandra Washington, how is life treating you?"

"I can't complain," I said. That's the understatement of the year, I thought. Here I was, sitting across the table from Matt Jones, the hottest hunk in the universe, staring into his exquisite brown eyes, and dreaming about what it would be like to kiss those inviting, luscious lips. What could be better than that?

Just then, Ivy Jackson walked in with two others from her crowd, Courtney Towne and Jewel Carter. I saw the startled looks on their faces when they caught sight of Matt and me, an unlikely pair by any stretch of the imagination. And, in that instant, I knew what could be better: Ivy Jackson, homecoming queen, could see Chandra Washington, geek, having dinner with the idol of Lincoln High. It was the most thrilling, proud moment of my life.

Out of the corner of my eye, I saw the trio sit down in a booth not too far from ours. I figured that I might as well milk the situation for all it was worth; there was no telling when I might get a chance like this again. I leaned forward and touched Matt's arm. Then I laughed uproariously, even though I hadn't the foggiest idea of what he'd just said. I could tell by the curious expression on his face that it must not have been funny.

Just then, Jewel sidled up to us. "Hello, Matt," she purred. I knew without turning around that the other girls were watching us from their booth.

"Hello there, Jewel. You look sensational this evening."

"So do you," she murmured.

For a moment she just stood there, transfixed, smiling at Matt. Her eyes stayed glued to his face. Then I think she remembered what she was there for, and she turned her attention to me. "And who might this be?" she asked, with raised eyebrows.

Even though I sat across the aisle from her in homeroom, she had no idea who I was.

"Chandra Washington," I said, extending my hand. She didn't shake it. It felt like a limp fish was hanging off the end of my arm, so I withdrew it quickly and placed it in my lap. "I'm in your homeroom."

"Oh, really?" She smiled like a barracuda.

"We just stopped in for a bite to eat," Matt said.

The waitress suddenly appeared behind Jewel juggling a tray full of food and three overflowing glasses of lemonade—one for me, one for Matt, and the extra one that she'd promised.

Jewel made no move to get out of her way. Gail glared at her back.

"Well, I guess I'll be going," Jewel said. "So long, Matt. Nice to meet you, Coral."

"Chandra," I corrected, but she was already gone.

"She's some piece of work," Gail muttered, looking over at Jewel. She set our plates and drinks down in front of us.

"I won't need this extra one," I said, pushing the extra glass away.

"Oh, that's okay, hon," Gail said. "It's on the house."

"Thanks, doll face," Matt said with a wink.

"Any time," Gail replied. "You folks enjoy your meal."

The potato wedges were seasoned, and they were delicious. I took a leisurely sip of lemonade. Then I took a big bite of rib. It was a mistake. Choking, I grabbed for the lemonade and gulped as fast as I could. Tears sprang to my eyes, and it felt like my mouth was on fire.

"Are you okay?" Matt asked.

"Fine," I managed to gasp.

"I could have Gail take it back and get you a milder sauce."

"I said I'm fine," I snapped, mortified, especially since I'd been so emphatic about having the hot sauce in the first place. I could feel my face turning red.

I took a look at Ivy's table. The girls were cracking up.

"Everything okay here?" Gail asked.

"Great," I lied, smiling at her weakly. My eyes were still watering.

"How are the ribs?"

"Delicious. Just the way I like them."

Matt guffawed. I ignored him.

"Well, if you need anything else, just let me know," she added.

"Will do," I replied. The minute she left, I gulped down some more lemonade. Matt was trying not to laugh, but it was a losing battle. He burst out laughing.

"Sorry," he apologized when he finally regained control. "You just looked so funny, with your tongue hanging out and your eyes all watery like that."

"Thank you," I said dryly.

I cut the rest of the ribs into bite-sized pieces and slowly chewed. Each small, delicate bite was accompanied by lots of lemonade. Even so, by the time the meal was over, I'd drained my glass of lemonade, the extra glass, and part of Matt's.

Matt was right when he'd raved about the ribs. They were the best I'd ever eaten, even with the hot sauce. As long as you had a gallon of lemonade handy, you were all right.

I didn't want the meal to end. Matt was surprisingly easy to talk to, and he was so handsome that he took my breath away. Move over, Brad Pitt, I thought. Matt's in town and he's looking good.

He had the whitest teeth I'd ever seen. He could've been

in a toothpaste commercial. I could just see it: "Razzle Dazzle Toothpaste for that Razzle Dazzle smile," the announcer would say. Then the camera would zoom in for a close-up of Matt's pearly whites. They'd never be able to keep that toothpaste in stock.

All in all, sitting there holding court with Matt Jones was pretty exciting. Of course, the more I talked to him, the more the little irritating quirks of his personality surfaced. Just by talking to him, you could tell that he was used to getting things the easy way. I doubted that he'd ever had to work hard a day in his life. He got by on his good looks and his considerable charm. He was kind of conceited, to tell you the truth, but that was to be expected. If you look like that, I reasoned, you have a right to be conceited.

He also had an annoying habit of looking over my shoulder every couple of minutes to check out who was there. And he was an incorrigible flirt. He flirted with every female within a ten-mile radius—the waitress, the bus girl, and even the little old lady in the next booth. All the women had the same reaction: They were flattered and delighted. Have you ever seen a seventy-five-year-old woman blush and giggle? It's not a pretty sight.

Still, who was I to criticize? Whatever he was doing, it was obviously working. Everyone was under Matt's spell. So what if there were a few flaws in his personality, a few chinks in the armor?

Matt offered to drive me home, and I almost took him up on his offer, thinking about what a coup it would be for someone like me to ride in the famous red Mustang. But then I thought of Mom and the thousand and one questions she'd have, so I decided to walk, instead. We made an appointment for tutoring the next night at seven.

"I won't be late," he promised.

It was a beautiful, starry night, and there was a little nip in the air. I pulled my jacket tight around me and floated home, remembering all the details of my date with Matt Jones. Well, it wasn't exactly a date, but it was close.

I dialed Jasmine's number the minute I got to my room. I was so glad that my parents had finally let me have a cell phone. It'd been a long battle, but I'd persevered. There are just some things that a girl needs to say in private, out of the earshot of her nosy parents.

"You'll never guess what happened!" I cried when she came on the line.

"What?" Jasmine asked eagerly.

"I just went out with Matt Jones!"

Jasmine shrieked. "Details, girlfriend, give me details," she begged breathlessly.

"Well, I was supposed to tutor him at five-thirty, right? And then he didn't show up. I was so mad—"

"Yeah, yeah," Jasmine interrupted. "Get to the good stuff."

"Well, I was just leaving when I saw him coming up the stairs. That's when he asked me to go to The Pit with him, to make up for being late."

"Oh, yeah, The Pit. Great ribs. Go on."

"So, I called my mom and asked her if I could go—"

"Yeah."

"And she said I could—"

"Right."

"So we went!" I finished triumphantly.

Jasmine shrieked again. "You went on a date with Matt Jones!"

"Well, maybe it wasn't technically a date," I admitted. "I mean, he didn't call and ask me out or anything."

"Did he pay for the food?"

"Yeah."

"Then it was a date!" Jasmine confirmed.

"And, guess what else!" I continued.

"What?" she asked breathlessly.

"Ivy Jackson was there."

"Get out!"

"Honest to God. She was there with Courtney and Jewel."

"Ivy Jackson saw you with Matt Jones?"

"Isn't it great?"

"It'll be all over school by tomorrow!" Jasmine predicted. "Courtney and Jewel will spread the word. You're going uptown, girlfriend, mark my words."

Jasmine was right. When I walked into school the next day, I noticed that people were buzzing about something, but it took me a while to realize that they were buzzing about me.

It was the strangest thing. One day I was the invisible girl, and the next day, everyone wanted to be my friend. A steady stream of visitors stopped by my locker. People who had never spoken to me before acted like we were long-lost buddies. The popular kids, who just the day before wouldn't have bothered to throw me a life preserver if I were drowning, were suddenly flocking around me and hanging onto my every word.

I looked forward to the lunch hour, when I could discuss this baffling phenomenon with Jasmine. She had a good head on her shoulders. She'd know what to make of it all.

I spotted Jasmine in the cafeteria and was headed over to her when Jewel Carter waylaid me.

"Come sit with us, Coral," Jewel said, steering me by my elbow over to Ivy's table—the one where all the popular kids sat.

"Chandra," I corrected automatically. I followed her reluctantly, trying to catch Jasmine's eye. When I did, I shrugged apologetically. I figured that I'd have to wait a little longer to talk to Jasmine.

Courtney scooted over to make room for me at the crowded table. I sat at the vacant spot next to Ivy Jackson. I'd never been that close to her before.

Ivy Jackson wasn't a mere mortal like the rest of us—she was an institution. She won everything—Prom Queen, Homecoming Queen, and Most Popular Girl.

Ivy turned to me. "You must be Lincoln High's best-kept secret," she said.

"What do you mean?" I asked, puzzled.

"Come on, don't be coy," she urged. "Give us the lowdown."

"What lowdown?"

"The lowdown on you and Matt Jones, of course."

"Oh." I laughed nervously.

"You two are quite the item. How long have you been seeing him?"

"Not long," I replied evasively. Well, that was true enough, I thought. I wished Jasmine were there. She was always good at fielding questions. I looked over at the table where she'd been sitting, but her spot was empty.

I was grateful when the conversation turned to other topics. My mind began to wander as I reviewed the amazing events of the day. Thanks to a false assumption regarding Matt Jones, my status was suddenly elevated in the eyes of the student body. Just yesterday I was a nobody, relegated to the sidelines, and today I was sitting at the popular table in the cafeteria. America is truly the land of opportunity, I thought.

I should've been delirious with joy, but surprisingly, as the lunch hour wore on, I found myself feeling restless and bored. I missed my old crowd. I knew that lots of kids would've given their eyeteeth to be in my position, but truthfully, I found the conversation artificial and contrived. I was actually relieved when the bell rang for us to return to class. In spite of the fact that I'd been surrounded by talking, happy teen-agers, it'd been a long, lonely lunch hour. I left the lunchroom flanked by Jewel and Courtney, my two new "best friends." I looked around for Jasmine, but she was nowhere in sight.

Jasmine wasn't waiting for me at my locker like she usually did after school, either. Usually, we caught a ride with her brother, Derek. I was beginning to get a bad feeling in the pit of my stomach. Oh, well, I thought glumly, I'll just have to call and straighten this all out when I get home.

I decided to stop in Room 101 to get my yearbook assignment. Several of us "shutterbugs" were taking pictures of student organizations for the yearbook. I located Reggie, the yearbook editor.

"Hi," I said. "I came to get my assignment."

He gestured to a bulletin board in the corner. "Over there."

As I was looking over the assignment sheet, he said, "I'm surprised that you have time to take pictures, what with your busy social calendar and all."

"I'm never too busy to take pictures," I said brightly.

Reggie didn't smile back. In fact, I was beginning to detect a definite coolness toward me. My suspicions were confirmed when he turned his back to me and silently went on with his work. I wondered what was going on. Usually, he was joking and laughing with me, but today, I could barely get two words out of him.

"Is something wrong?" I asked timidly.

"What could be wrong?" he replied icily.

"I don't know, you're just acting really weird."

"I'm acting weird, huh?" he spat. "I'll tell you who's acting weird—you are. You're the one who's acting weird."

"What are you talking about?"

"You. Dating that chump, Matt Jones."

"Well, I'm not really dating him exactly—"

"That's not what I heard," Reggie said. "I just never would've thought it."

"What?"

"That you'd be going out with Matt Jones. He's not exactly your type, you know."

"So?"

He shrugged. "So, nothing. It's just weird, that's all."

"What's so weird about it?"

"I thought you had better taste than that."

I stared at him. "Better taste than Matt Jones?" Is this guy nuts? I wondered.

"Yeah, I know. Everyone thinks he's so cool," Reggie said bitterly. "He's got everyone snowed. But I grew up around the guy. I've seen how he operates. He never does a lick of work if he can help it. He's a lazy, good-for-nothing loser. Sure, he's got a nice car and all the girls are crazy about him, but Matt Jones is all glitz and no substance. I thought that you, of all people, had enough intelligence to see through his game, but I guess I was wrong. You don't have any more sense than the rest of them."

I bridled. "One thing I can say about Matt Jones, is that he's always a gentleman. Too bad I can't say the same for you."

"Look, if you don't want to hear the truth, that's fine, but when he breaks your heart, don't come crying to me."

"I wouldn't come crying to you if you were the last man on earth!" I shouted. "You're just jealous, that's all."

"Jealous! Ha!" he snorted. "What do I have to be jealous about? It's not like I'm your boyfriend or anything. Go on, go out with the guy if you want to. It's no skin off my back. You're a free agent. You can go out with the wolf man for all I care."

"Okay, I will!"

"Fine!" He slammed the file cabinet shut.

"Fine!" I grabbed my book bag and marched out, only then realizing what I'd said. Okay, I'll go out with a wolf man? I shook my head. It had been a crazy day.

My conversation with Jasmine didn't go much better. Derek answered the phone, and I could hear him hollering for her in the background, but it took forever for her to come to the phone.

"Why didn't you wait for me after school?" I asked. "I ended up walking home alone."

"Oh, I figured that you'd get a ride with Ivy and her crowd," Jasmine replied airily.

"Look, I'm sorry about lunch. I was looking for you, but then Jewel Carter came and dragged me to her table."

Jasmine yawned. "Well, I guess that's to be expected."

"What?"

"That you'll be wanting to sit with them from now on."

"Now why in the world would I want to do that?"

"You're dating Matt Jones, aren't you?"

"It was just that one time, and it wasn't really a date."

"He paid for the food; it was a date," Jasmine replied flatly.

"Anyway, that doesn't have to change things between us," I pointed out.

"Oh, it doesn't?" Jasmine asked, sarcasm dripping from her tongue.

"Of course not," I assured her. "Come on, Jasmine," I cajoled. "Why are you acting this way?"

"What way?"

"Like you're mad because I ate with Ivy."

"What do I care who you eat with? You're free to eat with whomever you choose. In fact, you can eat with them tomorrow, if you so desire. I'm sure they'll save you a place."

"Jasmine, I don't want to eat with them," I insisted. "I'd much rather eat with you. You wouldn't believe how boring it is."

"Is that so? Well, I wouldn't know, because I've never been invited to eat with them."

"Believe me, you're not missing anything."

"Oh, that's my mom calling. Got to go." She clicked off.

I sat there on my bed, the receiver still to my ear. I knew that Jasmine was lying about her mom. I could always hear her mom calling for her in the background, but this time, there had been nothing but silence.

I sat in the library that night, dejected, and consulted the wall clock yet again. The library closed at nine; it was a quarter to. Okay, Matthew, I thought, you've got fifteen minutes to get your tail in here. I sighed. He was supposed to meet me at seven. I wondered what his excuse would be this time, if he made it at all—which at this point was doubtful.

The librarians were packing up and getting ready to go home. The last of the patrons were checking out their books and gathering their homework assignments.

Well, I thought as I hurried down the darkened stairs of the library, Matt didn't lie. He's not late; he just didn't show up.

As I walked home, I realized that, harsh as it was, Reggie's assessment of Matt had been basically correct. In spite of his astounding good looks and suave, sophisticated manner, Matt was indeed a selfish, good-for-nothing loser. I'd suspected as much when I'd talked to him at The Pit, but I'd been too taken with him to think clearly.

It's been quite a day, I thought. I could understand now why Jasmine was angry. After all, I'd stood her up in the cafeteria just like Matt had stood me up in the library. But why was Reggie so miffed? I wondered. He acted like my dating Matt Jones was a personal affront. Why did he care? And why did I care that he cared? Puzzled, I shook my head. Why did life have to be so complicated?

Matt stopped me in the hallway at school the next morning. "Chandra!" he greeted me heartily, just as if nothing had happened. "You're just the person I want to see."

"Where were you last night?" I demanded. "You were supposed to meet me at seven."

"Oh, Chandra, I clean forgot. I'm sorry. I hope you didn't wait long." He gazed at me apologetically with those sad, puppy-dog eyes. "I'll be there tonight, I promise."

"You may be there, but I won't."

"Come on, Chandra," he coaxed. "Help me out on this, will you? I've got a test coming up in a few days, and I'm really lost."

"You should've thought about that before you stood me up, twice."

"I said I was sorry."

"Sorry doesn't cut it."

"But my folks will be steamed if I flunk another course. They're threatening to take my car away until I get my grades up."

"That's too bad, Matt, but it's really not my problem."

He tried another tack. "We could hit The Pit again after our study session," he bribed in a silky voice. "They've got great ribs, remember?"

"Best ribs this side of heaven," I agreed, quoting him.

"So, you'll help me?"

"I'm sorry, Matt. You should try the after-school tutoring program sponsored by the math department," I suggested.

"But you're the best," Matt replied. "If it's the money you're worried about, my parents will pay you for your time. They're very generous. They'll even pay you for the two sessions I missed."

"That's not necessary."

"Please," he begged. "Pretty please, with sugar on top? I've really got to pass that test."

It took all of my willpower, but I looked him straight in the eye and said, "Not this time, Matt. You're on your own."

I left him standing in the hallway, a quizzical smile on his face. It was probably the first time anyone had ever said "no" to him.

I knew that it wouldn't take long for Ivy Jackson to deduce that Matt and I were no longer an "item." As soon as they got the word, I knew that she and her crowd would drop me like a hot potato. That was all right with me. I didn't enjoy being one of the popular kids, anyway. I'd much rather be me: a science misfit and oddball extraordinaire. Anyway, I didn't have time to worry about that right now. I had more important matters to deal with.

I found Jasmine at her locker and apologized for being such an idiot.

"That's okay," she said. "If it had been me that they wanted, I probably would've done the same thing."

"Is that so?" I said, cocking an eyebrow.

She grinned. "You bet your sweet life."

The final order of business was Reggie. I'd been thinking about him a lot since our argument, and I'd come to the conclusion that he really was jealous. Why else would he have acted like such a fool?

I found him in Room 101, hunched over one of the computers. He was editing a story for The Daily Voice, our school newspaper.

"I've set up the dates for the group pictures for the yearbook," I said. "All except Robed Choir. I haven't had a chance to talk to Mrs. Valades yet."

"Wow, that was fast," Reggie replied. He was in a much better mood than the last time I saw him.

I stood there awkwardly, not wanting to leave, but not knowing what else to say. "Uh, do you need some help?" I asked finally.

"Yeah, if you've got a little time, I'd really appreciate it."

"I've got all the time in the world," I assured him, pulling up a chair. Sitting so close to him, I realized that Reggie was every bit as handsome as Matt Jones was, but in a quiet, scholarly way. Matt might have had the flash, but Reggie definitely had the class.

Reggie turned to me. "Listen, I want to apologize for the way I acted yesterday. I don't know why I got so hot under the collar."

"That's okay."

"I know it's none of my business, but just the thought of you with that jerk makes my blood boil. You deserve better than him."

"Well, you don't have to worry. I don't think I'll be seeing Mr. Matt Jones anymore."

Reggie smiled. "No?"

I smiled back. "No."

"Well, I guess we'd better get to work. We're under a deadline, you know." We bent our heads over the computer. "Would you like to go out for a Coke or something afterward?" he asked shyly.

"I'd love to."

"Say," Reggie said, "if you're hungry, we could stop off at The Pit. I hear they've got killer ribs."

"Sure," I said, laughing. "Just make sure there's plenty of lemonade." THE END

NOTHING TO LOSE

Everything seemed to be my fault and I tried to eat my troubles away.

"Melissa, is that really you?" Angela, my next-door neighbor, said.

Angela had been traveling for a few months so she didn't know that I'd lost weight. "Twenty-five pounds today, thank you very much. And twenty-five more to go."

"You look fantastic!" she said.

"Thanks," I said, waving a hand as though to brush off my accomplishment.

But it *was* an accomplishment. Nobody loses that much weight without feeling proud. But I was also scared.

I could gain it back in a flash. I knew that.

Funny thing about losing weight. You think that once you've done it, you'll never have to worry about it again. But it's easy to slip back into old habits.

"How did you do it?" she asked.

"The old-fashioned way," I replied. "I just watched what I ate, especially in the evenings. And I walk to work now."

"I bet the men are really noticing, too," she said.

That was another thing about losing weight. People assumed you were losing it just to catch a boyfriend or a husband. But I had bigger reasons.

I smiled and shrugged, then set off for work. It took a big change in my schedule, but I was determined to get up at six o'clock each morning so I could walk to work. At first, all the extra activity was hard. Hauling around a body that was more than fifty pounds overweight made me exhausted by the end of the day. Some evenings I just collapsed into bed in my tiny apartment without even eating supper. And then the next morning it started all over again.

Men. Hah! If Angela only knew. I didn't have time for men.

One of the worst things about an eating addiction is that it consumes most of your time. Overeating is all about the negative voice inside your head. When you listen, you are like a captive audience. You feel like you have no choice but to sit there and listen to it over and over again. It's like a very demanding lover. It pushes out the good things in your life, like time with friends or walking along a beach and enjoying the feel of the water swirling around your feet. It crowds out those good things. Simple things.

The voice tells you that you're not good enough. You don't do your job well, or you look awful and no one would want to be your friend. It's a pushy voice, and what's worse, you believe it without questioning.

I realized that the voice was the quietest while I was at work and busy with other things. But after work—bam! I would go over and over the events of the day like a critic, blaming myself for everything from a mediocre performance review to a computer glitch. Then I'd grab a snack to comfort myself. And in those moments while I'm eating—just in those moments—the voice stops. That's why I ate.

For me, the voice sounded like my mother's—the person who had been the most critical of me. But although she might have started the cycle, I was the one who had let that negative voice stay in my head.

And I was the one who had to get it out. It wasn't easy, being nice to myself. It felt like pure indulgence. It was sad to think that I was actually getting comfortable with putting myself down every day. If I had a friend who treated me that badly, I would have dropped her like a rock.

It started slowly. After work, instead of berating myself for things that went wrong in the day, I immediately ran a bubble bath and soothed my tired muscles in the tub. It felt like heaven. And that was the trigger for a pleasant evening instead of one filled with torment.

I dug out hobbies and projects that I hadn't worked on in over a year. I began to rediscover my neighborhood, taking long walks after supper. It's amazing the people you meet when you're out walking. It felt good, and by the time I went to bed I didn't feel uncomfortable from a full stomach.

My life itself was full. On top of everything else I'd taken on extra shifts at work. Like with the weight loss, I had big plans for that extra money.

And wouldn't you know it, when you have big plans for anything, fate decides to jump in and try to wreck them. The money thing wasn't going as smoothly as I thought. Several unexpected bills came in—an increase in my rent and a couple of big wedding gifts to buy. And then, as Angela said, men were starting to notice me.

I worked with a lot of guys, but in the three years that I'd been at Lawton and Associates, I'd been practically invisible. That's what being overweight does to you. In spite of any achievements you have in your career, men seem to look past you and to the nearest attractive female. Well, that had been fine with me. I didn't need the complications of an affair right now.

I could ignore every man who had suddenly taken a passing interest in me, but I couldn't ignore Logan. He worked in a department on the top floor and I hardly ever saw him. But lately, it seemed like we were bumping into each other all the time—in the mailroom, the elevator, and even outside work as everyone was leaving for home.

"Hi, Melissa," he called out to me after work that day. "Heading for the bus?"

"No, I'm walking," I said.

"Walking? Do you live around here?"

I shook my head and tried not to act shy around him. I liked Logan. He wasn't like most of the other men who worked here. He'd always treated me with respect even when I was at my heaviest. There was a time when I thought he might ask me out. Then I went home and looked in the mirror.

"Why would he ask *you* out?" I said out loud to myself.

Everything, absolutely everything in my life was wrapped around my weight. If I didn't get a promotion, I blamed it on my weight. Being prejudiced against fat people seemed to be the last acceptable bigotry around. And hey, lucky me, I was fat.

And, okay, miserable. But it took more than that to get Melissa Phillips to lose weight. It took one huge scare.

"If you keep this up, you could be dead in two years," my doctor told me.

He'd been leading up to a lecture like this for a few years now. My blood pressure was high and I was borderline diabetic. He threatened to put me on all kinds of medication. But nothing had changed my habits until the day he told me to look in the mirror and think about planning my own funeral.

It was shocking. I left the office shaken, vowing never to come back to see him again.

But after I'd calmed down a little, I realized he was right. I just didn't feel good anymore. I ate all the time, except at work. It wasn't like I was hungry, either. No, I was an emotional eater. Any little thing that happened at work that day, I would brood on it when I got home. Everything seemed to be my fault and I tried to eat my troubles away.

That relief lasted just about the time it took to go through a box of cookies or half a cheesecake. Then the bad feelings came back and I reached for something else. No wonder my grocery bill was astronomical.

I used to look down on people who couldn't control themselves. How did I ever become one of them?

Those feelings threatened to overwhelm me each evening. And now, thinking about Logan and the brief conversation we had, I wanted to eat again. Even after just having supper. But I'd cleaned my kitchen of unhealthy food.

There was a little convenience store in the ground floor of my apartment building. I grabbed my keys and purse. I was halfway out the door, determined to buy something sweet and creamy to take my mind off the disturbing feelings that Logan had stirred up.

I stopped myself in time and went back into my apartment. I closed the door and leaned against it.

One thing I'd learned, the disturbing feelings don't go away with eating. It was like putting temporary freezing on a toothache. It would still be there, waiting for you and twice as bad, when the freezing wore off.

I had to think this through. I liked Logan. I liked him a lot. What was wrong with that? What would be so awful if he asked me out?

Why would he ask you out? Does he have a thing for fat girls?

That vicious voice in my head was always negative, always tearing me down. I went to the bathroom and looked in the mirror, trying to remind myself that I was looking good and was halfway to my weight goal. Not because I wanted to attract a man, but because I wanted to save my life.

If I wanted to get all psychological about it, I'd have to say that the bad feelings started with my mother. She was an unhappy woman in an unhappy marriage and she made sure each of us kids knew about her daily sacrifice of keeping the family together. When you don't have very good self-esteem, it's almost impossible not to pass those negative thoughts on to your kids.

"Melissa, I told you to avoid that school nurse. You don't need glasses! Where on earth are we going to find the money for that? Do you know that I haven't had a new coat in five years?"

Poor Mom. I didn't blame her. Now that I was an adult, I could see that she was out of her depth trying to stretch my father's small salary to feed and clothe six people. But for all her efforts, I didn't have many happy memories of her.

Yes, that voice in my head definitely was my mother's. That critical voice would be right there at the end of the day and that's when I would eat, eat, eat, to drown it out.

Not surprisingly, my love life had suffered. It was hard to get close to someone when the food came between you. Maybe it was time I did something about that.

The next day I went to the top floor at work and looked for Logan. I had to pass by several of his coworkers and one or two gave me an interested, curious look. I knocked on his office door.

"Come in."

I opened the door and he looked up from his drafting table.

"Melissa!" he said, his voice sounding pleased.

"Hello," I said, looking down at my hands and not knowing what to say.

"Come in," he repeated. "Have a seat."

In those few moments where he politely waited for me to tell him why I was there, I wanted to bolt out the door. I took a deep breath.

"I—uh, my neighbor gave me tickets to that new blues café. I wondered if you'd like to go. It's Saturday."

He looked at me as though he couldn't believe his ears.

Oh, boy, Melissa. You really screwed up this time. You'll be lucky if he doesn't laugh you out of his office.

"Saturday. . ." he said, looking at his computer calendar. "Let's see."

I sat there in embarrassment, thinking that he was just looking for an excuse not to hurt my feelings.

"If you're busy, I understand."

"No, wait a minute. It's the next weekend that I have to work overtime on a project. This Saturday's fine! What time?"

I stared at him, not believing it.

"Uh, two o'clock."

"Great! I'll pick you up."

I nodded and smiled and turned to leave. That had gone much better than I imagined it would!

"Melissa?" he said.

"Yes?"

"I think I'll need your address."

"Oh! Of course!"

Then he gave me the sweetest smile, one that said he liked me. I smiled back and he looked at me for the longest time, like he was just seeing me for the first time.

Wow. I left feeling like I was floating a couple of feet off the ground.

It felt strange and yet wonderful, going to that new café with

Logan. As we waited in line to be seated, his hand found mine. I could hardly believe it.

We didn't talk much as we ate lunch and listened to an incredible group of singers. I wasn't into jazz, but I loved the blues. It looked like Logan felt the same.

Afterwards we strolled along the streets downtown, still hand in hand. We sat on a park bench and I leaned my head on his shoulder. It just felt natural.

"I had a great time today, Melissa," he told me when we were back at my place.

"Me too," I said. I wanted to invite him in but I still felt shy.

"Well, see you at work on Monday," he said.

I was disappointed. He must have seen it in my face because he gave me a quick, unexpected kiss.

"We'll have to do this again. Soon," he said, and gave me the sweetest smile.

I was on cloud nine when I went into my apartment. Imagine, having a date with Logan! I was glad I had the courage to ask him out.

Of course he went out with you. He was just being polite.

No! I wouldn't let that negative voice destroy my memory of an almost-perfect day. I wouldn't.

I went downstairs to the workout room in our building and I really went at it. By the end I was sweating and exhausted, but I felt good about myself. I went to sleep that night feeling good, inside and out.

I didn't see Logan for the next few days at work. I tried not to think about the wonderful date we'd had. I wouldn't ask him out again. If he wanted to see me, he would have to be the one to approach me this time.

I didn't have to wait long. There was a small envelope on my desk on Monday morning. I opened it with trembling fingers.

Did I mention that I had a wonderful time on Saturday? How about we do something this weekend? Come to my place and I'll cook you supper. Logan.

I looked around, half expecting that this was a practical joke from someone. But it was real. I couldn't describe the feeling I had, one of excitement and untold possibilities. I really, really liked this guy.

But just like with dieting, there was always part of me that thought I might blow it. That I didn't deserve it.

I didn't try to contact Logan for a few days. He must have wondered if I even got his note because on Friday after work, he appeared at my office just as I was packing up to go home.

"So?" he asked, leaning against the doorframe. "Is the idea of my cooking so scary that you couldn't respond?"

"Oh, no, not at all!" I said, blushing madly. Just being around him was enough to get me tongue-tied like a twelve-year-old girl. "I'd love to come to dinner."

He beamed, detached himself from the doorframe, and went to my desk to quickly write down his address.

"And don't try to walk it, Mel. It's too far. Do you need a ride?"

"No. I do own a car," I said. "It's just that I need the exercise so I walk a lot."

He handed me the slip of paper. I knew where that neighborhood was. A very nice one. Logan must be doing well in the company.

"How about around seven o'clock?" he asked.

"That sounds fine," I replied.

I really wasn't ready for Logan's condo. It was absolutely gorgeous—high ceilings, hardwood floors, and bookcases that lined the walls.

"This is incredible!" I said, following him into the wide-open kitchen. "How long have you lived here?"

"About two years. I was lucky to find this, right downtown."

"You've got that right. How much did this cost—I'm sorry. That's none of my business."

"That's okay. And no, I can't afford this place on the salary I make at Lawton, although it's pretty good. No, I saved some money a while back and decided to put it into this place."

"Smart move," I replied. "I want to get a place of my own one day."

"You will," he said, handing me a glass of wine. "A toast. To us."

I nearly spilled my wine.

"Uh, of course," I managed to mumble, and we touched glasses.

Logan had made a gourmet meal with a special salad. I wondered if he cooked like this all the time.

"So tell me all about yourself, Mel," he said, using the nickname that I loved.

"Where do you want me to start?" I asked. "I skinned my knee when I was eight years old."

"I happen to find skinned knees fascinating," he joked. "Go on."

I laughed. He was so easy to be with. A part of me was thinking that I shouldn't be so open with someone I hardly knew, but it felt so comfortable talking to him. And yet, at the same time, my skin tingled when we accidentally brushed fingers as I helped him clear up the plates from the table. There was something there, all right. I was attracted to this man.

"How about you? What do you do for fun?" I asked.

He gave me a hot look, just for a moment, and I could feel

myself blushing. I seemed to do a lot of that around Logan.

"I like to travel. I do some rock climbing, but mostly I like taking long road trips in parts of the world where you really shouldn't take long road trips. It's the adventure, knowing that very few people have gone before you."

My heart started to beat faster. His adventure was pretty close to mine. I wondered if I should trust him with my dream. I'd kept it all to myself. A lifetime of having my ideas shot down had made me very cautious.

"I get the feeling that you want to tell me something, Mel," he said.

Slowly, I started to open up to him. "The reason why I'm trying to save money is because of a little place in Mexico that needs a new school. I found out about it when I was walking to work one day and passed a local church. They had a poster up asking for donations and people to go to Mexico and actually build the school. I want to take my vacation down there and help build that school."

"That sounds perfect!" he said. "When do you leave?"

"I haven't set a date yet," I hedged. The school project would start in about six months and would take at least a couple of months to build. "I still need to save the money." I didn't add that I still needed to lose all the weight, too. Before I could go to Mexico, I needed to get in shape to get ready for the physical labor, especially in such a hot place.

"If there's anything I can do to help, just let me know," he said.

"Thanks. Thanks, Logan, I'll do that."

I was surprised that I'd told him about that. It was a sign that I was slowly mending from my mother's harsh criticism of everything I did. It had been three years since she passed away. I was only now beginning to trust people again.

After supper, Logan showed me some of his books. He had a vast collection of everything from travel to investing.

He was handsome, he was successful, and he was very interesting. Then why wasn't he with someone?

He had some family pictures around his place, his parents and younger brother. But I couldn't see any of a young woman. I picked up the framed photo of Logan and his family.

"That was taken at my parents' cottage. Sid and I like to go climbing just a couple of miles from there."

"That's your younger brother?"

Logan nodded. I could tell he loved his family very much just by the way he was looking at the photo.

"He's not married?"

"Not yet. But there's a beautiful young woman who keeps showing up for family gatherings, so I get the feeling that it won't be long now."

I was dying to ask him about himself, if he had been serious about someone, or even married. But I didn't know how to approach the subject. After all, we didn't really know each other yet.

But it turned out that he was just as curious about me.

"What about you, Mel? Never been married?"

I shook my head.

"I looked after my mom for a few years. It was cancer, the slow kind. There was no one else to look after her. When she died, I guess I was just too used to being alone."

He took my hand and brought it to his lips.

"You don't have to be alone, you know," he whispered.

How I wanted to believe him! This was all happening so fast, this great guy who came into my life and my strong emotions about him.

Too good to be true.

That voice in my head was smug, like my mother's. The voice that said she was right.

It spoiled the moment for me. I slowly withdrew my hand from Logan's.

There was disappointment in his eyes, but he quickly recovered.

"How about some coffee? I make a mean espresso."

Logan must have felt that he was moving a little too fast because he didn't even try to kiss me good night. I wanted to tell him that it wasn't his fault, that I shied away from intimacy because of my own feelings of not being worthy. And with a man as nice as Logan, those feelings came on twice as strong. I just didn't feel like I deserved someone like him.

When I got home I stopped at the store and bought things I shouldn't have. I was halfway through a strawberry cheesecake before I even knew what I was doing.

Disgusted, I dumped the rest of it in the trash. Again, that automatic response had won out. I was binge eating.

But I stopped myself, I thought. I turned off that automatic switch for once. I had many reasons to be thinner. Most of all, my health. Then there was the project so close to my heart. I had to lose more weight in order to help build that school.

The amazing thing was, looking good for a guy was the last thing on my list these days. I liked Logan, I liked him a lot. But I had bigger reasons to be healthy right now. Stuffing my face to drown out the bad feelings just didn't make sense in my life anymore.

So instead of just walking to and from work, I started walking during lunch hours, too. I hadn't seen Logan in a couple of weeks, but I ran into him on one of my lunchtime walks.

"Mel! How have you been? I've been wanting to talk to you. Do you have a minute?"

"Sure," I said. We were near a little park and both sat down on a bench.

There was a pond where a little girl was trying to feed the ducks. It was more like she was assaulting the ducks with pieces of bread. Logan and I laughed.

"I love kids," he said wistfully.

I looked at him.

"You do? Then why don't you have any?"

The moment the words were out of my mouth I felt mortified. I had no business asking such a personal question. We still didn't know each other.

"I will, some day," he said, and looked at me for a long moment.

I looked away. The little girl was now leaving the park with her parents.

"So how are the plans for the school in Mexico?" he asked.

"Not bad," I said.

My savings were growing slowly for the project. My weight was inching down but not as fast as I'd like.

"Mel, I have something to ask you. I want you to know that if you say no, I'll understand completely."

"Sure. What is it?"

"I'd like to come along to your next meeting for that school project."

I turned to stare at him. He grinned a little self-consciously.

"You know I love to travel to out-of-the-way places. And I have some money I could use for a good cause. I've been thinking about your school ever since you told me about it. Do you think they could use another volunteer?"

My heart started beating faster. Logan, there in Mexico, with me? Part of me thought that would be fantastic. Another part remembered that this was my dream, to help out a community that wouldn't have that school unless volunteers went to build it. That should be the focus for me, not a budding romance.

But how could I say no? The project desperately needed more volunteers.

"The next meeting is this Thursday," I told him. There must have been some hesitation in my voice.

"Mel, if you'd rather I didn't go—"

"No, of course you should go," I said.

So that Thursday I introduced Logan to Mrs. Williston, the one who was heading the project for the school. Most of the members of the group were retirees, and Logan and I were about the youngest. Logan listened, fascinated, as the meeting progressed. We talked mostly about the finances and who would be doing what when we got to Mexico.

"So, Logan, how well do you swing a hammer?" Alex Cochrane, another of the retired members of the group, asked.

"I built a tree house once when I was eleven," he replied.

"He's hired!" Alex shouted, and we all laughed. I could tell they had taken to Logan right away.

But as Logan and I were walking back to my place after the meeting, he was unusually quiet. I invited him in for coffee.

"So, what do you think?" I asked.

"I think it's a great project."

"But?"

"But I think I'm going to pass on it this time."

"Why?"

"Melissa, this is your project. I like you very much and I want us to get to know each other a little better before we do something like this together. I've seen too many couples break up on trips abroad. I don't want that happening to us."

"Oh, Logan," I said, moving closer to him. "I—thank you. You're right. As much as I've come to like you, I was having second thoughts about the trip."

"Next year," he said, putting his arms around me. "Next year I plan that our relationship will be strong enough to withstand anything."

We kissed then, and all those old novels where the heroine can feel her toes tingle, that was me. It was a sweet, old-fashioned romance and I wanted it to last. Logan was right. Taking a trip together right now—one as demanding as the Mexico trip would be—should be saved for next year.

Next year. He was already seeing us together next year.

My bank account was rising and everything seemed on track. I was having more meetings with the church group to finalize plans. I probably wasn't looking at what I ate. Between dates with Logan and plans for my dream trip, my life was going so well that I didn't know I was actually gaining weight.

I stared at the scales. *No! I'd gained five pounds! How could that be?*

I immediately fell into a depression. Was I going to have to monitor myself like a prison warden the rest of my life? Well, that was that. I couldn't go to Mexico now.

Logan knew that something was wrong right away. I hadn't returned his phone messages and he sought me out at work.

"So what's up, Mel? You look awful."

Not the words a woman wants to hear.

"I haven't been sleeping. I think I may be coming down with something."

Yeah, Melissa. You're coming down with stupidity, the voice sneered.

"Want to get together after work?" he asked.

"No, I don't think so. I think I'll just go home and crawl into bed."

He offered to drive me home, knowing that I walked to work. But I declined, and in the end I took the bus home. It wasn't that I was really feeling sick. I was depressed. Depressed over having to cancel this trip of a lifetime. And all because I just couldn't stick to a diet.

About two weeks later, after I'd avoided Logan, someone buzzed my apartment.

"Mel, I know you're in there. I've just talked to Mrs. Williston at the church and she said you canceled the trip! She thought I knew. Let me in, Melissa, we have to talk."

Reluctantly, I buzzed him in. I quickly straightened up the apartment. I had stuff laying all around from packing for the trip days ago, when I thought I was still going. But not now. I hadn't wanted to do anything except eat lately.

"What's up?" he demanded when I opened the door.

"Nothing. I changed my mind. Is that all right with you?" I asked sarcastically.

"No, no it's not. And it's not all right with you either, Mel. What made you change your mind?"

I turned away from him and starting putting stuff away. He came to me and stood in front of me.

"You had your heart set on this trip. What changed?"

I wasn't going to get rid of him. I sighed. I didn't like talking about my weight to anyone.

"There were two things that had to be in place before I could go," I told him. "One was the money."

"And the other?" he asked.

"The other was, I had to lose a total of fifty pounds before I could go."

Logan looked puzzled.

"Your doctor told you that?"

"Not exactly," I said. "That was my goal. To lose fifty pounds. I was doing fine and then I started gaining weight again. I can't go now."

"Why not?" he asked, sounding incredulous.

He just didn't understand. Most men didn't. I shook my head.

"Seems to me like you're a perfectionist. If things aren't just perfect, then you don't want to do them at all."

I was surprised to hear him say that to me. But his words had a ring of truth to them that I didn't want to acknowledge.

"If I was a perfectionist, then I'd be perfect," I argued. "And I'm so *not* perfect."

"Let me tell you about being a perfectionist," he said. "It keeps you from enjoying life. Nothing is ever perfect, so you're never happy. You wake up each day believing that you are going to make things perfect, and it never happens. So you will never be happy."

"What do you know about it?" I snapped at him.

"I know about it very well," he said. "So well that I was in therapy for five years."

Logan? In therapy? I couldn't believe it.

But I thought about what he was saying. If a friend told me that she was canceling a trip because she had a few pounds to lose, I would have told her that she looked great just as she was. I would have told her to go on that trip.

"I learned to love the fact that life *isn't* perfect. I had the ideal job, the penthouse apartment, and girlfriends who looked like movie stars. But I wasn't happy. Looking back on it, I believed that if everything *looked* perfect from the outside, that maybe I could convince myself that I was all right on the inside. But I was a mess."

"But you changed," I commented.

"Yes, I changed. I quit that flashy job and took the one at Lawton. The firm isn't the best one in the city, but it gave me the chance to work on projects that actually help people, like designing schools," he said. "And my condo isn't in the best neighborhood, but I love it."

"Me too," I replied. It was cozy and it suited his personality. I couldn't think of Logan trying to be some hardnosed executive type.

I would never have been attracted to him if he was like that. I was glad that the Logan I met was happy being himself, a nice guy who enjoyed life.

And what about me? When was the last time I enjoyed life?

When I was planning this trip to build the school, that's when.

"You're not going to let me give up on this, are you?" I asked.

"Never," he said, smiling and giving me a big hug. "I'd never let you give up on something so close to your heart."

Alex was up on the roof of the new school, ceremoniously putting the last nail in. Below in the courtyard, the whole village had turned out. I stood with the church group that was responsible for this amazing thing and I cried.

There would be a week of celebrations before we went home. There were celebrations to honor us, the group of foreigners who had made all this possible. I thought of all the crazy TV shows that featured people going to far-off places to play survivor games. Building something lasting for people who really needed and appreciated it was much more rewarding.

I would never forget this place or the people.

And I would never forget the man who made it possible, the man who pushed me past my perfectionist ways so I would come down here. That night, I called him.

"It's done, Logan. The school is finished."

He let out a whoop so loud that I had to hold the phone away from my ear. He really was excited for me, excited for the project.

"So get yourself on the next plane," I told him firmly. "We are celebrating down here. And I can't think of anyone I'd rather celebrate with."

As I hung up the phone I thought about my struggles with weight and, yes, my perfectionism. But I'd pushed through all that to finish this project and I was so happy.

You did good, Melissa, the voice inside my head told me.

This time, it was my own voice. THE END

HE WANTED A SUPER MODEL

And I don't know how to be a blonde bimbo.

The music swept across the crowd, carrying the dancers with it. From a table at the edge of the dance floor, I watched a woman spin slowly, swiveling her hips. Her partner's eyes rested on her jeans. The woman caught the man's hand and they both smiled.

A waitress stumbled between the dancers, balancing a tray of glasses. Behind her, my boyfriend, Seth, made his way along the edge of the dance floor. His eyes were glued to the dancing woman. The waitress stopped at the table next to me and Seth bumped into her.

I couldn't hear what he said, but I saw his lips form the words, "Excuse me."

His eyes caught mine and he grinned sheepishly. "Did you see that babe on the dance floor?" he shouted into my ear.

I nodded.

"She's a piece of work. Look at that dork she's dancing with."

I nodded again. I'd heard him talk like that before, but I wasn't prepared for what came next.

"Grace, how come you don't look like that?"

I didn't know what to say. The woman on the dance floor was drop dead gorgeous and extremely sexy.

Seth went on. "See that picture over there?" He pointed to a poster hanging on a nearby wall. On it, a super model posed on a beach in a flimsy swimsuit. "That's the way a woman should look."

The lead guitarist crashed a final chord and the dancers walked off the floor.

Seth lowered his voice. "Check out that woman to your right, and observe that blonde on the other side of the room. She looks good too."

The women he indicated could have been photocopies of the picture on the wall.

"All women don't want to look the same, Seth," I informed him.

"Maybe not, but they could if they tried. Take you, Grace. You could stand to lose a few pounds—more than a few, actually. And your hair needs some work. You could get it styled and dye it blonde. You'd look great as a blonde. If you changed your makeup a little . . .well, you'd look like the model in the poster."

I couldn't have been more surprised if he'd thrown cold water in my face. Shock, hurt feelings, and anger fought for control of my mind. Anger won.

"I'm me, Seth, not a clone of some model," I snapped. "Life isn't about what you look like, it's about who you are. I'm not a blonde bimbo."

"I know that. But Grace, nobody will ever find out what you are if they don't like the way you look."

"So, you're saying I'm ugly?"

"No, I'm not saying that. I'm just saying that you should take more time with yourself. You could look a lot better."

"And what if I don't want to look like a model?"

Seth stared across the table and right into my eyes. "If you want to keep me, you will. Otherwise, I'm gone."

He didn't mention the subject again that evening, but I knew he was serious.

Oh well. What do I need with him? Obviously, he wasn't worth my time.

I had met Seth at a volleyball game down on the beach. I was standing on the sidelines watching the game when he came over and introduced himself.

"Did anyone ever tell you that you look a little like Nancy Malone?" he had asked.

Nancy Malone is a talk show hostess, and I don't resemble her at all.

"You have the same look about you," he had insisted. "You should make the most of it."

Instead of arguing with him, I had agreed that maybe I should.

"Say, I was just about to grab something from the vendor over there," he pointed to a lunch cart about fifty feet away. "Can I buy you a dog?"

Over hot dogs on the beach, I told him that I had come to California from the Midwest to be an actress, but I had ended up working for a rental car agency.

Before we finished our hot dogs, Seth had asked me out. That was six months ago. We were still dating, but lately things hadn't been going too well. The trouble started when I lost my job. For several weeks, I hadn't been able to find another one.

I could have gone home to my family, or I could have asked them for money, but before I had left home, Mom, Dad, and my brother Max had tried to talk me out of moving to California. They didn't like the idea of me becoming an actress, and when they couldn't convince me to choose another profession, they had reminded me that I could always return home if things didn't work out. I had been in California for less than a year. It would be a bad idea to call and tell my family that I had failed already.

Seth lived in a house with four other guys, so I couldn't stay with him—not that he had asked me to.

The weeks of unemployment had eaten up my savings. Plus, anxiety and fear had caused me to pig out on junk food. I had finally found another job working in a gift shop, but in the meantime I had let myself go. Now my boyfriend didn't like the way I looked.

I walked into the bathroom at the bar and I studied my reflection in the mirror on the back of the door. My body could use some work, and I did need a haircut. Still, I wasn't going to turn into a blonde bimbo, not even for Seth. It would be one thing to dye my hair because I had gotten a part in a movie that required me to be a blonde; it was something else for my boyfriend to expect me to make myself look like someone on a poster. After what Seth had said to me, I should have told him to get lost, but I liked him. Sure, he was shallow, but he could be a lot of fun when he wanted to be.

The entire next day, I thought about Seth insisting that people wouldn't get to know me if they didn't like the way I looked. Part of me argued that there were all types of beautiful women—all colors, all shapes, and all sizes. Part of me wondered whether my acting career would take off if I gave in and made myself look like a clone of someone else. The rest of me wondered if I should just dump Seth, forget about everything, and go home to Kansas.

I thought about it all day, and by the time the gift shop closed that evening, I knew I wasn't going to dump Seth, and I wasn't going home. Instead, I decided to visit a health club not far from where I lived. Before I gave up all my dreams, I decided to see what the health club could do for me.

Body Beautiful was bustling when I walked in the door. Men and women were working out on weight machines in a large, main room. Above the weight room, a second story built like a balcony held the treadmills, exercise bikes, and ski machines where club members ran, rode, and skied.

"May I help you?" came a voice from beside me.

I looked at a tall blonde in a bikini. "Uh, yes. I wanted to find out about joining. I want to get in shape."

She smiled. "Good for you. I'm Emma. Why don't I show you around and tell you a little about what we do here?" She led me past the weight machines and explained that I would be using weights to build strength and define my muscles. The treadmills on the balcony would develop my endurance and cardiovascular fitness. There were also two swimming pools, a sauna, and a hot tub located in another room on the main floor. Emma wanted to know my name and what I expected to gain from my workouts.

"I'm Grace," I told her. "I want to be strong and fit, and I want my body to be the best it can be."

"If you work with us," Emma said, "and stick with our program, I think you'll be happy with the results. But it won't be easy, and it won't happen overnight."

"I understand, but whatever I have to do will be worthwhile if I can wear a bikini like the one you have on."

"That'll happen," she assured me. "When do you want to start?"

"How about now?"

"That's what I like to hear. Follow me."

Emma led me into the women's locker room where she

told me to strip down to my underwear. First she weighed me. Embarrassment flooded my face when I realized how much weight I had gained. Emma didn't seem to notice my embarrassment. Instead of criticizing my weight, she wrote it down on her clipboard.

Then she began to take my measurements. She didn't just measure my bust, waist, and hips—her tape measure also surrounded my upper arms, thighs, calves, and even my neck.

"These measurements are so we can track your progress. Our program isn't just based on working out. We will also examine your eating and sleeping habits as well. We will teach you to cook low-fat meals, encourage you to drink lots of water, and push you to get eight hours of sleep every night."

We didn't start the program that evening. Instead, Emma explained that I would begin my workouts the next day. I was very excited when I went home that night. Emma had made me feel like I could reach my personal goals. In the future, I would wear a bikini, and maybe Seth would look at me like he had the picture on the wall at the club. Still, I drew the line at dying my hair blonde. I liked my brown hair.

Seth didn't call that evening, and I was relieved. Although I wanted to tell him I had joined the fitness center, I wasn't sure I should. I didn't want him to think that I was trying to change into the woman he thought I should be.

The next evening, I left my job at the gift shop carrying a duffel bag with my workout clothes. After changing, I went to find Emma.

"Ready to get started?" she asked when she saw me. I nodded and she motioned to a man nearby. He walked over. "Grace, this is Brady. Brady is going to be your fitness counselor."

Brady was tall with dark red hair and green eyes. A column of freckles marched across his nose. A tank top and jogging shorts showed off his lightly tanned body. Although he was quite muscular, his arms and legs didn't bulge as much as the body builders I had seen on television. He reached out and grasped my hands.

"Hi, Grace. Are you ready to work up a sweat?"

His eyes caught mine, and I felt my heart speed up. "Let's do it," I answered.

"We're going to start by stretching our muscles," he said.

I wanted to know how often I should work out.

"At least three times a week, but five times would be better."

"Are you a body builder?"

The smile he gave me lit up his face. "Not really. I do use weights for strength and muscle definition, but I'm more of an aerobics instructor."

That evening, I made up my mind that from then on, I would work out five times a week. The first week, I went home tired and a little sore every night. Brady had told me to expect the soreness, but he promised that it would go away in a few days—and it did. After a week, I couldn't really see any results, but the scales said that I had lost two pounds.

As the days passed, Seth didn't call or come by. At first, I was too tired to care, but when the weekend went by and I still hadn't heard from him, I began to wonder where he was. So, I called the shop where Seth worked installing windshields and auto glass. The boss told me that my boyfriend had taken a few days off. I couldn't imagine where he'd gone, but I didn't feel comfortable calling his house and asking his roommates. I knew his parents lived in Oregon; perhaps he was visiting them. However, as the days went by, his absence bothered me less and less.

Part of the reason I cared little about Seth was because I was paying more and more attention to Brady. For a couple of hours every day, he patiently taught me exercises, helped me adjust weight and fitness machines, and monitored my progress.

One Saturday, he took me to a special lunch and explained the benefits of good eating. We stopped by a salad bar and he followed me through the serving line, showing me which foods were good for me.

"You should never eat until you are full," he said after we sat down at a table. "If you feel full, you've eaten too much."

I giggled. "And if I'm stuffed?"

"Way too much."

"Do you promise that all this work and dieting will make me thin?"

His eyes caught mine. "Thin, strong, healthy, and best of all, you'll live to be old."

I couldn't pull my eyes from his. "Too bad it won't make me beautiful."

Brady reached across the table and took my hand. "Real beauty comes from within. If you want to be beautiful, you already are."

"You don't think I should dye my hair blonde?"

"Why would you do that? You've got pretty hair. Grace, I can help you develop your body, but I can't make you into someone else. A lot of women come to the fitness center to become someone else and they are always disappointed. I'm going to tell you up front that I don't understand why you'd want to be anybody else. You should try to be the best you can be."

I had been kidding about the beauty and the blonde hair. I hadn't been fishing for compliments, but the serious tone in Brady's voice sent blood rushing to my cheeks. Suddenly, I didn't know what to say.

"Then I don't have anything to worry about?"

"Not a thing."

I thought about my fitness counselor for the rest of the weekend. During our workout sessions, I had memorized everything about him—the rusty color of his hair, the playful light in his eyes, his crooked smile, and the way his clothes molded to his body. All those images danced through my mind.

I told myself to get a grip. Of course, he was attractive. Of course, he was patient and kind with the fitness center clients. It was his job. Being nice to me was his job. I knew that.

"Do you know a good hairdresser?" I asked my boss, Kaitlyn, one evening.

"Yeah. My sister." Kaitlyn fished around on her purse and came up with a business card. "Her shop isn't too far from here."

The shop was a fancy place with potted palms and waterfalls. Emma's sister cut my hair and suggested putting some highlights around my face. I told her to go ahead.

Brady noticed the change immediately. "Hey, what have you done to your hair? It looks great." His praise sounded genuine. "By the way, I've been meaning to tell you how pleased I am with the progress you're making. Are you busy this Saturday afternoon?"

His question caught me off guard. "What do you have in mind?"

"I thought we could get together for some inline skating. Have you ever tried it?"

"Yeah once, but I wasn't very good."

"Well, you know what they say, 'Practice makes perfect.'"

I agreed to try it again.

When Saturday came, we rented skates and glided down the walk that stretched along the beach. I must have fallen down five times in the first ten feet, but it wasn't so bad since Brady was there to catch me. After a few minutes, I managed to get my skates under me.

It felt good to be at the beach with Brady. Other women, some of them really pretty, tried to get his attention. Still, if Brady noticed their flirting, he gave no sign of it—he kept his eyes on me.

Seth had never treated me half as well. He would have been so busy looking at the other women, he would have never noticed if I had fallen flat on my face.

The weekend volleyball game was in full swing, and Brady and I stopped to catch our breath and watch it.

"Would you like a snow cone?" he offered.

I nodded and he skated toward the sidewalk vendor.

"Who's the dude?" a familiar voice asked.

I turned to see Seth standing beside me, his dark blonde hair floated around his shoulders and his cut-off jeans and tank top accentuated his deep tan. He looked like a Midwestern girl's dream of a California surfer. There was no jealousy on his face, only amusement.

"Where've you been? I haven't seen you in three weeks. I thought you were out of town."

He shrugged. "I was for awhile. I had to go and see my folks, but I'm back now."

"How come you didn't call?" I asked.

He gazed across the beach toward the volleyball game. "I didn't have a chance."

I followed his gaze to a blonde playing a position by the net. "She looks like your type."

He kept his eyes on the game and repeated, "Who's the dude?"

"He's a friend. I'll introduce you when he comes back." But by the time Brady returned, Seth had walked away.

He reappeared at the gift shop on Monday morning. "You didn't say what you'd been up to while I was away."

"No, I didn't. I've been up to the same old things, Seth. How about you?"

He ignored my question. "I was wondering if we could go out tonight."

"I'm sorry. I've got plans." He didn't need to know that I would be working out.

"With the guy from the beach?"

"Sort of."

"Then I'll catch you later."

After my workout that evening, Brady surprised me by asking me to dinner. It wasn't much, just a slice of pizza, but I enjoyed it.

The next day, Seth came by the shop again. "I forgot to tell you something yesterday," he said. "I like your hair that way." It was the first time he'd ever said he liked anything about me.

A woman walked into the shop right then.

"Excuse me, Seth. I've got to get back to work."

I started to move toward her, but Seth grabbed my hand. "Let your boss help her."

"I can't. Kaitlyn isn't here."

"Well, let the woman wait then. She's not going to buy any of this over-priced junk anyway. I want to talk to you."

I jerked my hand out of his. "I'm sorry. You're the one who'll have to wait. I have a customer."

"Let me take you to dinner tonight."

"Not tonight, Seth." I hurried over to wait on the customer. When I looked back, Seth had left.

The next time I saw Seth was a couple weeks later at the beach. He was chasing a skinny blonde across the sand. I was sitting on a blanket sipping a soda. They ran right past me and he never even glanced my way. He chased her out to the edge of the water and she shrieked when he splashed her. Sadness pricked my heart when I realized that he had never looked at me that way.

I picked up the novel I had brought and forced myself to focus on the words.

"Excuse me, Ma'am, but reading at the beach is illegal. Put the book down and smile or I'll have to give you a ticket."

As I looked up into the eyes of my fitness instructor, I suddenly forgot all about Seth. "Are you the beach police?"

"Yes, Ma'am, but today I'm on beach rescue. I'm here to rescue a brown-haired beauty from boredom and sunburn."

"Sunburn?"

He opened a beach umbrella and set it on the sand behind me. "Is this seat taken?" Without waiting for my answer, he stretched out on the blanket beside me. "So, Grace, how come you're not swimming?"

"I was planning on it. I just haven't gotten around to it."

He stood up and pulled me to my feet. Suddenly, we were splashing in the waves.

"How did you end up teaching fitness?" I asked. I expected him to tell me he was an unemployed actor who worked at the club until he got his big break, but his real story was nothing like that.

"I got my degree in exercise physiology from UCLA. I always wanted to come to California, because most of the people I saw on television looked like they stayed in shape. I've been working at the club for the past five years. Now that I'm in charge of the aerobics program, the pay is very good. But lately, I've been getting homesick."

"Where's home?"

"Somerset, Kansas. I'm saving to open a club in my hometown someday. Where are you from?"

"Bixby."

"Are you kidding? Bixby, Kansas? We grew up less than fifty miles from each other. What a small world. How did you get to California?"

"You won't believe it, but underneath this boring exterior beats the heart of a great actress."

Then, Brady asked what I had acted in.

"Nothing," I admitted. "At least nothing here. In Bixby, I was a regular at the Little Theater. But here, I can't get a part, an agent, or even a good acting coach."

"Don't give up. You'll make it. There's an old saying about something easy not being satisfying. I can't remember how it goes."

"'A task easily done leaves little satisfaction,'" I quoted. "My grandmother told me that."

"What would you be doing if you were still in Bixby?"

"Working at the bank."

We laughed and played on the beach all afternoon. Brady's attention was flattering, and when I looked around at the other women on the sand, I wondered why he'd chosen to spend the afternoon with me.

Mom called that evening. After telling me what had been happening with her, Dad, and my brother Max, she wanted to know how my acting career was going. I lied about having a few auditions. She asked about my apartment, and I made it sound like more than the furnished room it was. She wanted to know how Seth was, and I said I had decided to break up with him.

"I miss you, Grace," she said. "I wish you'd come home."

After she hung up, I cried myself to sleep.

"Will you come hiking with me this weekend?" Brady asked one evening after I had finished my workout. There's a special place I'd like you to see."

When I agreed, he told me to bring my bathing suit.

The weekend came quickly and Brady drove me to a secluded stretch of the coast. We left his car down by the beach and hiked up into the hills overlooking the ocean. He carried a blanket and a picnic dinner.

"I want you to see the sunset from here," he explained.

We sprawled out on the blanket, munched on fruit, cheese, and cold chicken, and watched the red sun sink into the water. As the sun went down, Brady's lips claimed mine in a long, sweet kiss. We sat there until the daylight had gone, and as the moon rose behind us, we gathered the blanket and remains of our picnic and moved them down onto the empty beach beside the water. There we waded, splashed, and chased each other through the waves, laughing like children.

"Do you ever wear a bikini?" Brady wondered when we stopped to catch our breath.

I was glad that the darkness hid my embarrassment. "Are you kidding? I've never been skinny enough to wear one."

"Well I think you'd look good, and if you're worried about being skinny, I'll teach you some exercises for your abdominal muscles that will give you a washboard stomach in no time." He slipped his arms around my shoulders and pulled me close to him.

We stood on the beach sheltered in each other's arms, our lips embracing, until Brady took my hand and led me to the blanket.

Gently at first, and then passionately, he claimed my heart and body. Afterwards, I lay in his arms, happy and content. As my eyes stared up at the moon, my heart reached out to Brady with all the love of my being.

"Will I see you tomorrow at the health club?" he asked early the next morning when he dropped me off at my place.

"Right after work," I lied. His goodbye kiss lingered on my lips long after I closed the door behind me.

I was in love with him. It had only been about three months, but I knew how I felt. Then, without warning, tears ran down my face and I stumbled toward the bathroom. There was no tub in the bathroom, so I turned on the water, stripped off my clothes, and slipped into the shower stall. Placing my back against the wall, I slid down and sat on the floor. With the water pounding my body, I surrendered to the tears.

I had come to California to be an actress, but so far, all I had been was a fool. First with Seth, who had wanted me to be someone else. When I had been with him, he had paid more attention to the women who passed us on the street. And Brady probably collected women from the health club like an athlete collects trophies. Last night, he had added me to the string of notches on his bedpost.

Mom called later that afternoon to ask how I was and to tell me again that she missed me.

"I wish you could come home, Grace," she said. "Max and Isabel have finally set the date—they're getting married on Halloween. They want all the wedding guests to come in costume and stay for a Halloween party afterward. I'm not sure it's appropriate, but they're so excited. I'm so happy for them that I've agreed to dress up like the good witch from the Wizard of Oz."

I giggled in spite of my soon-to-be-broken heart. "Oh, Mom,

you'll look great." She had been hoping that my brother and his girlfriend would get married since the day they had met in high school. I'm sure she had often imagined them tying the knot in a fancy June wedding, so a Halloween party wouldn't be her idea of a good time.

"The costume they want me to wear is very pretty," she admitted, "but I'm afraid I'll feel silly in it. Your dad will be dressed like the scarecrow."

I laughed so hard that, for the second time that day, tears streamed down my cheeks.

"Your dad loves his costume," Mom went on. "He was parading around in it last night. I think he's just relieved that he won't have to wear a tuxedo." She went on and on about the wedding, explaining that Max and Isabel were going to dress up as the Tin Man and Dorothy. Mom's words raised my heart back up from the floor where it had fallen.

I envied my brother and his fiancé for their love and their future life together. "Tell the happy couple that I'll be looking forward to their wedding, and I'll definitely be there. I wouldn't miss it for the world."

"I wish you could come home sooner. I know you have your heart set on being an actress, but if you change your mind—"

"I know, Mom."

After I hung up, I realized that my heart was no longer set on becoming an actress. My heart was set on Brady, but I refused to be his trophy. I didn't go to the club the next day or for the rest of the week. Brady called and left messages on my machine, but I didn't return his calls.

I did, however, continue to work out. I had worked hard to get myself in shape, and from now on, I intended to stay that way. Instead of running on the treadmill at the club, I ran through the park. I bought dumbbells and exercised with them in my room, and I stretched out morning, noon, and night.

Seth caught me at the gift shop on Wednesday. "Hi, Babe. How've you been?"

"Fine. How's the blonde?"

"Who?"

"The one I saw you with at the beach."

His eyes challenged mine. "She's probably about the same as the guy I saw you with. Anyway, she's history. I wanted to talk about you and me."

My eyes met his squarely. "There's you, and then there's me, but there's no you and me."

"There could be. Come on, Grace. You're looking great these days. We could be so good together. Give me another chance."

"Aren't you overlooking something? I'm not a blonde."

"I don't care about that. Please let me take you out tonight. I promise you'll have fun. Look, you went through all this trouble to get in shape for me. Now you won't give me the time of day. What gives?"

His pleading tone was flattering. "I didn't do it for you. I did it for me. Thanks, Seth, but no thanks."

"You're making a mistake."

"I seem to be doing that a lot lately."

I'd been moping around the shop all week, and by Friday my boss wanted to know what was wrong with me.

"I never thought I would be homesick for Kansas, but I am," I explained.

"Then maybe you should go home," Kaitlyn suggested.

"What about my job? I can't go and leave you in the lurch."

"You're a good worker, Grace, and I'd miss you, but I can find someone else to work here. Think about it over the weekend, and if you decide you want to go, just let me know."

Saturday morning, I walked along the beach and stopped to watch the volleyball game. This was where I had met Seth, but he wasn't there today. I found myself scanning the faces of the players and the watching crowd. Brady wasn't there either.

I really hadn't expected to see him, but my heart hungered for a glimpse of his face. I would have to forget about him, because as I stood there, an outsider amid that California crowd, I decided to go home to Kansas. However, I wouldn't be able to leave until Monday. I still had to tell my boss and my landlord, and I would have to tell Mom that I was coming and ask her to lend me the money for the plane ticket. In the meantime, I went back to my place and began to pack my things.

A sharp knock at the door interrupted me.

"Just a minute," I called and hurried to open the door.

Brady stood in front of me. I caught my breath in surprise, and in an instant my mind took a picture of him that my heart would always carry. His rusty hair hung over his brow, and his green eyes penetrated mine.

"Grace, is something wrong? I've been trying to get in touch with you all week."

"No. There's nothing wrong."

"Then where've you been? I missed you at the club. I've left a million messages on your phone machine. Are you avoiding me?"

I told him the truth. "Yes, I have been. You're a great guy, Brady, but I don't want to be your trophy."

He looked blank. "What are you talking about?"

"You don't need me to tell you how handsome and sexy you are. You know how to make a woman feel good about herself, and I'm sure a lot of your clients fall in love with you. I just don't want to be another notch on your bedpost."

"Is that what you think? That you're nothing more to me than a notch on my bedpost?" He walked past me into the room. "What did I do wrong to make you think that?"

"You didn't do anything wrong, Brady. You made me love you."

"You love me?" He glanced at my suitcases and clothes piled on the bed. "Then, where are you going?"

"Home. I'm leaving for Kansas on Monday."

He reached out and put his hand on my shoulder. "Look, I know that you've had it rough since you've been in California. Becoming an actress isn't easy. I brought you the card of an agent who was a friend of mine in college. He wants to talk to you." He held out the card, but I didn't take it. "I don't understand. Grace, if you love me, why are you leaving?"

"I told you. I don't want to be just another one of the clients you romanced for the fun of it."

"I don't romance my clients." He sounded surprised. "You're the only woman from the health club I've ever gone out with."

"Oh, sure."

"It's true. Please don't leave. Don't give up your dreams."

I sighed and looked into his eyes. "I've discovered that I don't really want to be an actress. It was fun acting as a hobby while I worked at the bank, but after being here long enough to see what is really involved, I don't want to follow acting as a profession."

"Are you sure? I love you and I'll help you with your acting career."

"I've discovered that I don't really belong here, Brady. I belong in a small town in Kansas."

His answer surprised me. "I'm so glad to hear you say that, Grace, because in this city of fakes and con-artists, there's nothing fake about you. Let's go back to Kansas and get married."

"You want me to marry you?"

He reached into his pocket, pulled out a velvet box, and popped open the lid to reveal an engagement ring. "I picked this up on Monday, and I've been trying to give it to you all week. I know we've only known each other for three months, but I want to spend my life with you."

Tears flooded my eyes. "Yes," I mumbled.

He took me in his arms and kissed me again and again. Then Brady explained that his best friend from high school had called and offered to be his partner in a fitness center in Somerset, Kansas.

"I was hoping to go back to Kansas myself," he explained. "Of course, I would have turned down the offer and stayed here if you wanted to continue acting."

"No, Brady. I want to go home."

"Then, would you mind living in Somerset?" he asked. "It's only about forty-five miles from Bixby. We could visit your family all the time. And Somerset has a Little Theater and a bank where you could work if I can't talk you into working at the fitness center with me."

We were back in Kansas with plenty of time to help plan the Halloween wedding of my brother and his fiancé. And Mom's wedding fantasies were realized when I married Brady the following spring in a fancy garden ceremony.

"Isn't it funny?" Mom asked just before Brady and I left on our honeymoon. "You had to go all the way to California to fall in love with a man from Kansas." THE END

I FEEL LIKE A TEENAGE FREAKSHOW

My only wish in life is to be able to look in the mirror without wanting to die, and if extreme plastic surgery is my only chance at happiness . . . I'm more than willing to risk my life.

"You were a beautiful baby when you were born," my mother and father told me so many times when I asked them why my face looked the way it did. "There was nothing to indicate anything was wrong," my mother always insisted.

So my questions went unanswered and I anguished over why I looked so weird.

Mom and Dad continued to reassure me that I was still beautiful. But on my tenth birthday I remember the worried looks on their faces as I blew out my candles on my birthday cake. After that, they took me to several doctors to confirm what they already knew—

My face wasn't developing "right."

"Her chin has stopped growing," specialist finally told us. "But let's wait and see what happens as she gets older."

What happened is—I was mercilessly teased and tormented by my classmates.

"Fran looks like a parrot!" a boy taunted.

"No, she looks like a duck!" another boy jeered.

And it wasn't only the boys. The girls mocked and ridiculed

me and most of them refused to be my friend.

Well, at least my grades never suffered. That's because I spent all my time alone studying; my social life—or lack thereof—was a total bust. After awhile, I simply was no longer the girl I was before my chin—or rather, the absence of my chin—became so apparent. At recess, I hung back hoping no one would even notice me.

One night I heard my parents talking. "She used to be so beautiful," Mom said, and I could tell she was about to break down and cry. "What is her life going to be like now?"

"I honestly don't know," my dad answered grimly. "The doctors are at a loss as to what happened and what they should do—how they should proceed from a surgical standpoint."

"My poor Fran!" Mom whimpered.

I fled to my room, not wanting to hear any more. Do they still even love me? I wondered then. Why don't they act like they used to when my chin was normal?

Of course they still loved me and kissed me and hugged me, but there was always that worried look or Mom's face and Dad tried not to look directly at me. I never thought I was "repulsive" to them, but my face was like a disease that no one could cure Even the specialists told us we would "just have to wait and see."

Sadly, my chin never started growing again and by the age of sixteen, I was seriously contemplating suicide, I felt I was a teenage freak show and that I would never marry or have a family and what kind of career could I have? But I kept all this from Mom and Dad; I don't think they ever really fathomed how desperate I felt.

As it was, my grades were straight A's, but I gladly would've traded them all for just one friend who wasn't ashamed to be seen with me. The girls at school shunned me, afraid that if they became associated with me, the boys wouldn't date them. The boys, needless to say, never even looked my way.

Somehow, I made it through graduation and even started beauty school, but my life was so awful that I couldn't think much about the future. Still, I did want to learn how to help make other people beautiful, even though I'd long since given up on myself. I mean, I always believed that people are supposed to like you for what's inside of you, but all of those seemingly wonderful slogans and platitudes don't really help—much less apply—when it comes to real life. And so church was my only refuge. At least there, I felt like I was loved.

I sang in the choir and taught Sunday school the little kids at least, accepted me as if I were just another person. Oh, they asked me why my face was "so funny looking" and things like that, but when I told them that my chin stopped growing when I was ten, they hugged me and told me they loved me and that I looked okay.

Then one day, the choir director took me aside during practice and hemmed and hawed around until he managed to say, "Fran, I really hate to say this, but although you have a beautiful voice, you're—well . . . a distraction—to the congregation. This Sunday we're having several visiting ministers and their congregations in attendance at our morning services and we would like the choir to look, uh—uniform, you see—in every detail."

"So, you don't want people having to look up into the choir loft and be shaken and disgusted by the sight of a freak? I get it, Mr. Fischback—and I won't bother to sing with the choir again. You can rest your fears."

I stalked off with all the dignity I could muster, but inside. I felt like dying. That's when I decided it would be best if I did.

Rummaging through my mother's medicine cabinet when I got home, I found a bottle of sleeping pills she used every once in awhile. The bottle was almost full.

I wrote a note to my parents telling them: I'm sorry, but I've got to end this misery. I don't know why God made me this way, but I can't live with it any longer. Please forgive me!

After swallowing the pills, I got into my bed and went to sleep forever. But when I woke up, I was in a hospital.

"Oh, Fran—why didn't you tell us you felt this horrible about yourself?" Mom wailed.

"We'll find an excellent plastic surgeon," Dad soothed quietly, wiping the tears off his cheeks. "You'll be as beautiful as you ever were, Fran; I promise you that, sweetheart. Your mother and I both love you with all our hearts and souls."

I smiled with that hope in my heart for the first time in a long, long while, thinking wistfully, Maybe someday, finally be normal. . . .

Frantically searching for just the right plastic surgeon, my parents had the surgery scheduled as soon as I was better, and I was thrilled beyond measure when the surgeon told me he could correct my receding chin with an implant.

"Are you sure?" I asked him, not quite able to believe that my imperfection could be corrected so easily.

"Yes; you'll be absolutely beautiful when I'm finished with you."

And when the bandages were off—it was true! I was so thrilled with my new face, I wanted to laugh and cry at the same time. I would never repulse anyone again.

I guess I thought life would change so much for me that I would never have another problem. Well, I was wrong. I made friends, started dating, began my career as a makeup artist, and loved every minute of it all. But slowly, I became aware that although they weren't visible on the outside, inside I bore the scars of the previous ten years of my life.

When I met Brad at a party given by one of my many new girlfriends, he was immediately drawn to me and I to him. It wasn't just his good looks and bright smile that appealed to me; I really appreciated his wonderful personality right from the start—he was always so upbeat and happy all the time. I tried to be the same way, but there were times when my past rose up to haunt me and I felt like the ugly duckling I used to be all over again.

"What's wrong?" Brad asked me one evening after dinner when a pensive mood came over me.

"Nothing," I lied, but privately, I was wondering why my life still seemed empty. I knew I was falling in love with Brad and he with me, but I still felt like something was . . . missing.

When I took him home to meet my parents, I cautioned them in advance to remove the photo albums bearing my photographs from the age of ten until my face was restored to its former beauty. Mom took down every family portrait from that period and all that was left were my early pictures and those taken after my surgery. Brad is observant, however, and he pointed out the discrepancy.

"Did you go on a trip or something when you were a kid, or did space aliens abduct you'?"

"What do you mean?" I asked innocently.

He glanced at my parents and my mother blushed while Dad stared at his cocktail.

"I mean, I see pictures all over the house of the family when you were small, but there seems to be a gap here somewhere. Was there a fire or something?" Brad looked directly at me. "You've shown me photo albums from your babyhood until you were about nine or-ten, but then nothing. Excuse me if I'm being too inquisitive, but . . . what happened?"

The emotional scars were so deep that I hated having to bring up the trauma of those years when my chin stopped growing and kids made fun of me. I wished I could tell him that there was a fire or an accident—or that I went on a long trip—but I knew even then that, sooner or later, I'd have to reveal the truth.

Slowly, haltingly, I began the story of my misery and my parents helplessness when my chin stopped developing naturally. Brad sat there transfixed, and I just knew then that he was going to stop loving me.

"May I see the pictures that you've hidden?" he finally asked.

Mom sprang from her chair when I nodded and produced the photos she had hidden in a closet. Brad looked them over and then gazed into my eyes.

"You don't have to be ashamed, honey. I love you for what's inside of you; that's the only thing that really counts."

Clenching my teeth, I tried not to argue, but lost the battle. "But if I had looked that way when you met me, Brad ... you know as well as I do that you never would've given me a second glance."

"Then it would've been my loss, because Fran—you are truly a wonderful person." He sighed deeply and took my hands in his. "Honey, if it bothers you so much, why don't you form some kind of support group for people who have issues with their appearance?"

"What a great idea!" Mom said.

Inspiration struck—and I did exactly that. I formed a group called: Inside Out. Because even after my life-altering surgery, still, when I looked in the mirror, I realized that I still saw the same miserable child without a chin looking hack at me, I knew then that surely others were suffering from the same sort of issue.

Indeed, even after I married Brad and we had our little girl, that horrible feeling of inferiority still occasionally plagued me. When I met new people in my work as a makeup artist, I often found myself wondering self-consciously, Are they looking at my chin?

My insecurity was so ingrained in me that the only way I could help myself, I realized, was to help others. So I joined with the plastic surgeon who restored my face and asked him to refer people to me who still had issues deep inside, even after their "outsides" were "fixed."

My slogan became: "Every woman is beautiful in her own way." And at my seminars, I taught that very thing. I thought I believed it myself, but sometimes I remembered the choir director and the kids who taunted me and all at once—no matter where I was and no matter how well my life was going—I'd feel that terrible touch of that old despair.

Still, working with women who came through terrible accidents and birth defects did a lot of good for me—maybe as much, if not more, than I did for them. When I worked, seldom did I find myself dwelling on my own imperfections in the face of such tragedies. Many of these women were horribly disfigured and yet, they had sunny, hopeful smiles on their faces and they didn't whine or cry or dwell on their misfortunes. The hours I spent with them taught me that loving yourself and others will bring you out of the "mully-grubs" as we called them.

"If you sit around and pity yourself," one girl told me, who was in an awful boating accident and literally had her face torn off, "you will never rise above your circumstances. But if you think of how grateful you are just to be alive, you get over yourself."

From her advice I screen-printed thousands of T-shirts with the message: Get Over Yourself! and they sold like hotcakes. With the money from this enterprise, we were able to pay for the services of plastic surgeons for people who couldn't afford it for themselves.

I thought my life was finally on an even keel. Embracing who I'd become and not who I was, I finally felt empowered to live my life to the fullest. Or so I thought. My daughter, Claudia, was a beautiful and sweet four-year-old and Brad was the love I'd only dreamed of in my girlish daydreams before my face was disfigured.

Yes—everything was perfect in my life until I came home one day from work and found Brad in our bed with another woman. Claudia was with my mother that day, and I intended to serve Brad a candlelit dinner before going to pick her up. Needless to say—all of my foolish, romantic dreams flew right out the window, along with my newly acquired, strong self-image.

"How could you?" I screamed as Brad jumped from beneath the covers and threw on his briefs.

The woman with him cowered by the bed, as naked as the day she was born. As I charged at the two of them, fists flying, she scrambled for her clothes and ran past me to the door.

"Fran—it was just a fling—that woman means nothing to me!" Brad cried, trying to hold me by my shoulders as I raged and clawed at his face with my fingernails.

"But you—you told me you loved me—!"

"And I do, honey—I do! Britney and I were just—just having a couple of drinks after we closed a deal at the office and—one thing led to another and then—"

"And then you brought her home to our bed and—"

I couldn't say the words. But the image of her lust-filled face and naked, flagrant body were etched in my brain forever. As it was, I knew she was prettier than I, and her figure was gorgeous. I felt so worthless suddenly—so unwanted. How can I ever compete with all of the beautiful women in this world? I wondered in vain. I opened my heart to Brad. I showed him the pictures of my face before the plastic surgery and now—now ... I feel so violated. I trusted him and this is how he repays me?

"Get out!" I shouted. "Get out and don't come back!"

He could see I meant business. Immediately, he started gathering his clothes into a suitcase, along with his shaving kit from the bathroom. "You'll regret this, Fran. I'll get custody of Claudia and you'll be all alone."

Almost to the door, he turned and sent one last volley in my direction:

"You've got problems, Fran—serious, disturbing problems. Oh, sure—you look fine on the outside, but inside—you're a complete and total mess. You'll have a hard time getting another man—that's for sure!"

"Get out before I call the police!" I screamed.

He was long gone before I collected myself enough to drive over and pick up our daughter. When I told Mom and Dad what happened, they were floored.

"Maybe you can still get him back," Mom finally said fretfully, wringing her hands in her grief and anguish.

Her words stung. Maybe she thinks, like Brad does, that I can't get another man. "I don't want him back," I told her curtly, feeling my whole body straighten with rigid decisiveness. "He's tarnished what we had and it will never be the same."

Dad nodded. "Forget about him, precious. If he cheated once, he'll do it again. You've got a good life now and you'll bounce back. Don't let this get you down for even a second."

Easier said than done, I thought dismally later that night. I couldn't sleep in the bed Brad had shared with his lover, so the next morning I decided to look for another house. I knew that if I lingered and let myself weaken, I would either slip back into the sludge of self-pity or despair—or, in the darkest hour, I might even call

Brad and beg him to come back to me. And that wasn't going to happen!

That day at my job behind the scenes on one of the most popular daytime talk shows in the country, I was making up a lady's face when she suddenly drew back as I tried to apply her lipstick.

"I never wear the stuff," she protested. "My lips are too thick."

I leaned back and smiled at her. "Who told you that?"

"My first husband. He told me I look like a clown when I wear lipstick."

"Well, he's dead wrong," I told her, "and he's an absolute fool, and I'm going to show you just how wrong he is!"

Carefully, I applied lipliner slightly inside the outline of her lips. Then I selected a shade called "Cantaloupe" that brought out the curve of her lips without accentuating their natural fullness. She was thrilled with her new look and cast off all of her feelings of insecurity about her mouth.

"Roger used to tell me that my eyes are my best feature, and that I should downplay my lips, but suddenly, well—I think he's full of it!" she exclaimed, happy tears running down her cheeks.

I laughed. "I agree! Every woman is beautiful in her own way."

"I like that," she mused. "You should put it on a T-shirt."

From that discussion came a whole line of T-shirts with inspiring, uplifting messages of hope and healing for women in every walk of life, faced with all kinds of bridges to cross. Along with the first one, Get Over Yourself!, the proceeds for the new shirts that followed were used to help women afford the plastic surgery and therapy they needed to get over issues about their appearances.

I threw myself into my work and the rest of my time was spent with Claudia and my parents. Brad gained visitation rights through our divorce proceedings, but sadly, once the divorce was finalized, I have to admit that he seldom bothered with our daughter. I decided then that even if I were beautiful all my life, Brad still would've cheated on me, eventually. The defect lies in him, not in me. Indeed, slowly, I was emerging as a whole human being and I felt the scars were really and truly beginning to heal.

Before I grew to this point, Brad's betrayal would've devastated me and I would've been in the valley of despair for only God knows how long. Somehow, though, I was able to pick myself up and move on with my daughter toward our bright, new future together—without Brad. The last hurdle I knew, deep down, that I needed to overcome was the dating scene, but I honestly really didn't want to try again. Even without the hurt of my former appearance, loving someone so much and having them toss that love aside for a mere fling was devastating in its own right.

How could I go out there and open my heart to someone new?

Church was something I gave up when I was nearly twenty. After the divorce, though, for Claudia's sake, I started attending again. Of course, since we'd moved nearly thirty miles away from my parents and the church I used to attend, there was little chance that I'd be recognized by anyone who knew me "back then."

The pastor's sermon that first Sunday that Claudia and I attended was about loving the "unlovable" and forgiving the "unforgivable." It hit close to home with me because when I thought of all the children who taunted me so long ago, deep down, I knew it was still hard for me to forgive them. But in my heart, that Sunday, I finally began to try.

The following Sunday the pastor stood at the pulpit and greeted us with exciting news: "We have a wonderful choir visiting us today." As he gave the name of the church and its choir director, I suddenly felt ill.

The man who hurt me so badly that day when he asked me to vacate my position in the choir was rising from his seat up front at the head of the sanctuary . . . and the choir from my previous church was filing into the choir loft!

Holding my head high, I tried to tell myself that I'd forgiven that man. But the anger inside me toward my tormentor was enormous. All at once I wanted to cry and I wished I could slap him and kick him like a child having a tantrum.

Urging myself to settle down, I finally decided that at the appropriate moment, I would find Claudia and leave the sanctuary. Forgiveness is just fine and dandy in concept, I found myself thinking bitterly, but what that man did to me is unforgivable!

As this man took the podium and gazed out over the congregation, I knew the precise moment his eyes fixed on me. There was a moment of hesitation in his speech, and then he carried on. Turning to the assembled choir, he conducted a wonderful selection of hymns—I have to give him that much credit, at least.

Composed, I sat there and listened, and even tried to enjoy the music. Afterward, I found Claudia in her Sunday school class and quickly ushered her out to our car, parked in the church lot.

Halfway there, that man—the choir director who crushed my soul and drove me to attempt suicide—rushed to confront me in the parking lot.

"Fran, I'm sorry," he said urgently. "I want to apologize to you with all of my heart. If it's any consolation, I have felt terrible every day of my life since I was so unthinkably cruel to you." His hand reached out then, and somehow connected with mine.

"You have my forgiveness," I told him, and I knew in that moment that it was true; I held no more bitterness inside of me because of his mean-spirited and unthinking words.

After making his peace with me, he walked away and I bundled Claudia into the car and we went home. Somehow, I was free. The anger, the bitterness, the wounds

It was all behind me, once and for all.

Today, I have a wonderful man in my life and I travel around the country holding seminars that heal people who've been hurt by the reactions of others and their own insecurities about their appearances. I sell my own line of T-shirts and beauty products, with most of the proceeds going toward charity cases. I still do makeup on a professional basis, but now, it's for victims of crimes, accidents, and those scarred by other horrors.

I no longer think of myself as a freak. Indeed, my confidence is through the roof these days, and when I look in the mirror, I don't see the little girl without a chin—I see something else.

I see my true beauty. And it comes from loving and accepting yourself as you are, and from loving and accepting others as they are. THE END

True Love Knows No Pounds. . . .

I'M LARGE AND IN CHARGE

So where's my lover boy?

For as long as I can remember, I'd always been the short, heavy girl with zero confidence who was the butt of everyone's jokes. To this very day, I can still hear the taunts and teases, and feel my face flush with anger and bitterness from all the misery they caused.

But when puberty set in and the pounds somehow melted away, I was amazed at how differently people treated me. My weight was no longer an issue. And the men—the same men who wouldn't give me the time of day when I was fat—suddenly paid attention to me.

I was thrilled. Soon, I rarely stepped out of the house without makeup on, and I fussed over my hair constantly. I began to carry myself with the confidence and charm I'd always known that I had, but had always kept buried. In the many years following those magical days, I've looked back and wondered who that girl was, and what happened to her.

What happened to that girl? I asked myself as I stared at the round, chubby, yet still attractive, face in the mirror with hair flying in twelve different directions. She used to take such good care of herself.

I shrugged my shoulders as tears began to form. I'll tell you what happened to her: two children, an endless stream of abusive relationships, years of fighting for survival, and pounds of food is what happened. Maybe I've always wanted it this way—to be so big that no man will ever want me, even though I hunger for a good, satisfying relationship—one that won't leave, taking a small part of me right along with it until I fear that nothing remains.

"Mommy, why are you crying? What's the matter?" Sean, my five-year-old son, asked from the doorway. I quickly turned around.

"Sean! What are you doing out of bed?" I demanded, frantically wiping the tears away so he wouldn't see them.

"I have to go potty."

"Well, then—go! And then get back in that bed!"

"Okay, Mommy."

I inwardly chided myself for snapping at my innocent son, but the diversion was a welcome one. I was afraid to turn back to that mirror, so I turned off the dresser light and crawled into bed with a bowl of heavily buttered popcorn beside me and a movie in the VCR—my favorite escape.

The next day, pushing a shopping cart full of bagged groceries, I stopped in front of the bulletin board near the grocery store exit to check on anything of interest. There were numerous diet advertisements posted promising a slimmer you in thirty days—I needed another diet like I needed a hole in my head, local yard sales, driving lessons—the usual nonsense tacked to a bulletin board. Then something caught my eye.

It was a schedule for continuing education classes sponsored by the local community college. I plucked off the leaflet and read through the offerings.

"Me? Go back to school? After all these years?" I muttered

under my breath. Then I stopped myself.

After all these years!

I was only twenty-nine, for God's sake!

I adjusted my glasses and cupped the side of my full face absently. I did see one class that I wanted to take. And the classes weren't all that expensive. And I knew that Chanel, my next-door neighbor, would watch the kids for me, seeing as it was only one night a week.

I stood there for a good couple of minutes, weighing the pros and cons in my head. Then I grabbed a piece of paper out of my bag and quickly jotted down the number for the college.

What did I have to lose?

Three days later, after the kids went to bed, I looked over all the courses and their descriptions from cover to cover in the catalog I'd received in the mail. The more I read, the more interested I became.

Why shouldn't I go back to school? I asked myself. After all, what's the harm? Perhaps, if I did well, I could take more classes that might even lead to a degree—get a better-paying job so I wouldn't always be scrambling financially and just scraping by.

Can I honestly pull this off?

"Of course you can do it!" Chanel said enthusiastically when I put the idea to her. "I think it'd be great for you, as a matter of fact! And I'll gladly watch the kids for you!"

"I don't know, Chanel," I said, glancing at the leaflet for the umpteenth time, dog-eared from all my perusal. "I don't want the kids to think I'm neglecting them or anything. . . ."

"Don't be silly, Tamika," she said, nudging me slightly. "You worry too much. You need to do this for you. As it is, you have no life!"

"Thanks a lot, Chanel," I said, pulling myself up off the couch.

"No, I'm serious! I think that taking this class will be just the thing you need in your life right now. And if you do well and feel comfortable, you can take two more. And who knows? I may even attend your graduation if I'm invited!"

I laughed.

"Your kids will be fine," she assured me. "They're in good hands. And it's about time you got out and did something constructive. You're too young to be. . . ."

"To be what?" I snapped defensively.

"To be lookin' the way you do! All you do is go to work, tend to the kids, and then you sit in front of the TV eating! You may do your hair every once in a while, maybe put a touch of color on your face, but that's it! Girl, I look at you and I'm like . . . damn! Why does she look the way she do?"

"Gee, Chanel, what would I do without your never-ending support?" I said sarcastically.

"I'm just telling it like it is, Tamika. The truth hurts, baby, but there it is."

In that split second, I wished that Chanel, with her slim body, perky attitude, and responsibility-free life would just disappear off the face of the earth. I could barely tolerate me holding a mirror up to my face, let alone anyone else doing it.

"And I know you're excited about this. I can tell, Tamika. You have a whole new glow about you since you've brought this up."

I eyed her suspiciously. "A new glow? I'm glowing? You sure it's not sweat?"

She gave that sigh she always gave when I exacerbated her nerves and threw a pillow at me.

Scraping up the money for tuition proved easier than I'd thought. Although I filled out the financial aid forms a little later than what was recommended, the report I received concerning possible aid was enough to get a deferment for tuition until the college awarded aid.

I tried not to stare at all the young kids surrounding me as I bought my necessary supplies from the college bookstore. But as I stood in front of all the college merchandise—T-shirts, sweatshirts, caps—I suddenly thought to myself: What on earth am I doing here? What business do I have going back to school with all these kids? I have children to take care of!

I took a deep breath, and as I glanced over my shoulder, I spotted something—or should I say, someone—interesting. He was standing a few feet away in the notebook section with a confused look on his face. I judged he was close to my age—medium height with dark hair and eyes, he stood there scratching his goatee in indecision. Then he glanced my way and I immediately felt embarrassed and self-conscious, quickly turning away. I snatched a T-shirt off the rack, but before I could make an escape, he approached me.

"Excuse me? Could you come over here for a second? I need your help for a little bit."

"Oh . . . I don't work here. I—I'm a student."

"I know. I still need your help, though."

I followed him over to the notebook section, and holding up a couple of notebooks, he asked, "Which one do you think is better? I don't know why I can't decide. When I shop for my daughter, it's nowhere near as difficult."

I smirked. "That's because as long as the notebook has their favorite cartoon character on it, they couldn't care less about what's between the pages."

He laughed in understanding, and as he replaced the notebooks, I noticed that his ring finger was bare—me being Miss Nosey Rosey.

"So you're a student, huh? What's your major?"

I explained that I was currently undecided, only taking one class to get acclimated, and he said, "You'll like it here. This college is perfect for people like you and me who're older and going back to school. Don't go thinking you'll be surrounded by teenyboppers all the time."

I gave a slow, easy smile. "Good. Then I won't feel as old as I'm feeling right now!"

"How old is old—if you don't mind me asking?"

"Twenty-nine."

"Twenty-nine's not old, lady, and if you don't mind me saying so, you don't look it."

"Believe you me, I don't mind you saying it! And just so you know, my name's Tamika."

"Nice to meet you, Tamika. I'm Renel. Say, do you have to go somewhere?" he asked shyly.

I could feel my mouth open slightly in surprise, and he quickly said, "Well . . . I mean, if you're in no hurry, I thought you might like to join me in the lounge for a cup of coffee or something."

I looked down at my feet and was absolutely mortified to realize that I was wearing a pair of beat-up sneakers without socks that showed my ashy ankles. I had no makeup on, my hair was jammed into a baseball cap, and had I remembered to put on deodorant? My underarms felt wet and I couldn't very well sniff for inspection purposes, could I? Why did I have to pick this particular day of all days to look a fright? Chanel's past words about keeping up appearances swam in my head and I silently cursed her for being right—this time.

"You know," I said hurriedly, "on any other day, I would, but I have to pick up my children soon, so. . . ."

"How many children? I have a little girl, myself."

"I have two . . . two boys," I said, wanting desperately to leave.

He must've sensed this, because he said, "Well, I won't keep you, then. I know the stresses of childcare so . . . I hope to see you around soon?"

"Renel, it's a big campus; anything's possible," I said, trying to sound noncommittal—and failing.

He nodded.

In my effort to make a hasty retreat, I ditched the things I was going to pay for and exited the building. I ran to my car, huffing and puffing along the way. All I wanted to do was just crawl back into my shell, my lonely shell.

Nighttime was quiet time for me. Stepping out of the shower, I glanced at my naked body in the mirror.

Ugh!

I gripped at the "tires" of thick flesh that surrounded my middle and slapped my cellulite-riddled thighs. I held one heavy, bare breast in my hand and made a face in the mirror.

I wasn't always like this, I thought to myself. Once upon a time, men sniffed around me like I was a flower with sweet nectar. All I had to do was flash a smile—that's all it took.

I felt that if I only lost some pounds, I would once again be that vivacious, flirtatious individual, full of life and charm. Then I stopped myself. Would I ever be that person again? More importantly, did I ever want to be that person again?

I'd been younger back then, with no responsibilities on my shoulders. I'd been able to go out at a moment's notice, party until five in the morning, go to the bathroom without some little one knocking on the door, calling my name about some sort of nonsense.

But you decided to have these children, Tamika, I thought to myself. You wanted to take responsibility for your actions. You made your bed, now lie in it. No one ever said it would be easy.

No, they certainly hadn't. And though the children might be a heavy responsibility, they were also my blessing. Their childhood innocence never failed to put a smile on my face and love in my breast.

But they'd also failed to mention the many lonely nights I'd spend because guys I was interested in thought I was looking for a father for my children. No one had ever mentioned the dates I'd have with nary a word from them afterward—the phone calls I'd make in vain, trying to get the truth out of guys who just didn't want to see me anymore.

So I'd happened to meet a man—a single parent at that, or so I suspected—who'd actually engaged me in conversation, and I'd run like a scared rabbit! Figures!

Tired of looking at my naked body, I dressed in my underwear and nightgown and slipped into bed with thoughts of Renel to lull me to sleep.

I was a nervous wreck my first week of school. Absentminded to the point of self-strangulation, I sent e-mails to the wrong people, forgot minor items in the kids' lunch boxes, and walked around in a cloud of confusion. Doubts as to whether or not I could actually go through with school surfaced night and day.

On the first day of class, I rushed home from work to heat the kids' dinner, make their lunches for the next day, give them baths, and take a shower myself. Like Napoleon, I barked and snapped orders at the kids:

"Any homework? Are you sure?"

"Eat your dinner!"

"Go brush your teeth!"

"Stop fighting! I don't want to hear it, just stop!"

By the time I jumped into my car, I thought the final nerve that was holding me together had finally snapped. I arrived at the college campus and again felt old seeing such younger people around me. Using the campus map that had been sent to my home, I found my classroom building and tried to slip in as quietly as possible.

All tensions and doubts dissipated as the professor spoke about things I felt strongly about, seeing as I argued these points with my coworkers on a daily basis. On several occasions, I wanted to speak, but I decided to stay quiet that first day. I figured I had the whole semester to shoot my mouth off. Then the professor cut us loose for a ten-minute break, and I went out into the hallway to get a soda from the vending machine.

"Hello, there," said a voice I faintly recognized.

I turned, and there Renel stood, grinning at me.

"Uh . . . hi!" I sputtered. "How are you? Do you have class in this building?"

He smiled. "You must not have seen me. I'm in your class."

"You are? Gosh—I haven't noticed much of anything lately. Listen . . . I really didn't mean to cut out so quickly on you the other day. . . ."

He held up his hand to stop me. "It's forgotten. You left in such a rush, though, that you forgot some things." From his backpack, he pulled out the items I'd intended to purchase that day. I gazed at them, wide-eyed.

"Renel, you—you didn't have to do this," I stuttered. "I would've come back for them. I mean, what if you'd never seen me again? I feel so embarrassed now! How much do I owe you? I'll write you a check right now. . . ." I began scrambling inside my purse for my checkbook, but he stopped my hands from their hasty action.

"Tamika, don't worry about it. It won't break me financially. And I knew I'd be seeing you again because you dropped your class schedule when you left."

"Thank you, Renel. This is very nice of you," I said, accepting the merchandise from him. Then, more shyly, I said, "You know, now I feel really bad about turning you down for coffee."

He grinned. "I guess you'll just have to make it up to me, won't you? Perhaps after class?"

I nodded, smiling shyly.

We chatted some more after that, showing each other pictures of our children. Renel confirmed my suspicions about him being a single parent; divorced over a year, he shared custody of his daughter with her mother. I found him quite easy to talk to, actually. Perhaps it was the fact that he was able to relate to my woes of single parenting and was making a big leap in furthering his education, like myself.

After class, I called Chanel to tell her that I'd be a little late getting home. When I told her the reason behind it, she exclaimed, "You go, girl! Your first day at school and you already snagged a man!"

"Stop it!" I admonished.

Once Renel was able to reach his baby-sitter, I followed him to the local doughnut shop, where we talked more over steaming cups of coffee.

"I shouldn't be drinking this, you know. I'll be up all night," I remarked.

"Is that such a bad thing? That way we can talk more!"

I laughed and shook my head. "I have children to go home to, and so do you. I thought you knew—single parents don't have personal lives."

"Life is what you make of it, Tamika, and you only get one.

If you're unhappy with the way your life is right now, then you need to examine what you're not doing to make yourself feel better."

"It's a little too late in the night to wax philosophical, Renel. Besides, it's different for you. You have an ex-wife to leave your daughter with. I don't. My sons' father doesn't care one iota for them, so it's all on me. I never get a break."

Renel was studying me intently, and right then and there, I wanted to crawl into a black hole and die. I hadn't meant to sound so bitter, but there those words were, lingering in the air, and I knew I couldn't take them back.

"Renel, I really should be going now," I said, placing money for my share of the bill on the table. "I have to get up early tomorrow and it's been a long day for me."

"Did I say something wrong? Am I that boring? Is it my breath?"

I laughed. "It's not your breath!" I managed. "No, no—you're very nice to talk to, actually. I can't remember when I've been so at ease with a man. Anyway, it's nice to know I'm not the only single parent out there."

His eyes sparkled as he looked at me, making me feel special and . . . dare I say it . . . attractive. He tore a piece of paper from his notebook and wrote down a phone number.

"Call me sometime, okay? Since we're in the same class, we can be study buddies."

I grinned and folded the piece of paper, placing it in my purse. "I will. And thanks for the adult conversation. I'll see you next week."

"You will, definitely. Good night, Tamika."

He squeezed my hand and I sighed inwardly.

Renel sneaked into my life through the back door when I

wasn't looking. Perhaps I did leave that door open just a crack, after all—enough for him to fit his foot through. Suffice it to say that Renel had a way about him that allowed me to open myself up to him a bit and talk, really talk, about my life and my fears. I admired how much he was in control of his life, how he let nothing stand in the way of his goals and hopes for the future. He wasn't bitter about his divorce; he believed it'd just been a bad decision to marry his ex-wife because of their incompatibility, but hardly regretted the daughter they'd produced.

Renel had a self-confidence and inner peace about the way he looked at life that I envied. When we would talk, there were brief moments in which I wanted to tell him everything—my fears, my insecurities—just everything. But I knew I'd only scare him away if I did, so I held back—held back just a little, but gave just enough to be polite, so I wouldn't seem too difficult. I knew that he was trying to get to know me as a person, but deep inside, I doubted his sincerity, doubted his motives. Although he never mentioned sex and had never disrespected me by even remotely getting sexually suggestive, I felt I had to protect myself.

Still, after a month of dates, I'd finally relented, and so here I was, in front of my full-length mirror, trying to find an outfit that would make me look slimmer. I raced around my bedroom, mumbling to myself as the boys watched me curiously from the doorway. Then the doorbell rang suddenly, and I told the boys to answer it.

"Mommy!" my five-year-old yelled.

"What? What?" I yelled, exasperated, "If it's Chanel, just let her in!"

"It's not Chanel!" they both yelled in unison.

Now what? I rushed to the door—and there stood Renel, grinning down at my two little boys.

"Renel! You're very early!"

"Nice to see you, too," he quipped.

"Oh, I'm sorry—come on in—have a seat. I'll be done in a minute. These are my crumb snatchers, by the way—Sean and Jamari."

"Hey, little men!" he said, holding up his hand for high-fives.

I rushed my beautification—as best I could—and quickly rejoined Renel on the couch as he played and roughhoused with my sons. He had a way with the boys, that's for sure. They responded well to him, but then again, it probably had something to do with the fact that they had limited contact with men. Chanel arrived soon afterward, and then we were off on our date.

I hadn't realized how much time had passed since I'd last had a real, honest-to-goodness date. I felt so awkward suddenly, and my weight made me extremely nervous and self-conscious. I didn't know how to act, really, and I found myself fumbling for words at times. Renel and I had never had trouble with conversation in the past, but that night was different. We were "officially" on a date, and I think he felt the pressure, as well.

"You really look beautiful tonight, Tamika," he said during a lull in the conversation. "I meant to say it earlier, but I didn't want to sound too bold or like I was trying to run a line on you."

I bowed my head to hide a shy smile. "Thank you, Renel," I said quietly. "It's really nice of you to say that."

"Sounds like you don't believe me."

"No, that's not it."

"Don't you believe that you're beautiful, Tamika?"

"Wait. Before you start waxing philosophical again, let me order a glass of wine."

"Stop trying to change the subject, Tamika. You know, when I look at you, I see a very attractive woman. I don't see what you see."

"And what do you think I see?" I snapped.

He drew back suddenly, and then leaned in and said, "Honestly? I think you see a heavy woman who doesn't possibly think that she could attract a man or find any kind of happiness unless she loses weight. You use your children as a shield, as an excuse as to why you haven't had a decent relationship," he snapped back.

All of the defensiveness of my childhood immediately reared its ugly head.

"After a month of coffee and conversation, you think you know me? You don't know anything about me, Renel! When you start carrying some extra letters after your name signifying some credentials, then maybe you can make some observations about me!"

"I don't need a degree to see what I see, Tamika. You're so pessimistic about life and all that can possibly lay in front of you and I don't understand why. You're not stupid; anybody in our class can tell you that. Just because you have two kids doesn't mean that your life has to stop. And if you'd just let me get to know you and get past all those layers you hide behind, I know I'd like you even more."

Bitter tears began to spring to my eyes. "Renel, you don't know a damn thing about me. You don't know how I've struggled to keep a roof over my sons' heads and food on the table. There were times when I had five dollars to last me until payday and I'd have to hock my jewelry so I could put gas in my car to get to work. I've had to stay strong and build up all these 'layers,' as you so delicately put it, to protect myself, to keep myself from falling apart because if I do . . . if I fall apart, the price I pay will be losing my kids and I can't let that ever happen." I snatched the cloth napkin off my lap to wipe my eyes.

"What makes you think that I want you weak, Tamika? I don't want a weak woman; I want a strong woman. I'm not asking to marry you; I just want a chance to get to know you."

"For what? So you can get what you want and then leave just like all the rest? Been there, done that, have the T-shirt."

"Is that what you think of me? Is that what you think I'm all about? Have I ever given you any indication that I want to just hit it and run?"

"Oh, so now you gonna act indignant? Are you saying that men aren't capable of trying to gain a woman's confidence until they get what they want and then leave?"

"We aren't talking about all men," he said, slightly raising his voice. "We're talking about me. And all I've ever wanted was a chance to get to know you, Tamika. I've never cared about your weight or the fact that you have kids."

He sighed in defeat and threw his napkin on the table. "Come on," he said, signaling the waiter. "I'll take you home. I don't want to waste any more of your time—or mine, for that matter. I can see that this is going nowhere."

I swallowed the lump in my throat and held my head high as we walked out of the restaurant.

Never let them see you cry, sweetie. Never let them see you cry.

Renel coolly dropped me off at home and quickly sped off, leaving me standing alone at the curb. Sadly, I walked upstairs to my apartment to meet Chanel. When she saw the look on my face, she knew I wasn't in the mood for chatter, so she just gathered her things and offered me her ear if I needed it before leaving.

On the verge of tears, I undressed and took a shower. In my shower, I could finally break down and cry, my tears mixing with the water spray.

What was the matter with me? Why couldn't I believe that a man as handsome and smart as Renel could find me wonderful to be with?

I'd always said to friends that I was a hell of a woman, and that it would take one hell of a man to handle me. So here was Renel, all ready to be there for me with all my warts, and I was trying at every turn to push him away!

Deep down, I knew that Renel wasn't like the other men in my past. He liked my mind and my sense of humor and had never once mentioned my weight or done anything to make me feel bad about myself. He always met me with supportive words and good advice about how to just go with the flow and not push against it, for that created discontentment and difficulty.

But I hadn't listened. I was doing the exact opposite of what he'd tried to convey and was pushing against the flow. And this time, I was pushing out a person who could very well be a positive force in my life.

Fear and shame made me miss two weeks of classes. I couldn't face Renel because I felt it would only mean reliving that terrible night. Besides, I wasn't too sure that I had enough courage to face him. Imagine that—me—not having enough courage when I lived my whole life bracing for a storm.

So many times, I wanted to pick up the phone and apologize for my words and behavior that night—to tell Renel that I wanted to give him a chance if he still wanted it. But my pride got in the way. I would've let three weeks go by, but Chanel chided me on how I was only cheating myself from attending a class that I really loved. She insisted that I pick my behind up and get back to class before I fell too far behind in my coursework.

That first night back, I purposely arrived early so I could sit inconspicuously in the back of the classroom. When it was time for our break, I bravely approached Renel at the soda machine.

"Hello," I said quietly.

"Hello, Tamika," he said coldly. My feet desperately wanted to run away, but I knew I had to face this.

"Renel, could we talk for a moment? Just hear me out for a sec?"

He toyed with the cold can in his hand and said, "I'm listening."

I sighed and closed my eyes. "I want to say that I'm sorry for the way I treated you at dinner. You didn't deserve my hostility and you're right—you've never given me any indication that your intentions were anything less than . . . honorable, for lack of a better term."

He continued to stare down at the can in his hand without saying a word.

"And you're right—I do have some issues about my past relationships and my weight and my kids and my life and . . . and I took them out on you because I had no one else to take them out on. I flipped on my defense mechanism and just let all these things come flying out of my mouth because it's a way of protecting myself."

He looked up at me. "You don't need to protect yourself from me, Tamika."

"I know that . . . now. I don't know—maybe I've always known it—and it scares me."

"Scares you?"

I looked down at my feet. "Maybe I'm scared that for once in my life, I've finally found a good man to be with . . . and I'm not equipped to handle him."

He tilted my head so that my eyes met his searching gaze. "The class missed you, you know."

I gave a little laugh through my tears. "They didn't miss me."

"I guess I should be more specific, then. I missed you."

I closed my eyes and smiled. "I missed you, too, Renel," I croaked.

He wiped my tears away with his thumbs. "Quit that crying, girl. Where's that strong girl that I'm attracted to?"

I stared into his eyes. "Weak and vulnerable in front of you right now."

"So don't be afraid to show me that look every once in a while, Tamika. It's not a bad thing, you know."

"Does this mean—does this mean that we can try dinner . . . again?"

He put his arm around my shoulder, and as we walked back to class, he said, "You name the time and place and I'll be there. I'll always be there."

That time, I believed every word he said. THE END

I HAVE BECOME ONE OF THE BEAUTIFUL PEOPLE

I went from being the ugly girl to being one that turns heads.

I can't even start my story by telling you that I was average looking as a child and a teenager. I was not a pretty baby. In the pictures that my aging mother proudly pulls out for any and all guests, I look remarkably like a little meatball with arms. She points to my brown curly hair and dimpled cheeks and says, "She was the sweetest baby; never a problem to anybody!"

I couldn't have been a problem because every time I opened my mouth to complain about something, Mama shoved some food into it. The fatter I got the more she praised me. I wanted to make her happy because when Mama wasn't pleased with something she made sure that nobody was happy or had any chance of peace and happiness until she had received an apology, rebate or other 'making right' of the situation. Everyone in the neighborhood feared Mama. Her reputation for "taking care of business" had neighbors reciting her name like a prayer when they stood before car dealers or merchants that tried to pull a fast one. If Ma thought someone was trying to take advantage of her or someone she loved, she'd scream and carry on so that every manager within earshot was called to calm her down. It was nothing for her to cry, throw herself on the floor and lie prostate as she wept, or to pound the chest of some innocent bystander all the while shrieking at the top of her lungs that the manager was a shyster.

As an adult I sometimes call it performance art. As a kid I was terrified and never wanted Mama to throw a fit on my behalf. So I ate everything put in front of me, and everything she insisted I try. I wobbled when I walked, but hey, Mama was happy.

Mama's happiness came to a screeching halt when I entered school. One of the wee little girls standing in the kindergarten classroom eyed me suspiciously when Mama and I entered. "Well Jade," the teacher said. "You have a friend now. Jade, this is Crystal Rose."

My first thought was that I wished I had been given a lovely sounding name like Jade. One pure syllable—although I was too young to know what a syllable was—and a quick ending. My two names, which Ma insisted went perfectly together, seemed to hang in the air forever.

Jade took one look at me, sniffed dramatically and declared, "She's fat."

"No!" Mama said as if she'd been stung. "Not fat, healthy! What is a skinny thing like you going to do if you get a fever? You'll fade away—"

Miss Barker thankfully cut Mama off before she could terrorize Jade. I went over to where the boys stood. My cousin Rupert and I played well together so I figured I'd be safe and play with the boys.

"She's fat and she smells!" one of the boys said at recess.

I hated school. I hated Mama for making me go. I hated Papa for telling me that someday I'd lose my baby fat and be beautiful. The only thing I excelled in was lunch and it wasn't hard to do that because everything in the cafeteria looked interesting to me. Ma was so accustomed to making everything from scratch that I hadn't savored the salt-grease combination of French fries, or the spiciness of Buffalo wings. I was thrilled and begged Mama to let me eat at the cafeteria every day.

I suppose Daddy wanted to try and help me compensate for my looks so when I graduated from high school he gave me a sporty new convertible. I loved that car. It even helped me make a few friends, but after they got their own automobiles I didn't see them again. It hurt to know that they'd just been using me all that time.

College was even worse than high school because it meant that there were even more people that could reject me. I hid in the library, sat in the back of class and only spoke when spoken to. Somehow I managed to stay for the two years necessary to get an Associate's degree. I went to work right away.

Mom and Dad decided to retire in Arizona so I ended up having to find an apartment of my own. I found a cheap place in a building that used to be a big mansion but had been turned into individual apartments. It was an old Victorian structure and although my room even had a bay window I didn't appreciate it because I was too busy feeling sorry for myself. I felt that I was the loneliest person in the world.

The work week always went by very quickly. I convinced myself that I was being frugal by purchasing black khakis and white shirts to wear to work. The office I worked in had a casual business dress policy. Every day I wore the same type of thing, with my only choices being between whether or not I wore a long or short-sleeved blouse with my standard black pants.

"I don't believe I've ever seen you in a dress," My landlady who lived right downstairs said once. "You'll never get a boyfriend if you don't advertise a little."

I grimaced, "I don't need a boyfriend," I said as I pushed my hair out of my eyes. "Men are more trouble than they are worth."

"Surely you want a family," she insisted.

I shook my head, the tears welling in my throat too much to make speaking possible. "Never!" I finally managed. "I am so over that idea!"

"You could change your mind," she smiled. "With a nice haircut and some makeup and a dress or two you might be surprised at how the boys will suddenly appear in your life."

I hurried away as soon as I could. I didn't need that old biddy butting into life. I was happy. I went to work, I went home. I watched television until late at night. On the weekend, when there wasn't much on TV, I rented movies. Sometimes I went out to dinner alone. Mostly I ate cookies or potato chips while I watched television. I didn't need anything more than that, did I? A man would have interfered with my interest in current events. At least that's what I told myself.

A promotion at work brought me additional responsibilities. It also meant that I sometimes had to attend meetings chaired by the president of the company. Whenever I had to answer a question or address the group my knees shook and my voice trembled. I knew the material, but I was so embarrassed to have all of those eyes on me that I just wanted the floor to open up and swallow me.

"You're such a good worker," my boss told me on more than one occasion. "You know if you'd just look up from your notes once in awhile you'd find that we're not all out to get you."

"I know that," I told her. "I just don't like speaking in front of people."

"You'll get better at it," she assured me.

I didn't get better at it. If anything I got worse.

"What you need is a dose of confidence," she finally said after one particularly awful presentation. "How about you and I go shopping?"

I shook my head. "I'm still paying off my student loans," I lied.

"My treat," she insisted. "A haircut, a facial—"

She was talking about things that horrified me. I struggled to find the right words to refuse her generous offer.

"My mom and I are going shopping this weekend," I stated. "I'll come back on Monday with a new look. I didn't want to say anything before because I don't know how it will turn out."

She patted my hand, "I can't wait to see it."

I'd lied to her and now I had to do something. On Saturday morning I dragged myself into a haircutting place and told the stylist to do whatever she wanted with my hair.

When I left I have to admit I did feel a little bit better. My hair was short and its natural curls seemed to frame my face. I went to a department store and found a couple of sweaters that I liked. I bought them because they were the only things I could remember the other women in the office wearing. It never occurred to me to ask for help. Why would a woman that looked like me want to spend money on something as frivolous as clothing? I couldn't justify any further expense.

"Very nice," Bernice said. "I like the new 'do."

I blushed and stammered a thank you. I was relieved that she had noticed because I didn't want to disappoint her. Neither did I want to spend a day shopping with her and pretending that I knew how to do the sorts of girl things that I saw women doing on television. Shopping seemed like an unnatural act to me, and I was a klutz when it came to things like makeup and anything other than getting a brush through my hair.

Maybe it was my new look or maybe it was just the full moon but the very next day a man named Mark who worked on the floor above ours invited me to lunch. He made me laugh. He made me feel good about myself. When he invited me to his place for dinner a couple of days later I happily agreed. We had a wonderful evening, and when he took me to his bed, I responded the way a woman in love will. I thought he might have opened the door to happily ever after for me.

"I'll call you," he said the next morning as he put me in a cab.

He didn't call. In fact, I didn't even see him at work anymore. I wanted to know if he'd been fired, but I was afraid to ask. I tried not to let my disappointment show, but once I was at home at night I'd cry and wonder what I'd done wrong.

One of the things I liked to do late at night when I couldn't sleep was get behind the wheel of my car, drive into the country where I'd really let loose with a few wild screams and my foot heavy on the gas pedal. I once clocked myself going 97 miles per hour. I quickly realized that I had a very good chance of getting myself killed, or getting a ticket so I slowed down to a more reasonable 80 miles per hour.

When I was behind the wheel of my car I felt beautiful. Maybe it was that old feeling I had when I was in high school driving the pretty little car Papa had given me. All I knew was that I liked to drive at night because all of the hard edges and things that I had to deal with in life became soft in the darkness. Nighttime felt safe to me, and I reveled in the absolute freedom of being able to be a part of everything around me without taking my daytime troubles into it. Sometimes when things were tough at work I'd mentally relive one of my drives and I'd calm down. A girl who can take a curve at 70 miles per hour can probably handle a cranky boss, right?

I drove a lot while I was trying to recover from my short affair with Mark. In the morning I'd haul my tired self to work and hope nobody noticed.

"She smells," Kirsten was saying as I came around the corner at work. "That hair is a wreck and I swear she smells."

"Hi there!" I said as I neared. "How are you today?"

The guilty looks on their faces made me realize my worst fear. They were talking about me. I strode to my desk, barely hearing their muttered, "Fine" and "How are you?"

Did I smell? I bathed every day, but as I'd gained weight I'd noted that I perspired much more. Also, the heavy folds of fat often trapped perspiration and sometimes I did note a certain odor. I forced myself not to run from my desk. During my lunch break I went into the bathroom and doused myself with perfume. I went back to my desk feeling absolutely disgusted with myself and everyone around me.

That night I went to a nearby burger place, ordered an entire bag of hamburgers and greasy French fries and two large milkshakes. Maybe in a few days I'd go to Weight Watchers, or one of those Jenny Craig centers to lose weight. In the meantime, I intended to eat whatever I wanted because I'd be deprived soon enough.

As soon as I pulled away from the fast-food place I was stuffing a hamburger in my mouth. I cried as I drove through town and out into the country. Once I hit the main road I began to speed up. I promised myself that I'd lose weight, learn how to dress provocatively and I'd show Mark what he'd given up. When I'd had enough self-pity I slowed down and began the drive back to town. I was actually going the speed limit and savoring the last of the chocolate milkshake when my life changed forever. I never even heard the car that streaked through a stop sign and broad sided me.

It was horrifying to wake up in a hospital nearly completely encased on a body cast and barely able to move. I couldn't speak because my jaws were wired shut. Feeding was done intravenously as it had been for nearly 10 days while I'd been in a coma.

"You're lucky to be alive," Mom told me. "The guy that hit you was drunk."

I tried to speak but a nurse quickly came into the room and ordered Mom out. She explained that I'd suffered a head trauma and that I needed to take it easy. She gave me a shot and I dozed.

For the next week I slept off and on; waking up just long enough to receive another shot for pain, or to have the nurses try and clean me up. I was still too fragile to do anything for myself.

"I have good news and I have bad news," A doctor said as he stood beside my bed. "The good news is that you are well enough for the surgery. The bad news is that we can't put your face back exactly as it was before."

I'd been up from my bed only twice with a tremendous amount of assistance from the medical staff. I'd glimpsed myself in the mirror once and decided not to ever do it again. I hadn't asked if I'd be undergoing any type of surgery. I had been ugly most of my life so it never occurred to me that anyone would try to repair the damage. I planned to just live my life with the scars. Trying to make myself understood with my tongue stitched back together and my jaws and teeth wired made speaking seem like more trouble than it was worth.

"No surgery," I insisted.

"You don't have a choice," he said softly. "If I don't fix your nose you'll have trouble breathing for the rest of your life. Also, if we don't fix your left eyelid your vision will be impaired."

I could feel tears leaking out of my eyes. I was in pain physically and emotionally. I'd gone from being a fat, smelly girl to a hideous ogre with a swollen face and no real hope for improvement.

The doctor showed me several photographs of women and asked me to select a certain type of nose and a certain type of eye. Between the drugs I was on and my inability to think about anything other than my nearly-constant paint, I barely glanced at the pictures. I made my selections by nodding when I saw one that looked okay to me. I would never look like the models in the pictures so why try to pretend that I would?

It took a team of four specialists to reconstruct my face. I was still black and blue from the surgeries when I was finally sent home to recuperate. Mom stayed with me while I recovered. I was grateful for her presence.

Since I couldn't eat anything that wouldn't fit through a straw the weight just fell off of me. As the swelling went down on my face I actually began to be pleased with my new emerging features. I had a nice straight nose, cheekbones that I could actually see, and my eyes seemed bigger and more expressive. I wasn't beautiful, but I wasn't hideous either.

It took months of rest, physical therapy and continued medical care for me to be well enough to even venture outdoors. One of the first things Mom and I did was go shopping for some clothes that would fit me.

We got to the store and I immediately headed over to the plus-size clothes; the ones marked with sizes in X's and not real numbers. "Where are you going?" Mom asked.

"To find something in my size," I said.

"You aren't that size anymore," she reminded. "I'd say you're pretty far from it."

I spent the next hour trying on clothes that I had only dreamed about owning. Each time a small pair of pants, or skirt easily came up over my hips I felt a shiver of pleasure. I was thin—thin at last and I could wear anything that I wanted.

"Well, look at you!" Terri, my physical therapist said when I showed up in sleek black exercise pants and a cropped little T-shirt. "If I didn't know better I'd say you decided to live."

"What I've decided to do," I said as I lay my crutches against the parallel bars. "Is go back to work."

"Certainly," she smiled. "I've been waiting for you to ready to take that step."

"I'm more than ready," I told her. "I'm sick of staying home."

"To work it is," she said. "But you'll need the crutches for awhile longer. We haven't built your muscles up enough for you to be able to completely support yourself all of the time."

"I only notice trouble when I'm tired," I reported. "But most of the time I do just fine."

"I'd feel better if you'd keep them with you until our next session."

Reluctantly I agreed. The following Monday I returned to work. I went slowly, because walking was still difficult for me, but I made my way to my desk. There was a sweet welcome back card on my desk from a girl that I barely knew. I turned on the computer and began to work. Everything seemed surreal because it had been so long since I'd sat at that desk. I was so busy entering numbers and information that I completely lost track of time and was oblivious to the commotion going on around me.

I had just completed a lengthy report when I overheard two men talking about someone new to the company. I wrinkled my nose in disgust as they discussed the poor girl.

"She's hot!" one of them said. "I mean really hot. I had no idea."

"With assets like that, she won't have to work another day in her life," his friend stated.

"I'm more of a breast man myself," the first one said. "And she's got everything in just the right places as far as I'm concerned."

"I'd ask her out but my wife might complain," the other one chuckled. "It's one of the most amazing things I've ever seen. She's absolutely striking."

I resisted the urge to stand up, look over the divider that separated my desk from where they were standing and tell them to get back to work. I felt sorry for the woman they were discussing. She was being eyed like a piece of meat. It made me want to vomit, but I stayed put, mindlessly inputting the data that would eventually come out into a fine report showing the buying trends of our repeat customers. I'd heard that kind of talk before and it always angered me.

It wasn't until I took my lunch break that I figured out who the men had been talking about. I'd just gone into the break room for a soda when Clifford, one of the guys from accounting ambled in. He stopped in his tracks. "Mama!" he called out. "You are so hot you're giving me a sunburn."

I looked around to see if he was talking about someone else. I suddenly realized that it was me in the heels, short tight skirt and stylish blouse. I tried to ignore him but he stepped too close to me and whispered, "I had no idea such a tigress was hiding under the woman that used to sit at your desk."

"There is a lot about me that you don't know," I said as my soda thumped into the tray at the bottom of the soda machine. "And if you don't get away from me, I'll make sure your wife finds out a few things that you'll wish she didn't know."

He blushed, stammered some sort of apology and backed away. I grabbed my drink and raced back to the relative safety of my desk.

I suppose it was naïve of me to think that by taking control of the situation I had made it clear to him and all of the other men in the office that I wasn't there for anything more than to do my job. Although he stayed away from me, the other men came around and did everything they could to get my attention.

I would arrive at work and find flowers on my desk, or funny cards. During the day I'd be interrupted by e-mail from men asking if I wanted to go to lunch or dinner with them. In the break room they'd make it clear that if I just nodded once in their direction they'd follow me anywhere. In just a few short months I went from being the girl that blended in with the carpet to being one that turned heads whenever she walked into the room. My wildest fantasy had come true and I hated it!

For a few weeks I tried to make the best of things. I reasoned that eventually the people I worked with and even strangers would realize that I was all-business and not looking for a date. Even if I wanted a boyfriend, I wouldn't have chosen anyone from my work because those men had been downright rude to me before my accident. One of them had even called me a fat cow to my face.

"Get out of my way, you fat cow," he barked one morning when I was getting my coffee.

I jumped back as if he'd physically slapped me. He never apologized even though I know some of my coworkers told him that I spent most of the morning crying over his insult. It was hard not to say something equally crude to him when he now smiled suggestively at me and when he loudly announced to everyone within earshot one morning that he'd brought me coffee because I was "a babe."

The novelty will wear off soon, I thought. Everyone would just do their jobs and I wouldn't be pestered by lecherous men anymore. A few weeks went by and I began to sense that this wasn't a temporary problem. I'd be working away and suddenly a man was at my desk asking an inane question, or offering to take me out to lunch or dinner. Just when I thought I was getting something done, my boss would hand my work to someone else; usually someone who hadn't been at the company as long.

"Is there some problem with my work?" I confronted my boss as he was relaxing in his office after a particularly busy day.

"Why do you ask?" he sat up a little straighter.

I listed the projects that he had taken away from me. "If you aren't pleased with my work, you need to tell me so that I can improve."

He was twisting his pen in little circles on the note pad on the desk in front of him. After a long silence he said, "It's not that you're not doing your work well. It's just that I've been concerned about your concentration. Every time I look up it seems as if you have someone standing at your desk."

"That's not my fault!" I cried. "I'm doing everything I can do discourage that!"

"Really?" his voice was full of disbelief. "Perhaps you could dress a little more conservatively."

I stared at him. I was wearing a gray suit consisted of loose pleated pants and a jacket. Underneath the light wool jacket I wore a buttoned down white shirt. All of the buttons were buttoned."

"Exactly how much more conservative would you like?" I asked. "If I added a tie you and I would be wearing the same outfit."

"Maybe it's the way you walk," he suggested. "Or the way you talk. I just don't believe that you aren't sending out some kind of signal."

I turned on my heel and left before I could say anything ugly. I was still working very hard, but no one was taking me seriously. Being beautiful seemed to have dimmed my credibility.

Things got tougher at work. One of the young trainees that was given one of my reports before I was finished failed to check all of the numbers and consequently cost our company thousands of dollars. My being let go was anticlimactic. I'd been expecting it for months.

Even though Mom had returned home months earlier, she called nearly every day to ask if I was dating anyone or had any prospects. "I just don't understand it," she said "You have everything going for you. I don't know what's wrong with men these days. You'd think they'd have the sense to recognize quality when they see it."

Had she ever loved me for who I am inside? I was afraid to ask. Mom had always put looks before the inner qualities of other people, so I suspected she based her assessment of me the same way.

Each morning I dressed as if I still had a full-time job. Then I devoted myself to looking for a new position. My resume opened a lot of doors for me, but once I met with the Human Resource representatives, I would come away feeling that they didn't like me. I went dressed in severely tailored suits, my hair pulled back from my face and absolutely no makeup on in an attempt to present the appearance of one who cares more about the products than her appearance. No one made me any offers. I began to think I was horribly flawed. The only thing I kept up with was my physical therapy. Everything else fell by the wayside as I let myself fall into a dark depression

"For someone who is getting around just fine these days without crutch or cane, you look horrible!" Terri, my physical therapist said. "What's the problem?"

How could I look otherwise? My life was in shambles. I looked great on the outside but on the inside I was a boiling caldron of outrage and worry. Although I didn't know Terri very well, I trusted her enough to tell her my story.

"I understand," she said when I'd finished. "In fact, I know some other people that are going through the same experiences. They too are confused and hurt by what has happened to them."

"You do?" I was genuinely interested in hearing more because I'd felt alone in my pain. "Can I meet them?"

"I can try to arrange it," she said. "But you have to be open-minded enough to understand that there are people who are coming at this from a different way than you. Some of them were beautiful before a disease or an accident took their beauty. Where they were admired and sought after before, they are now left alone to deal with their pain. One man no longer has much of a mouth or a nose. He can't go out in public without people gawking at him. Another woman has large burns over her hands and arms and part of her face. Children sometimes say horrible things to her. And several of the patients have scleroderma, a crippling disease that literally freezes the bones and muscles into place.

"I need that kind of a group," I said as I wiped a tear from my eye. "I need to be with people that understand what I am going through."

She gave me the details and I went to the group's next meeting. I wasn't sure what to expect as I walked into the room. Right away a little person came toward me, offered her hand and showed me where the coffee was.

"I'm not sure what your story is," she smiled. "But nobody comes here by accident."

There was a model who had lost an arm in a motorcycle accident, a former police officer who had once posed for some beefcake pictures for a calendar that now had the scars of having half of his face blown off by an escaped convict. There were men and women with scars, deformities, and a woman like me whose looks had changed so drastically that her children no longer recognized her. She was beautiful, but she said her life felt hopeless and out of control. I understood every word that I heard.

With the encouragement of the group I went to work for a temporary agency. Working boosted my self-esteem and moving around from company to company gave me an up-close view of how other managers treated their most attractive employees. What I learned is that moderately attractive people seem to be treated better than those society considers unattractive or too beautiful. I sometimes felt sorry for myself because I'd lived in both extremes. The members of my support group reminded me to take things one day at a time and to focus on friendships that were based on something far deeper than looks.

My entire life changed when the agency sent me to work for Lee Hollis. I arrived expecting to be working with a man, but was surprised when one of the most beautiful women I had ever seen greeted me.

"Wow!" I exclaimed as I sat in the chair she indicated. "You're gorgeous!" I immediately felt like a fool. I blushed and stammered and did my best to assure her that I was not a lunatic or lesbian.

Lee laughed and told me to stop apologizing. "I could say the same thing about you," she noted. "I'll bet you hear it often."

I was supposed to be at a job briefing, but I found myself telling Lee how I'd come to be one of the beautiful people. "I don't feel beautiful inside," I stated. "I feel angry and hurt. Where were all those men when I wanted a date?"

"You have two choices," Lee said thoughtfully. "You can let this defeat you, or you can use it as energy to fuel your real dreams." She opened a desk drawer and removed a photograph album. "This is my personal brag book," she said as she handed it to me. "I've walked in your shoes."

The first picture revealed a woman who was extremely overweight. The second one showed the woman as an even fatter version of the first photograph. And then there was a series of pictures in which the woman seemed to shrink right before my eyes. "I can't believe what you've been through," I said. "Your hair is different now and you look as if you've always been petite."

Her smile told me that she'd heard that more than once. "I had to have surgery to remove the loose skin after I lost so much weight," she said. "I went to the doctor on my twenty-seventh birthday and he told me that I was going to die if I didn't lose weight. I had tried everything—and I do mean everything—to lose the pounds. I didn't know what else I could do. He gave me a referral for a specialist. I decided to have my stomach stapled so it would be about the size of a mini-muffin."

"Amazing," I said as I looked at the charming self-confident woman in front of me. "How did you deal with men coming on to you and people treating you differently?"

"It was tough, but worth it," she said. "Like you, I was a good employee and I knew my job. When I became thin and started taking care of myself the people that I'd been working for suddenly decided that I didn't have a brain in my head, and I was too pretty for the good assignments."

"What did you do?"

"Held on to that job until I could start my own business," she said. "It wasn't that simple of course, but I sat down with a blank sheet of paper and began drawing up a business plan for myself. I had a new body—basically a new life. I needed to determine how I was going to live that life.

"I realized that my dream was to own my own accounting firm and to work for myself. For two long years I worked on raising enough capital to finance the opening of this place. I didn't know if I'd be able to make a go of it, but I didn't want to reach the end of my life without finding out. Sometimes you just have to take a leap of faith and do what your heart tells you to do."

I worked for Lee for 3 weeks. She gave me her support, stories of other self-made women and encouraged me to try and find my passion. Slowly I began to have some ideas about what I'd like to do full time. Between my group and Lee I was developing a new kind of confidence. A weekend Assertiveness Training course was especially helpful. I learned how to deflect backhanded compliments and outright insults with humor, firmness and the clear signal that I wasn't about to be taken advantage of.

When my contract with Lee was up I decided to take that leap of faith that she talked about.

It was frightening going into the heart of what was considered the worst part of town. I was welcomed at the local mission and given an apron and told to serve food. The supervisor said we'd talk after we fed the lunch crowd. I saw men and women and young children down on their luck and grateful for a hot meal. I saw women that had once been beautiful, now wearing the wrinkles of depression, poverty and various addictions. I saw people that had the shakes from withdrawal so intense they needed someone help them steady a cup of coffee.

Over coffee after the lunch crowd was gone I pitched my idea to the director. She immediately called several of her staff together and we began to plan out how my idea could come together. I had to live on my savings until the non-profit organization I founded made enough money to pay me a small salary. With the help of the mission we opened a clothing bank for men and women that are going back into the work force. Along with the clothing we have hair stylists, manicurists, and counselors who work on building up the client's self-esteem. No paycheck from a corporation can ever compare to the feeling I get when a woman I've sent out on an interview comes back crowing that she got the job.

Best of all, I'm working to help other women feel beautiful. When a woman who has never owned a good suit comes out of our little dressing room in a previously owned suit that looks as if it was tailored made for her, I can see how her self-confidence is boosted. I have seen women that were completely beaten down by life take on an air of assurance that even an abusive husband quickly realizes can't be bullied away.

So of course, just when I was feeling that I had achieved my goal to provide women with good quality clothes and assistance in securing employment, I ran into Mark—Mark the one-night stand who had dumped me so horribly.

"You look—ah, you look fabulous," he stammered when he saw me. "I should have called you."

"Really?" I feigned surprise. "Why?"

"Well, you're such a babe," he cooed. "I mean you're just beautiful now. I don't know what you're doing but it really agrees with you."

"Thank you," I said. "I've really got to be going."

"Don't you want to know how I am doing?" he asked. "We could have a drink—"

"Honestly no!," I smiled. "It's nice to see you, Mark, but you had your chance and blew it." I walked away and never looked back. THE END

NOWHERE TO HIDE

Sometime you just have to face the facts.

"Hey, Lauren! Grab a handful of that popcorn and pass it down this way."

With a flick of my wrist, I sent the basket twirling down the bar. "Help yourself, darling!" I said with a wink. Aidan Jones, the best looking man in the plant where we worked, grinned at me over the heads of the three people between us.

"Oh, no! You first," he teased. "Even I'm not stupid enough to eat something that Lauren Evans won't touch."

I forced myself to keep smiling, but inside I cringed. No matter how loud I laughed, fat jokes really hurt. And, no matter how horrible I felt about being fat, there was nowhere for me to hide.

A woman with hair bleached so blond that her brain must have been pickled smiled and snuggled her stick-sized body closer to Aidan. I wanted to die.

I wanted to speak my mind so badly. "So what if I am fat?" I wanted to shout. "At least I can think for more than five seconds without collapsing from exhaustion. I can also carry on a conversation without saying "duh" even once. And I can make love to a man without giving him bruises from bony protrusions."

Still, I wasn't simply overweight anymore. At three hundred

and twenty four pounds, I was morbidly obese. I had become a doctor's nightmare. And even though I was smart, articulate, and a lot of fun, most people didn't get to know me because of the way I looked.

Well, all that was going to end. The next morning, I was scheduled to have gastric bypass surgery. My stomach would be whittled down to the size of a thimble, and I wouldn't have to worry about overeating. I wouldn't have the ability to overeat ever again.

I'd already accomplished a task I hadn't been sure I could do—I hadn't had a bite of food in over twenty-four hours. Now, only twelve more hours and I would be ready for the surgeon. I was more than ready; I was ripe!

Aidan didn't seem to notice the blond stick at his side as he reached past her for my hand. "Well woman, if you're not going to eat, let's dance."

"You bet!" I grinned as we twirled onto the floor. I loved to two-step, and Aidan was amazingly good. He was tall, with arms long enough to spin someone as fat as me around the floor. At that moment, he made me feel beautiful and magical, like Cinderella at her first ball—not a bit the dancing hippo I knew I was.

He pulled me as close as my bulk would allow. "So why the hunger strike, Lauren?"

I fell back on my wit, as usual, for my answer. "Hey, the owners offered me a deal—all the free drinks I want and the best looking guy in the place to dance with if I don't eat them into bankruptcy tonight. It sounded like a good plan to me."

"Yeah?" he teased. "How'd they know I'd want to dance with you?"

I could feel the fat in my cheeks jiggle as I laughed back at him.

"Are you kidding? The owners were talking about Fred when they made me that offer. They didn't even know you'd be here." Fred was passed out near the corner of the bar, drool dripping from his chin.

Aidan's smile softened a little. "I'm always here and I always want to dance with you. You know, you're more fun than all those other girls put together."

If that was the case, I wondered why Aidan had never asked to take me home from the bar. I knew it was probably because he'd rather be with one of the skinny, blond bimbos who bruise men with their hip bones. I might be more fun to dance and tease with, but when it's time to be alone together, I'm not the right girl.

As the music ended, I slipped away and headed for the ladies' room. Then, when I was certain that Aidan was on the dance floor with someone else, I hurried back to where I'd left my things and got ready to leave.

But just as I was going out the door, Aidan caught my elbow. "Going home already? It's early yet."

My arm tingled where he touched me. Clearing my throat, I nodded. "I'm going on vacation tomorrow, so I want to get to bed early."

He widened his eyes. "Going to bed early and all alone?" he joked.

"Yeah. All alone," I choked out.

Leaning back against the doorframe, he let his hand slide to my wrist, but didn't let go. And there was no way I could force myself to walk away from him. "So where are you going on this vacation?"

Suddenly I wished I'd jerked from his grasp and run for home. There was no way I could tell him what a failure I was. Not only had I tried every diet in the book—and a few that weren't—but I'd gained weight with each one. This was my last chance. If I didn't lose weight this time, the doctors had assured me that I was going to die. And what a horrible thing to have on my death certificate: Lauren Evans—victim of overeating, commonly known as hand-to-mouth disease.

Unable to tell the truth, I joked to hide the pain. "I'm going to fat camp, and I'm the counselor!" Then, while he threw his head back and laughed his guts out, I slipped my arm from his grip and headed for my car, finally excited about going through with the surgery.

Early the next morning, dressed only in a gown and covered by a warm blanket, I waited for the surgery to begin. I nibbled on my already short fingernails. What was wrong with me? Why was I doing this?

Elective surgery meant that I had a choice. So why was I deliberately putting myself out there for a doctor to slice open? What if I had a reaction to the anesthesia and died? What if Dr. Cozens's hand slipped and I died? What if I started bleeding in the recovery room and no one noticed and I died?

Fighting the fear that threatened to overtake me, I took my finger from my mouth, got out of bed, and crossed the room to get my Vaseline from my purse. After I walked back to the bed, I had to rest a moment to catch my breath. I crawled under the covers and tried to draw my knees up, but the pain in them was too great. Besides, I knew from experience that I wouldn't be able to get my arms all the way around them.

That was the reason I was doing this. Because if I didn't die in surgery, I was going to die soon anyway. My weight was wearing out my heart, my blood pressure was as high as any I'd ever heard, and my joints were wearing out much faster than they should. I was only thirty-four years old.

Just as I made up my mind—for the hundredth time that morning—the nurse, holding a needle and bag of fluid, came into the room. "Almost time," she said with a bright smile.

"Good." I settled back on my pillow and bravely held out my left arm.

Before long, Dr. Cozens, dressed in scrubs, came into the room and gave me an encouraging smile. "Are you ready?"

I lifted my chin and held back the fearful remarks that were on the tip of my tongue. Nervous emotions still circled in my brain like gnats around old fruit. "You'll never know how ready."

"You'll do great." He patted my shoulder, and then glanced at the clock on the wall. "You should be in recovery by two o'clock, and back in your room before they deliver the supper trays—not that you'll be getting one. By this time tomorrow, you'll be trying out that new stomach of yours. Is anyone here with you?"

I shook my head. "No. Everyone had to work."

He frowned, concern evident on his face. "But there will be someone to take you home and help out for a few days, right?"

"Oh, yeah. But I didn't want her to have to take off any more days than she had to." And I wasn't sure I wanted anyone there with me. The doctor had told me that with the pain medication they'd be giving me for the next few days, I would sleep most of the time. I really didn't want Samantha, my best friend, sitting by my bed staring at me lying there like a beached whale.

After a moment, he smiled and nodded. "Well, let's get this show on the road."

He stepped out and a pair of nurses came to push me, bed and all, into an operating room. The room was cold, and I shivered as I moved from the bed to the surgery table.

Before long, the room started to swim. "You've given me

something, haven't you?" I asked.

"Yup, you must not have paid much attention back in pre-op," the young anesthesiologist answered, his eyes twinkling above his mask. "You should be asleep pretty—"

I never heard him finish, and the next thing I knew, I was in the recovery room.

After a few days in the hospital, I went home as was planned. Samantha took some time off from work to help me. She worried about eating in front of me, but it didn't bother me. For the first time in my life, I wasn't hungry. I didn't fantasize about what I was going to eat. In fact, food didn't even smell good anymore.

After almost three weeks, the day came when I had to go back to work. Samantha had promised not to tell a soul that I'd had surgery, and even though the management at the plant would know, I wasn't worried that they would spill the news. After all, they wouldn't want their insurance to have to pay for others to have the same surgery.

At lunch, I pulled out a thermos of broth. I almost groaned out loud when Aidan sat next to me with his lunch box.

"Hey, girl! How was your vacation?"

I tried to dredge up some enthusiasm. "It was fine."

He took a big bite of his sandwich and chewed a moment. Then, after a sip of soda, he set the can down, and looked closely at me. "What's the matter, Lauren? Have you been sick?"

I shrugged, trying to look unconcerned. "Oh, you know how it is at camp—sick kids show up and share their illness with everyone."

Frowning, he grasped my chin and turned my face toward him. "Well, you must have been sick the entire time you were off because you've lost a lot of weight. Have you seen a doctor?"

Aidan had noticed! He was the first person who'd told me that

I'd lost weight. I was so happy; I would have danced on the table if I hadn't been positive it would buckle under my weight. I tried to keep the grin off my face, but that was impossible. "Yeah, I saw a doctor."

Aidan lifted a brow and teased, "From the look on your face, he must have been good looking. Don't try to make me jealous, Lauren. I don't want to have to kick some doctor's skinny butt."

Aidan was a good guy, but everybody knew he was just being nice to me. He was the kind of guy who women flocked to. Plus, I'd never seen him pick a fat one out of the crowd.

Soon our table was filled with pals of Aidan's, and the few women who worked on the floor. While I slowly sipped my soup, I listened to the chattering around me. Usually I was the biggest duck in the puddle when it came to give and take, but I was still regaining my strength. Wishing I could lie down for a nap, I got up and headed for my locker.

"Where are you going?" Aidan called after me.

"To the little girls' room," I shot back, giving him the first answer I knew would shut him up.

"The little girls' room?" Mike Williams, a friend of Aidan's, echoed in a loud voice. "Then they won't be letting you in, will they?"

I was so used to cutting remarks, I ignored his and hurried on. After I stashed my things in my locker, I glanced at my watch. With fifteen minutes to spare, I decided to exercise, and I went outside to walk around the parking lot. I took it slowly, but made it around the entire enclosure twice before my time was up. After that, I took my broth with me to drink as I walked the lot. With knees as bad as mine, I couldn't move very quickly anyway, so it was easy to kill two birds with one stone.

A few months later, I was typing invoices when Mr. Mathers, my boss who was well into his sixties, stopped at my desk. "Would you please come into my office, Lauren?"

As I nodded, I reached for my steno pad. I followed him into the room and shut the door behind me, then I moved to the chair in front of his desk.

"Wait," he said before I could sit down.

"What is it?" I asked, surprised.

He didn't quite meet my gaze as he asked, "I don't mean to embarrass you, but would you mind turning around for me?"

My stomach cramped as I turned. Then, at his nod, I sat in the chair.

"Lauren, you look wonderful. How much weight have you lost?"

As I lowered my chin, I realized that the fat which used to bulge there was gone. "A little more than fifty pounds, Sir."

"Well, I must say, I'm impressed. I was afraid this surgery would be like the time you had your jaw wired shut or the time you went on the liquid protein diet, but you're really doing well."

I wanted to tell him that I didn't have a choice. Since my surgery, I didn't have a place to put any food. Still, I didn't want to be rude to him. I nodded my thanks.

"I've looked into that surgery, and I know there are women who have it who don't lose weight, like that one on TV for instance. But I see you out there, walking around the parking lot everyday at noon and drinking soup for lunch. I think you're going to make it this time. I'm proud of you!"

"Thank you," I whispered, wishing I had a coat or jacket to button up so he couldn't stare at my body.

"I'm thinking about having an employee's gym built here at the plant so you won't have to walk in the snow this winter.

And, to show you how proud I am of you, I'm going to give you a bonus and a little raise. You need to buy some new clothes that fit a little better."

Why was he giving me a raise? I certainly wasn't a better secretary just because I'd lost weight. In fact, I probably wasn't as good an employee with my lower energy levels and all the time I'd taken off for doctors' appointments. Feeling uncomfortable, I glanced down. For the first time, I noticed that my clothes were too big for me. I shrugged and smiled at Mr. Mathers. After all, a little extra money couldn't hurt.

The next week, after spending my time off buying clothes, I went to work wearing some of my new items. I immediately wished for a long coat to wear. It wasn't so bad when other women came up to me in the ladies' room, but having the men stare at me was horrible.

Feeling as if I'd been stripped naked and shoved out into the world, I wanted to run and hide. I was vulnerable to anyone who wanted to look at me. When I wasn't at my desk working, I kept my arms crossed in front of me, but crossed arms couldn't hide my new body.

Why did the simple task of losing weight make me feel so exposed? Women did it everyday, some did it year after year, and it didn't bother them. Besides, my excess weight had shamed me for so long. I was more than ready for the change.

One day as I went into the break room, Mike Williams caught my arm, and spun me around in front of everyone. "Wow, woman! You're looking fine. I may have to find a way to sneak out of my wife's bed one of these nights and pay you a little visit."

With all eyes focused on us, I struggled to draw a breath. I didn't want anyone paying me a visit. My throat closed and sweat broke out on the back of my neck. As I fought for air, the room started to dim. Pinpricks of light danced in my vision as my hands and feet started to tingle. Very soon, I was lying on a cot in the nurse's room surrounded by several of my fellow employees, including Mr. Mathers.

"She'll be all right," Sophie Bridges, our company nurse, nodded confidently. Then she made a shooing motion. "Now, get out of here. She needs a minute to recoup."

Once the room cleared, she came back to take my pulse and blood pressure. "Are you seeing your gastroenterologist as often as you're supposed to?"

Surprised that she knew about the surgery, I stared at her a moment.

"Mr. Mathers sees to it that I have access to all the employees health records in case something like this happens. So, are you making your appointments?"

"Yes," I whispered, shivering as the sweat that covered my body cooled me.

Sophie got a blanket and tucked it over me. "Are you following all his instructions?"

I nodded. "To the letter."

"I think you hyperventilated. Any idea what caused it?"

I tried to swallow as I thought back, but I couldn't. Although the doctor had warned me to be ready for it, remembering the look on the men's faces as they stared at my body was almost too much. I pulled the blanket tighter under my chin and wished I could hide there for the rest of the day.

"I-I don't—" Not only did I have to fight to breathe, I couldn't make sense of the thoughts spinning in my head. It was almost as if the gastric bypass had also been a lobotomy. I wanted to tell Sophie that I didn't like the way the men looked at my body;

that it made me feel naked, dirty, and cheap, but the words wouldn't come. All I could do was stammer, "I d-don't know."

Although Sophie's gaze was filled with compassion, she nodded briskly. "Okay. Why don't you lie here until you feel better and then head home—unless you want someone to drive you?"

"No, I think I'll be fine," I whispered.

I left the plant by the back door. It was farther to the parking lot, but I didn't want to see anyone—especially Aidan. I could just imagine the jokes that had gone down the line after I fainted. Thinking of him hearing those gross insinuations—and possibly laughing with the others—was more than I could handle.

At home, I went straight to bed. When the phone started ringing, I put the pillow over my head. I knew it was probably someone from work, and I'd made such a fool of myself. How could I ever go back?

Samantha, my roommate, had already left for a short trip that weekend, and I was glad to be completely alone. I didn't know what I was going to do, but I had to do something to rectify the horrible mistake I'd made. How had I been so ready for the surgery, but not prepared to live my life as a thin person?

I stayed in bed the entire weekend, getting up only to bathe. I couldn't eat, talk to anyone, or leave the house. All I could do was think. Finally, late Sunday night, I asked myself why I'd had the surgery. I listed the reasons on my fingers—for my health; because my heart couldn't handle the stress it had been under; because my joints were wearing out way too fast; and because I was tired of being the fat chick.

And now that I'd lost all that weight, I wasn't happy. Why not? Because, if I was no longer the fat chick, then who was I? Nobody.

I sat bolt upright in bed. That wasn't true. I was Lauren Carol

Evans. I was a human being who was intelligent and easy to talk to. I was a good cook, a great two-stepper, and a lot of fun. Or at least I used to be, before I lost my pride along with all that weight.

Getting out of bed, I ran to my closet and pulled together the outfits that I would wear the next week. Not having taken the time to buy many new clothes, I didn't have much to choose from. Still, what I did have would look the best it could. Next, I tried on each outfit and stood in front of the full-length mirror in Samantha's room. "You look wonderful!" I said out loud. "Absolutely mah-velous."

I looked at myself really hard. I was thinner, but it was still me. There were fewer bumps, lumps, and humps, but it was still me. I shook less when I laughed, but it was still me.

I was lacking, of course—now I had only one chin and no swinging wings on the backs of my arms. Another thing lacking was laughter. I wasn't having as much fun as I used to, and I'd stopped going dancing.

I was determined to have fun, no matter how people looked at me. I was going to laugh again and go to dances, because somewhere out there a man was waiting just for me—a man who'd never seen me as fat; a man who could love me without remembering the old Lauren; a man I could have a whole new life with.

More resolute than ever, I sat down and wrote myself a letter. In it, I listed the reasons why I'd lost the weight. I explained what it was about myself that I liked—and not a word of it had anything to do with my body. Then I outlined a plan for a whole new life.

I would go to work every day with my pride intact. I wouldn't duck my head, no matter what anyone had to say about my body.

I would go shopping until I had a whole new wardrobe. Then, as a symbol of my whole new life, I would give away all my fat clothes.

And on Friday night, I would go back to the Stables Lounge and I would dance to every song—all night long.

I hadn't been out since the night before the surgery, so I was sure many of the people who frequented the place wouldn't recognize me. But even if they did, I still planned to have a great time!

During the next week of work, I wondered if I should buy earplugs so I wouldn't have to hear the crude comments some of the men made. Instead, I solved that problem by wearing a walkman when I wasn't at my desk, and turning the music up loud when Mike Williams was around.

Finally, Friday night arrived. Although Samantha offered to go with me, I wanted to handle it all by myself. After dressing in my new, not-for-little-old-ladies dress, I slipped into Samantha's room for a look in her mirror.

I almost didn't recognize myself. The dress was sassy, sleek, and made me look like a million dollars. I wasn't sure if my eyes sparkled because they'd stopped being surrounded by fat, because of the new eye makeup I'd bought, or because I was ready for a good time, but they lit up and made me smile. And my hair, which I usually kept back in a ponytail, now curled around my shoulders.

I swallowed hard, forcing my timidity down, and then I put on a smile. "Look out, Stables! Here I come!"

After driving to the bar, I had a moment of uneasiness as I watched several young women slip in the door together. I thought that I probably shouldn't be in there with them. I was different. They're used to being skinny and having men chase after them, but I was just a fraud.

But before I allowed myself to put the car in reverse, I pulled my letter out of my purse. Turning on the overhead light, I unfolded it and read it from beginning to end. Then, I read it again.

I do belong here, I thought. As much as anyone, and more than most.

After taking a long, slow breath, I opened the door and forced myself to get out. I locked the car, and then stepped up on the sidewalk and headed for the entrance. Before I'd gone three steps, I heard someone running to catch up.

Glancing back, I saw the blond stick who'd been flirting with Aidan the last time I'd been at Stables. My heart sank, but I pasted a smile on my mouth.

"Hi. I don't know you, do I? I'm Katie, and I just hate walking into places like this alone, don't you?" She stopped talking just long enough to emit a high pitched giggle, then she stuck her arm through mine. "If we walk in together, we won't feel so lonely. After I get my first beer under my belt it's not so bad, but I just hate walking into places—"

I stopped listening because she'd started repeating herself. Instead, I glanced at her face. She had on enough makeup to plaster walls. It was caked onto her cheeks in an effort to hide old acne scars. Maybe Katie didn't have all the confidence in the world; maybe it had been my total lack of self-worth that had made her seem worldly.

When we got inside, the usual crowd was at the bar, laughing, drinking beer, and eating popcorn. I ordered a light beer and expected to see Katie stop next to me, but she made a beeline for Aidan.

Rather than smile down at Katie, Aidan was watching me.

Without a word to her, he picked up his drink and walked over to me.

"Hey, Lauren."

As usual, his deep voice sent a shower of tingles down my spine. "Hello," I murmured.

Before he could say another word, a cowboy I didn't know grabbed my hand and jerked me onto the dance floor. As we two-stepped, I tried to watch Aidan over the stranger's shoulder, but I began to get dizzy. After several long, painful minutes the song ended and I staggered back to the bar.

All of my beer remained, and I couldn't drink more than a little bit, because I'd been warned it might cause me to get sick. Rather than chance it, I waved for the bartender. He skidded to a stop in front of me. "What can I get you, sweetheart?"

"A glass of water?" I asked, worried that the request would make him angry. After all, the bar didn't make any money serving water.

"Coming right up, beautiful."

Surprised by his reaction, I reached into my purse and pulled out a bill to drop in his tip jar. "Thank you."

"Hey, you don't need to tip me. Just getting to see your beautiful—" his gaze dropped from my face to my body, then moved back "—face is enough."

The old feeling of humiliation started to creep out, but I hiked my chin and my chest and shoved that feeling right back down. I had no reason to be ashamed!

After a blessed sip of cool water, I set my glass down and noticed Aidan waiting beside me. "Hello again."

I started to answer, but before I could speak, another cowboy started to approach. Aidan grabbed my hand and took a step closer, settling himself like a wall between me and the other man.

"Hi, Aidan," I finally answered.

"Would you like to dance with me?"

I nodded.

When we made it to the floor, Aidan drew me into his arms. "Why have you been ignoring me lately?"

Unable to tear my gaze from his, I had to wet my lips before answering. "Because I knew you were just being nice, and I couldn't stand for Mike Williams to tease you about being my friend. I know what he thinks about me."

Aidan frowned, his jaw hardening. "I don't care what Mike says or thinks. I just want to be with you."

Aidan hadn't wanted to be with me when I was fat. I wanted to cry. I wasn't good enough then, was I? I was just fat Lauren Evans who ate anything that didn't bite her first. I had been a buddy to pal around with and someone to drink with. I could just as well have been one of the guys.

Afraid I would break into tears right there on the dance floor, I broke from Aidan's arms and ran outside. Blindly, I made my way to my car. Before I could open the door, Aidan was beside me. He turned me around and took me in his arms.

"What is it, Lauren? Aren't I good enough for you now that you got skinny? I've cared deeply about you for a long time—since before you started losing weight. I love the sweet spirit you have inside. I love your laughter and your kindness. I love your imagination and your quick wit." His voice dropped to a whisper. "I love the person you are.

"And if you hadn't been so skittish," he continued, "I'd have told you so the last time I saw you here at Stables. But you ran off that night, and I was stuck fighting to keep Katie from attacking me."

With the pads of his thumbs, Aidan wiped tears from my face.

"Oh, Aidan," I whispered, unable to find enough breath to say more.

He pulled me closer. "Lauren, I want to be in your life. I want to be your best friend, your confidant, and your lover. You're the only woman I've ever wanted to spend my life with."

Finally, I'd found home. I knew that no matter what happened in the future, even if I became old, bent, and wrinkled, I knew that I would always be loved. And when I was feeling a little down, I would have the perfect place to hide—right there in Aidan's arms. THE END

She Had To Learn The Hard Way:

"BEING SKINNY DOESN'T MEAN A THING"

Especially when your hot, MTV-ready body attracts the wrong kind of guys.

On the first day of spring, I was sitting on the bleachers with my friend, Clarisa. We were the outsiders, watching the other kids have fun.

When we became sophomores, I expected things to get better, but so far, high school was still a drag.

"When's the fun going to start?" I asked Clarisa.

She studied me through squinted eyes. "Maybe you could make it start for you, Jenna—if you'd lose a few pounds and do something with your hair."

If anyone else besides Clarisa said that, it would've made me mad. But Clarisa's my best friend and she understands me, just as I do her. In fact, I look at her in the same critical way. Clarisa isn't overweight; she's actually a little on the skinny side, but she's not pretty. Her teeth protrude and her features are uneven, her nose a little too long.

"You'd look a little more curvy in skirts," I said. "And maybe it would help if you got highlights. Makeup can work wonders, too."

She shrugged disconsolately. "I'll never be pretty, but you could be. You have the bone structure and that beautiful face."

"You really think so?" I asked.

Looking into my little compact mirror, all I saw was a pudgy face; I knew the "bone structure" she talked about was hidden under excess pounds and it all seemed so . . . hopeless. Every time I tried to lose weight, I gave up in desperation and ended up at the snack bar, stuffing myself because I was so hungry.

But Clarisa couldn't seem to take her eyes off of me and she was still studying me without blinking. "You really could do it, you know, Jenna."

Maybe just the fact that she believed I could was what made me try again. "I'll do it," I said. "I'll lose the weight and then we'll see what we have to work with. I'll be a different girl when school starts in the fall."

As it was, there were only two weeks left until school was out. I figured three months of summer vacation would give me plenty of time to lose twenty pounds.

Just then, the football team was coming out of the locker room and Justin's the one I was watching, Justin—with the sandy-blond hair, blue eyes, and that devilishly innocent sideways grin. Just what a Greek God would've looked like, I mused. Clarisa knew I had a crush on him, but even she didn't know the depth of my feelings for him. I'd fallen in love with him the year before and it didn't seem like I would ever get over it. As it was, I thought about him all the time. He was coming toward me and my heart was beating like crazy; if I had to say something to him, I was sure I'd stammer. But he didn't even look at me—just walked on by.

He stopped to talk to Cara, a cute, little cheerleader. She was smiling up at him and he was beaming down on her, showing nice, white, even teeth.

I couldn't bear to watch.

Thankfully, just then, my bus pulled into the loading zone, so it was time to go. I picked up my books, waved good-bye to Clarisa, and got on the bus. Nate motioned for me to sit next to him, but I stuck my tongue out at him and sat in an opposite seat. I won't sit by him and have the other kids tease me, I thought. He should know that by now. Anyway, we get off at the same stop to walk the rest of the way home together.

Nate's been my friend ever since we started kindergarten together. Nate Lightfoot is half-American Indian. He has an Indian name, too—"Little River," but he prefers to be called Nate.

"I'm going to lose some weight," I told him that afternoon. "Before school starts again, you'll see a whole, new Jenna."

"Why would you want to do that? You look just right the way you are."

"You're just trying to be nice," I said, thinking, Of course he really couldn't mean it.

Back in those days, Nate never seemed ready to go home. As it was, I'd only been to his house a few times. It's awfully quiet there, compared to the activity around my house. Nate's dad is a Mohawk Indian, but his mom's white. His dad died when Nate was just a baby and he and his mom live in a small cabin that's been weathered to a soft, worn gray. Nate's bedroom is the loft upstairs. His mom speaks to him in soft tones, calling him River, the only time I ever hear him called by that name.

We came to the fork in the road where I turn and he goes on. "I could walk home with you," he offered.

"If you want to." I handed him my books.

Nate's dad and my dad used to always do things together. Before Nate's dad died, they were building a chicken coop, and they hoped to have it ready by summer. Now, most evenings, Nate worked on it alone. He planned to raise broilers and share the profits, with Dad furnishing the capital and Nate doing most of the work.

We walked down the lane not saying anything and soon, the little, rock house I call home came into view. It's nestled against the hill behind it and always, when the house comes into sight, I have to stop for a moment in wonder. I love that house, just as I love the hills around it. I don't have anything to compare it to, but I cannot imagine a better place to call home.

"This is the best place to live in the whole, wide world—right here in the Ozarks," I declared suddenly, and Nate nodded. He knows how I feel about our little corner of the world. He feels the same way, too, I know.

We came to the house and headed into the kitchen. The wonderful aroma of fresh-baked cookies filled the room. "You two will want some milk with your cookies," Mom said as she set a plate of warm, gooey chocolate chip cookies on the table.

"Not me," I said. "I'm not very hungry, actually. I'll just have an apple." I polished the red apple against my jeans.

Mom looked at me like she thought I must be sick. "At least Nate won't say no to my cookies."

Indeed, he took four from the plate and straddled a chair. That's when I realized that it wasn't going to be easy, losing weight with all of the tempting, tasty food that Mom cooks, and the way she always encourages me to eat, eat, eat. Still, all of a sudden, I was determined. I had only to bring Justin's face to mind to know that I could do it.

Afterward, Nate went to work on the chicken coop and I called old Lancelot, my Collie, and went out to run a mile. I made it about halfway before I collapsed in a heap. With all the fat I was carrying, I was huffing and puffing for breath; I honestly still don't know why I ever let myself gain so much weight. I guess it probably started with too much inactivity through the winters and too many sweets. It all kind of slipped up on me over three years.

After school was out for the summer, I got earnest about the weight loss. Once Mom realized I was trying to look better, she really started helping and supporting me. She bought fresh vegetables and fruit, and there was always something good to eat in the house that wasn't loaded with calories.

Nate and Dad worked every day on the chicken coop, so I tied on a carpenter's apron and climbed on the roof to pitch in. I don't have brothers, so I've always pitched in to help when needed; anyway, I really enjoy outdoor work. Those days, the sun was warm on my back and I felt in tune with nature and with Dad and Nate as we worked together. The hard work firmed my muscles and my jeans started to fit a lot looser as the summer wore on.

My birthday is the twentieth of May and the strawberries are usually ripe just in time for my birthday. That year, Mom planned on having strawberry shortcake with homemade strawberry ice cream for my birthday celebration, but I told her, "I don't want a dessert. I'll be happy just having the berries. I want to be a size eight."

"How can we have a birthday celebration without cake?" Mom wailed.

I shrugged. "Make an angel food cake and I'll eat a small piece without icing; anyway, fresh-picked strawberries are delicious without sugar and whipped cream. The rest of you can enjoy the cake and ice cream."

We didn't have a party—just the family and Nate. I don't know if Mom invited him or if he just assumed he was welcome; as it was, he was around so much, we all kind of just thought of him as part of the family. For my birthday, he gave me a little emerald heart on a silver chain, my birthstone.

I noticed Mom didn't eat the cake and ice cream, either. "My clothes are getting a little too tight. It wouldn't hurt me to drop a few pounds, too," she said.

The summer went by before I knew it. I didn't do anything special, really; Nate took me to the movies a couple of times and we went skating on Saturdays. The rest of the time we spent on the farm; we went horseback riding once a week and fishing when we felt like it. Nate's a natural in the woods. One of his uncles, a Sioux Indian, was teaching him the ways of Mother Earth and sometimes they let me come along. It was a real compliment to be included, Nate assured me. Then he taught me things he learned when I wasn't with them.

By and by, the twenty pounds I set out to lose were gone, and then I had a brand-new figure. If Nate noticed, he didn't say anything, but I knew the kids who hadn't seen me all summer would notice it. Mom took me shopping and she had to buy me a whole new wardrobe; she was so proud of me that she didn't seem to mind. I got a cute, little, short, flared, denim miniskirt at Old Navy that I would never have worn the year before, and the boot-leg jeans I bought were exactly the size I wanted them to be; I was a perfect eight. Mom took me to the beauty salon for my first professional highlighting job and I got a makeover, too—also a first. Mom's strict about what she considers to be "in good taste," so it was light and subtle and very natural looking, but that was okay with me; I didn't want to be too obvious since I never bothered with makeup before. As it was, that afternoon, after my "transformation," I passed a storefront and caught a glimpse of myself in the window and so help me—I didn't even recognize myself!

Back in school, all of a sudden I got a lot of attention, but I didn't once forget what I did it for. All along, I knew I just wanted to impress Justin; as it was, I still did. But Justin still didn't seem to know that I was alive, even though I saw him almost every day. Because he was a senior, I didn't have classes with him, so I only saw him in passing in the hallways, the library, or the cafeteria. Somehow, I thought, I have to get him to notice me, to really look at me. I figured if I were as striking as my classmates told me I was, it shouldn't be too hard.

I planned it for days. I know where the seniors hang out after school—a Johnny Rockets close to campus—and I decided I would hang out there, too. As it was, a school dance was coming up and I really, really wanted Justin to ask me. So I enlisted Clarisa to help me, seeing as I couldn't very well "just show up there" all by myself. That would be too obvious. No, I decided, Clarisa and I will just saunter in really casually and sit in a booth near him. Maybe I'll even ask him to pass me the salt or something.

Clarisa didn't want to at first, but she finally relented and agreed to help me. "After all," she said, "you've gone to a lot of trouble for this guy. He must be awfully important to you. I just hope he's worth it."

"He's worth it—you'll see. If you knew how I feel about him, you'd totally understand."

Clarisa just sighed and rolled her eyes heavenward the way she does when she's exasperated.

The next evening we strolled into Johnny Rockets. I saw Justin as soon as we went in; he was seated in a booth with another guy and two girls.

"This doesn't seem like a very good time," Clarisa whispered to me. "He seems busy with his friends."

Having gone this far, I didn't mean to be dissuaded. I slid into the booth behind theirs, facing Justin, and Clarisa slid in on the other side. I could easily see over the back of the booth. Justin saw me looking at him and smiled. Clarisa and I ordered cheeseburgers, fries, and cherry Cokes.

"Would you pass the salt, please?" I did actually ask him that.

Justin grabbed the saltshaker and came to our booth, sliding in beside me. "You're a junior, aren't you?"

"Yep. I'm Jenna and this is my best friend, Clarisa."

He nodded in her direction. "You're a hottie," he said to me. "I remember seeing you around last year, but I don't think you looked like this."

Clarisa just kind of sniffed. "Well, beauty isn't the only thing in the world, you know. Maybe you'd like to know if she has any brains."

Justin ignored her. "I have to get back to my friends, but give me your phone number and I'll call you tomorrow."

I wrote it down on a napkin and he stuck it in his pocket.

Clarisa and I ate and left. Once we were outside, though, I couldn't contain myself a second longer. I gave out a big, "Yesss!"

Clarisa didn't look very convinced. "You may be in for a big letdown, you know," she said sourly.

I wondered why she couldn't just be happy for me. After all, I thought, she's the one who pointed it out to me in the first place that to be in on the fun, you need to be good looking.

Justin did call the next day, just as he said he would. "There's a party at this girl's house tomorrow night. Wanna go?"

Would I? I took a deep breath, thinking about just how long I'd waited to hear those words. "Yeah; sure."

"Good. I'll pick you up around seven."

My mind was working as fast as it could, thinking of all the city girls he dated and wondering what he'd think of where we live, so far out in the country—not to mention the fact that the road isn't too good after you leave the main road.

"It's a long way out to my house, actually. I could stay at my grandmother's and you could pick me up there. How would that be?"

"Great. You can tell me tomorrow how to find her house. 'Bye, now."

I hung up the phone very gently.

I told Mom I had a date and wanted to stay in town to save the boy the trouble of having to drive such a long way. She said, "Okay, but have him come in for you, just as he would have to if he called for you at home. I hope he's a nice boy, but of course he is, or you wouldn't go out with him." She kissed me. "I trust you, Jenna."

I didn't tell Clarisa about the date. We always said that when we had our first real dates, we'd double-date together. I wasn't counting the casual outings I had with Nate as dates, and thought of this as my first real "date." Still, somehow, I couldn't bear to tell her. After all, I knew there was no way she'd be included.

The next evening I took a lot of time fixing my hair and nails. I wore one of my new outfits—the denim miniskirt with a wide, funky-looking, retro-style belt, and this really cute, embroidered, pink peasant blouse with big sleeves. I checked myself out in my grandma's full-length mirror and paced restlessly while I waited. Finally, I saw Justin drive up in his black BMW convertible. He honked the horn and I went to the door and motioned for him to come in. He acted slightly impatient, but he complied. I introduced him to Gram. She smiled and held out her hand to him; she always tries to be nice to my friends, but almost instantly I got the distinct impression that she disapproved of Justin.

When we got to the house where the party was being held, there were already cars lining the street on both sides. Three girls were there with their dates and we made eight. I knew all of them, but only slightly; they were all seniors except for one girl from my class. Cara was the hostess.

"Have something to drink," she said, indicating a cooler full of beer.

"Where are her parents?" I whispered to Justin.

"Oh, I think they're out of town, so it's pretty safe for us to be here."

"But they have drinks—and we're underage," I whispered back.

He snorted, making a face. "It's just beer, girl. One bottle isn't going to hurt you." He popped one open and handed it to me.

Maybe he's right, I reasoned. One bottle can't hurt, and anyway—I don't have to drink it all. I took a sip, not wanting to seem "different."

We sat on the floor or wherever we could find a seat and Cara put a movie into the DVD player. I only had to watch it for a few seconds before I realized it was hardcore porn, but still—what could I say? I wanted to conform; I wanted Justin to like me; I wanted to be his girl. So when he slipped his arm around me, I relaxed against his shoulder. He didn't move except to get another beer.

An hour later, there was nobody in the room—just Justin and me. "Where did everybody go?" I asked him.

"Probably looking for a place with a little more privacy," he said. "Looks like we've got this room all to ourselves."

He pulled me against him and I could feel the hardness of his body and the smoothness of the muscles in his arms. His breath was warm and sensuous against my mouth and I wondered suddenly, How long have I dreamed of that moment? Then he opened his mouth on mine; before that moment, I didn't even know that people kiss like that—I was honestly that naïve. I knew I should pull away—do something to stop him—but I was powerless to do so. He slipped one hand into my bra and I still didn't push him away. He ran his hand up the back of my leg.

"I'm glad you wore a skirt," he said.

And I still didn't push him away. His kisses were as intoxicating as the beer and I didn't want him to stop. It was only when he started removing my pantyhose that sanity returned. I jumped up, pulled up my hose, and buttoned my blouse.

"You don't have anything to worry about," he said. "I have protection."

I have a lot to worry about, I thought. Most of all—my own actions. Already, I can see Mom's face before me, telling me she trusts me.

"I think I'd better go home." I grabbed my purse and headed for the door. It didn't matter then that I'd dreamed of being with this guy for what seemed like my whole life, I felt nothing then but shame.

Justin followed me. "Hey—I understand—it being our first date and all. I guess I was moving too fast."

But he didn't understand that it was my first date with anyone. How many girls have already yielded in his arms? I wondered then.

I saw him the next day. He sought me out after school while I was waiting for the bus and acted as if nothing happened.

"Want to go to the game with me on Friday?" he asked. "I have to play, but I could find someone to sit with you and afterward, we can join the gang at Johnny Rockets. If we win, there'll be a celebration. If we don't, we'll have a condolence party."

I did want to go. Given time to think, I didn't think he was as much to blame for what happened at the party as I was willing.

I decided I would just have to be more careful from now on.

And indeed—I made it work. I got really good at keeping him at arm's length, while still giving him the impression that it was "only a matter of time." And I admit—I was so proud to be seen with him. The girls who snubbed me before were all of a sudden actually anxious to be friends with me! Deanna, Hilary, Cara, and Jessica took me into their circle—the "magic circle" I'd admired for so long and never thought I'd be a part of. I tried to include Clarisa in our fun, but she didn't want to be included and they didn't act friendly toward her the way they did with me.

And then there was Nate. Sometimes he still walked home with me, but all of a sudden, we seemed to have nothing to say to each other; gone was the easy camaraderie we always enjoyed. I tried not to let my loss of friendships with Clarisa and Nate bother me, though; after all, I was popular. Suddenly, I had everything any girl could want. But for some reason, I felt I didn't really belong in the crowd—not really, anyway. Too often, I still felt restless and unhappy.

Cara was having a slumber party and I was invited. It was easier for me to go home with her from school because I live so far from town. Mom said it was okay, but added, "I think it's time for you to bring your friends here so we can meet them. We've never even met the young man you're dating, and Dad doesn't like you going out with someone he's never met. Maybe you'd like to have a party of your own some night."

"Okay; I will soon." But even as I said it, I knew I wouldn't. It suddenly occurred to me that I didn't want them to see the country home where I live. All of a sudden I realized I was ashamed of our house, and it came as a real shock to me to realize it—I'm ashamed of the cozy, loving home I've always loved so much! Unfortunately, compared to the big, brand-new, McMansion-style houses my new friends lived in in the new developments outside of town, our place sure didn't look like much.

The night of Cara's party, six girls showed up. We had popcorn, Cokes, and brownies—no beer because her parents were home. We watched TV and played games, but soon settled on the floor in our sleeping bags, "just to talk."

It was not what I expected. When they talked about sex, I thought it would be with curiosity—the same kind of curiosity I had raging inside of me most of the time. But these girls already knew a lot about it from their own experiences. And when I had nothing to contribute to the "tell-all session," they started teasing me about me being a virgin.

"I'm only sixteen," I finally said, blushing miserably.

Cara snorted. "I was fourteen my first time. We did it in the backseat of my boyfriend's car."

"You did?" I asked in astonishment.

She shrugged, rolling her eyes as she painted her toenails with gold, glittery polish. "Why not? Everybody else is doing it. Anyway, you've gotta get it over with—sooner or later—right?" She blew a big, pink bubble and popped her gum.

"But, I mean—did you think about what could happen? Did you use protection?"

"Nah. It was completely spur-of-the-moment the first time. But I wouldn't do that again,"

Then Hilary said, "You can act as high and mighty as you like, Jenna, but sooner or later, you'll come around to it. I mean, even if you're not crazy about the idea, the guy expects it. And if you won't do it, he'll just find someone who will."

"I wanted to do it," Cara insisted proudly, sipping her Coke and giggling. "I wanted to find out what I was missing—and I'm sure glad I did. It's totally awesome!"

"But if a boy really loves you, won't he be willing to wait?" I asked, embarrassed by my "country bumpkin" stupidity.

They all just stared at me with blank expressions. "Not Justin," Jessica finally said. "You've just snagged the most popular boy in the whole school, you know. He can have just about any girl he wants and he's not gonna wait around for you to grow up and put out, girl."

Deanna finally changed the subject and I was glad. We spent the rest of the night discussing movies we'd seen, the latest hairstyles, and of course—guys. No one brought up sex again, and I was relieved.

But the seed was sown. I believed them. After all, I reasoned, they're all older than I am, and what they say seems to jibe with Justin's actions. Already, as it is, he's starting to become impatient with me. In my heart, I know it's only a matter of time before I have to give him what he wants or he'll dump me. I can't even bear to think about him dumping me . . . I think I'm in love with him, even. Never mind that I plan to go to college and I promised myself that I wouldn't get seriously involved with anyone in high school. When I'm with Justin, his kisses are all that matter. I want to be in his arms forever and when I'm away from him, I can hardly wait until we're together again. As it is, I already have a hard time thinking about life without him.

He called me the next day. "Hey, you know what? We always seem to have a crowd around, and I thought it'd be nice if we went somewhere together, just the two of us. How about a picnic if the weather holds out? We could drive up Lookout Mountain and spend the day. The leaves are turning and it should be a great time to go."

"I'd love to!" I gushed, I was thinking, I'll have him to myself for the whole day. There was no tomorrow then; I lived for the moment.

I met him in town, which had become my habit. As it was, I still wouldn't let him come to my house.

He had the top down on the convertible. I laid my head against the back of the seat and let the wind blow through my hair, musing, I've never felt more carefree in my whole life. This is how it will be from now on—just the two of us in his gorgeous BMW—never going back to school, or to work. Just holding hands and smiling at each other. . . .

Justin brought the car to a stop beneath a giant oak and came to my side to open the door for me. Instead of letting me get out, he put his arms around me and lifted me out. He spread a blanket under the tree and put me on it. Then he sat beside me and kissed me—first on my forehead and cheeks, and then on my mouth. After awhile he started to unbutton my blouse and all of a sudden I was completely happy and willing to let him do whatever he wanted to do.

It's what I want, too, now, I realized.

What I felt next was pain—terrible pressure and this tearing, burning pain. All of a sudden, I no longer enjoyed the lovemaking, but I didn't tell him to stop. I just closed my eyes, squeezed out the tears, and let him continue—let him finish, to put it bluntly. I decided then that I was "doing it for him"—doing what Justin wanted—what he "needed." When it was over, he groaned and cried out and then collapsed on top of me. After a few moments he groaned again and rolled over to lie on his back next to me on the itchy, wool blanket.

"Wow," he said. "You're an awesome lay, girl."

I realized then that he didn't even seem to know how much he hurt me. As it was, I was sobbing quietly beside him, but he didn't reach over to comfort me. After a few minutes—after he caught his breath and wiped himself off and buckled his jeans—he just got up and walked away, leaving me to deal with the pain—and the aftermath—alone. When he finally came back, he handed me a Coke from the cooler he brought and poured Jack Daniel's in it. "Drink this," he instructed. "It'll make you feel better."

I drank it, then another—and then another—until I could no longer feel the pain. To tell you the truth, after awhile I didn't feel much of anything, but even as I knew I was getting drunk—make that: bombed—I promised myself I wouldn't drink again until I was of legal age.

And maybe not even then, I thought suddenly.

My whole life changed that day—

And I wasn't ready for it—

Not by any stretch.

We stayed there until late evening—until we were both sober enough for him to take me back to town. Even though Justin seemed weirdly indifferent suddenly, I was sure then that in the end, everything would be okay. After all, I thought, now I'm his girl and his alone. By giving my virginity to him, I've sealed our love and now we'll be together forever.

The next day was a Sunday. I waited anxiously by the phone, but Justin didn't call.

On Monday, I could hardly wait to get back to school so I could see him again. I was sure something had happened on Sunday to keep him from getting in touch with me. But in the cafeteria, he saw me—I know he saw me—and yet he still went to sit with another group, and he didn't even look my way—not even once.

I thought for sure than that he'd come to talk to me when

school was out, like he usually did, but he didn't. I went home and waited for him to call me that evening, but still no phone call. After a week, I finally had to accept the fact that he was through with me . . . and that he wasn't even man enough to tell me so.

I just thought I had troubles then.

A week later, I missed my period. I waited anxiously for two more weeks before I finally called Justin. "I have to talk to you," I told him urgently, quickly—before he could hang up on me. "It's very important and I wouldn't have called if it wasn't, since you don't seem to want to talk to me anymore."

At first he argued that he "couldn't" see me. Then I told him, "Well, then—I guess I'll just have to go to my dad, and he'll talk to you. Would you like that better?"

Only then did Justin agree to meet me.

That afternoon at Denny's, Justin already knew what I was going to tell him before I told him.

"Why didn't you protect me?" I asked him with tears streaming down my cheeks.

"You didn't tell me that I had to use anything! I thought you were on the Pill or something!" he snapped viciously.

"But—didn't you know? I—I was a virgin, Justin!"

He snorted and gave me the nastiest, meanest look. "A virgin can take the Pill, dummy."

"What are we going to do?" I wailed.

He shrugged like we were debating whether to watch Star Wars or The Empire Strikes Back. "I'm not gonna do anything. I suggest you talk to your mom; maybe she'll know where you can get a cheap abortion."

As I watched him walk away, a part of me died—the part of me that trusted.

I knew I'd never be the same again.

I didn't talk to Mom. I just wasn't ready to do that and I couldn't bear to think of the pain it would cause her.

The person I did finally talk to is Nate. As it was, he could already tell that something was wrong—just by looking at me—and when he finally confronted me and asked me about it, I just blurted it all out. Then I burst into tears.

"I oughta break his neck," Nate muttered, clenching his fists at his sides. "What kind of guy would do that to a girl like you?"

He put his arms around me while I cried and cried until I was finally quiet in his arms.

"Well, if it's true, then I'll marry you," he finally declared. "That is, I mean—if you'll have me. I'd be proud to be your husband and the father of your child."

I didn't answer him. In that moment, I could find no words to express what I was feeling.

As it was, a month had gone by since I last had my period and I didn't think I was going to have one, but that night, I woke up with a familiar pain in my abdomen: menstrual cramps. I ran to the bathroom and sat there on the toilet for the longest time, tears of pure and utter relief streaming down my cheeks. After all the worry I've been through, I thought, I don't know how I could ever be so lucky. Dear Lord, I've been so incredibly stupid, but I don't intend to ever be stupid again.

I didn't tell anyone else about what happened—except Clarisa. I knew I could tell her and my secret would be safe. After Justin dropped me, the girls who'd been my "friends" suddenly didn't want to be "friends" anymore. After having neglected Clarisa for so long, I found out the hard way that she's my best friend—and always will be. All along, despite the way I mistreated her and took her for granted, she always cared about me, she was always faithful—always the kind of person anyone would be lucky to have for a friend, just like Nate is.

We went on to be seniors and Justin and the girls who pretended to be my friends graduated. Since then, I've put it all behind me (I think, for the most part) and I'm planning on college next year. If anything good came out of this experience, it's that I learned to be careful about what kind of people I trust.

A few weeks ago, I got off the school bus and walked with Nate to where he usually turns off to go to his house. "I could walk home with you, you know," he suggested suddenly—the first time in ages.

"If you want to," I said, and handed him my books.

"Will you go to the senior prom with me?" he asked.

I grinned and turned to face him. "I thought you'd never ask."

He reached for my hand and we walked home together. THE END

WEIGHT WOES

Seeing past the pounds.

I rushed across the parking lot of the local gym, wondering why I had complicated the one experience I dreaded most by being late. I had managed to avoid places like this for all of my twenty-eight years, a record that would never have been broken if my sister hadn't announced her upcoming nuptials.

The very thought of standing next to my petite sister in front of the condemning eyes of our family while wearing a fitted bridesmaid's dress had broken my resolve. Calling the gym to make an appointment with a trainer had been my first priority. If I had to rush headlong into the fitness world, I might as well have a guide.

Pushing through the double doors, I asked a leotard-clad woman at the front desk which way to go. Panting from exertion, I sped down the carpeted hallway and took a quick left. In my haste, I didn't notice the man until it was too late to stop. Colliding, we toppled to the ground in a tangle of arms and legs.

The man recovered first, jumped to his feet, and leaned over to offer me a hand. As I rose, I pushed my wavy brown hair back from where it had fallen over my eyes. Instant mortification engulfed me like a heat wave.

The man before me was gorgeous. Dark brown hair framed a strong face and his eyes were a lighter shade of brown and flecked with black. He was a good seven or eight inches taller than me and his body toned and taut. I pulled at the hem of my oversize T-shirt. Please, don't let this be my trainer, I thought.

"Paige Henderson?" he asked.

As soon as the words passed his full lips, I sighed in defeat. Life was cruel. I just had to make a complete and total fool of myself in front of my new trainer, my new hot trainer.

"Yes," I said. "I'm so sorry about that. I was running late—" the words drifted off at his smile.

"Literally," he joked. "Running, that is."

I cringed inwardly as he motioned me into the room. Introducing himself as Alex Night, he began the session as if everything were normal, as if speeding clients ran him down everyday. With his looks, I thought clients probably ran after him a lot.

I followed him through the gym, listening intently as he described equipment and the classes.

Last chance, I thought. If this didn't work, I was doomed to be pointed out as the chunky girl in my sister's wedding photos.

"So, let's weigh in and set up your program," Alex said.

Weigh in! Why hadn't I requested a woman?

With a deep, fortifying breath, I blocked out the world around me and stepped onto the scale. I watched with detached horror as Alex moved the markers up and up. My eyes snapped shut. When I heard him start to write, I cracked open my eyes a little. It was better to get off the scale while he wasn't looking. Thank goodness that part was over.

"Tell me what your goal is," Alex said.

I sighed. The embarrassment would surely continue. I mentioned an impossibly small number, my sister's weight. Alex fixed his eyes on my face, his smooth brows drawing together.

"Do you think you can maintain that?" he asked.

I choked back a laugh. Maintain? Who said anything about maintaining? I'd feel lucky just coming close. After years of trying every diet under the sun, my expectations of lasting change weren't very high.

"To be honest, Paige, I don't think that's the right weight for your build and height," he said.

"Why not?"

"Because at that weight you'd be nothing but skin and bones," Alex replied, his face serious. "You need to take into account your body build and height, not what weight you think you should be at."

"What would you suggest?" I asked, feeling lost. I had spent most of my life being compared to my sister, who was at least two inches shorter than me and made me feel like a clunky elephant standing next to a delicate deer. I could wrap my hand all the way around her wrist with space to spare. I'd never considered the thought that I might be made bigger.

Alex named a number about fifteen pounds heavier. "Trust me. That's better for you." Maybe, but it still left me with a good thirty pounds to lose.

I pondered Alex's words as I walked my golden lab in the park the next evening. A lifetime spent chasing my family's idea of perfection, wrapped up in my sister's image, had led to frustration and awkwardness. It was way past the time when I should have stopped comparing myself to others, but that was much easier said than done.

I would have to start all over again, not just relearn how to eat and exercise, but learn how to think about myself, how to be happy with myself. Was freedom from all these negative feelings worth the effort?

"Paige," the hesitant voice caught my attention. Turning toward it, I spotted Alex.

"Hi," I said. "What are you doing here?"

"I just moved into an apartment nearby. Mind if I walk with you?"

As if I would turn down the chance to spend time with such

a handsome man, one who was nice to me too. We set off along the path, talking and getting to know each other. I felt at ease until Alex brought up my program. "What made you brave the gym?" he asked with a hint of a smile.

"Brave the gym?"

"You weren't exactly happy to be there," he said.

"Was it that obvious?" I asked, frowning.

"Let's just say, I noticed."

My teeth sank into my lower lip. I hardly knew this man. Could he even begin to understand how complicated an issue this was for me? But a shy glance into those earnest brown eyes gave me the courage to take a chance.

"My sister's wedding. In six months, I have to stand with her in front of three hundred people. She's always been the small one. I was desperate." I turned my head to hide the tears welling in my eyes.

"Hey," he whispered, his hand turning me around to face him. "There's no reason to feel that way. You are a beautiful woman."

"I've never felt beautiful." I sniffed quietly, unable to stop a lifetime of inadequacies from surfacing.

"I mean it. Being willing to do something you don't enjoy so you can be there with your sister is amazing. I admire it."

He reached out and gently squeezed my hand. I saw my own surprise mirrored on his face before he pulled back. Cupping the hand that was against my stomach, I closed it, as if to preserve the tingle generated by his touch.

"Women come in all shapes and sizes. Trust me, I know. Still, having what people consider the perfect body on the outside doesn't make what's on the inside any prettier. You learn that really quickly in my line of work."

Several weeks later, I walked through the doors of the gym, an action that had become so routine I no longer experienced the nervousness I encountered on my first visit. I'd made it halfway across the foyer before the woman behind the counter called out.

"Ms. Henderson?"

"Yes?" Eyebrows raised, I wondered about this change in routine. "Is something wrong?"

"No. I just wanted to let you know you've been switched to Maria today. She'll meet you in room four."

Another trainer? "Is Alex sick today?"

The girl shrugged her bony shoulders. "No. He's in the weight room."

I turned back to the hallway, my steps much less confident this time. I'd just seen Alex last night in the park. He hadn't said anything about wanting to switch me to another trainer. We ran into each other several times each week, and he seemed eager to join me on my walks. We got along well—maybe too well.

I knew my feelings for Alex had moved beyond friendship. Besides being drop dead gorgeous, he exuded a boyish charm and southern kindness, creating a cocoon of appreciation around me that had been singularly lacking in my family.

Still, I wasn't foolish enough to act on my feelings. I didn't want him to know I was attracted to him, thereby risking an embarrassing rejection and my only hope of getting in shape for my bridesmaid's dress. With Alex's looks and wonderful personality, he could have anyone. An obvious choice would be one of the thin, beautiful women he worked with every day. He'd never mentioned a girlfriend, but I knew he must have one. Of course, that didn't stop me from dreaming.

My thoughts shut down as I entered the training room. Maria

rose to meet me with an outstretched hand and a smile on her pretty face. Unlike the woman behind the front counter, my new trainer was about my same height and, while fit, could never be classified as skinny. I relaxed slightly as she talked, realizing her style and manner was a lot like Alex's. At least he hadn't thrown me to the wolves.

Though the session went well, confusion and hurt cropped up during my time with Maria. I couldn't help wondering why he'd given me up as a client. The least he could have done was said something. Of course, he probably didn't consider it a personal issue as I did. I decided to ask him about it anyway. It would be better than continuing to obsess about the situation.

Drawing on some of my newfound confidence, I approached the weight room after my session. My thoughts escalated once again. Had I overstepped the bounds of trainer/client protocol? Had I in some way made my attraction obvious? Did I make more out of our relationship than was really there?

Catching sight of him talking to another employee, I eased across the room. Spotting my approach, Alex waved off the other man and came to meet me.

"So, what did you think about Maria?"

His nonchalant smile both melted my heart and evoked a rise in anger. Obviously, he didn't think this was any big deal. Biting my lip, I struggled with the decision of whether to continue this conversation at all. Of course, I was already here, but did I really want to make a total fool of myself?

"What's wrong?" Alex's strong brows met in a frown. "Didn't you like her? I thought she was someone you might feel comfortable with."

With a deep breath, I decided to take the plunge, fighting my natural instinct to avoid any type of confrontation. "Well, she was fine. I just wish you had told me you were switching me to another trainer first."

His wince told me I'd hit a sore spot. "I'm sorry, Paige. I should have told you first. I actually meant to introduce you myself, but I got called into the manager's office at the last minute."

Well, that was better than nothing. "I just don't see why I needed a new trainer. I thought we were getting along just fine." That was as far out on a limb as I was prepared to go. Chicken.

With a quick look around the crowded room, Alex reached for my arm. "Why don't you let me walk you to your car?"

I let him lead me away, a sense of doom closing in around me. He probably didn't want to set me straight in front of all of his friends and colleagues. Now I wouldn't even be able to enjoy the strolls through the park.

Stepping out the front doors, Alex paused on the sidewalk instead of heading straight for the parking lot. I looked up to see the wind ruffle his hair before finally meeting his eyes. He took a deep breath.

"Paige, I hadn't planned to get into this right now, but maybe it's better this way."

Oh, God. I must have been too obvious. Now he feels he has to get rid of me like some lovesick teenager who won't go away. My face heated with embarrassment. I was going to have to find a new gym.

"To be honest, I switched trainers because I'm interested in dating you."

My mouth fell open at his sheepish grin. "What?"

He glanced back at the gym doors. "I'm sorry. I guess that was a little aggressive of me, but I'm attracted to you and wanted to ask you out. Unfortunately, it's against company policy for a trainer to date one of his clients, so I switched you to Maria."

My heart pounding, I blinked. He actually wanted to date me, just like I wanted to date him. Wow.

"Why didn't you just say something before, like last night in the park?"

He ran a quick hand across his face. "You were doing so well with your training. I didn't want to interfere with your goals, which I know are important to you right now. So I figured we could still meet outside of the gym and at least develop a friendship. Then, after the wedding, I could ask you out."

Pushing aside the shyness and fear of rejection that had followed me all my life, I decided it was time to take a risk. "But I don't want to wait that long."

"You don't?" He grinned. "Good. Great. I mean, I'm glad you feel the same way." He reached out to rub his hand down my arm. "I really am sorry I didn't talk to you about this last night, or even last week."

I had to laugh. "Me too. I really do like my new trainer, and now I can meet my goals and date you."

"Sure can." We shared a smile filled with the excitement of our budding attraction. "Well, I need to get back to work. Can we meet tonight in the park? Maybe continue this conversation?" He squeezed my arm.

"I'll see you then."

I refused to let my happiness slide into my ever-present doubts as he went back inside. I was making much needed changes to my body, thanks to Alex's instruction and help. It was time to change on the inside too, but the only one who could help to do that was me.

Between our walks together and our dates, our relationship quickly moved from friendship to romance. We had a lot in common and sparked each other's interests.

That spring, we would often meet to walk in the nearby park, the dusky sunset a perfect backdrop for our intimate conversations. Alex continued to encourage me in my exercise program, though Maria had taken over my training. I found that his interest in me was serious and persistent. He helped me discover types of exercise I actually enjoyed. We even took a healthy cooking class together!

I had never had more fun losing weight in my entire life.

In no time at all, I found myself introducing Alex at my sister's wedding reception. The twenty-two pounds I had lost made my fitted sapphire bridesmaid's dress more comfortable. Alex said my confidence in myself had shown as I walked gracefully down the aisle.

I didn't know whether I was more proud of all my hard work or of the wonderful man at my side. Alex had given me an incredible gift—he helped me learn what I was capable of, which revealed my strength. I no longer had to live in my sister's shadow.

I knew my face glowed as I introduced Alex to my family, but I reluctantly led him to my grandmother, conscious of the woman's habit of speaking her mind.

"So," my grandmother said, "you're the one whose been helping Paige get her weight down. That's so nice of you. She needs all the help she can get."

A moment of surprised silence met this remark. My cheeks flooded with color as my grandmother moved away.

Alex took my arm and led me to the dance floor. He studied my face, looking closely, as if searching for something beyond the surface.

"I can't believe they don't see it," he said.

"See what?" I asked.

"How beautiful you are," he replied. Lingering doubt must

have shown in my eyes.

"You are beautiful," he insisted. "These past few months, you've changed—and not just physically. You're not the nervous, self-conscious woman who ran me down in the gym."

We shared a smile before he continued.

"You trust your body and have relaxed enough to be yourself. A self I love."

Those words, spoken with tender certainty, brought tears to my eyes. For once, I didn't care what my family thought. Coming to a full stop in the middle of the dance floor, I reached up on tiptoe and boldly kissed Alex on the mouth—right there for everyone to see.

Alex had spoken the truth: I am happy with myself, and that has made all the difference. THE END

LOOKS CAN BE DECEIVING

I stood in front of the full-sized mirror hidden on the inside of my closet door, and for the first time in a long while, liked what I saw. I turned sideways, admiring my profile. My rear was nice and tight, my chest was not too big, not too small, and thanks to Victoria's Secret, where it was supposed to be. My new size 8 jeans hugged my hips and thighs in all the right places, and my size medium blouse accentuated curves I had thought at one time had turned to permanent rolls. Yep, the woman in the mirror smiling back at me was a far cry from the size 22 she used to be. Two years and a hundred pounds later, I was ready to take on the world!

At least start dating again, anyway.

I went into the bathroom and gave my spiral curls another blast of spray, touched up the lipstick again, then let out a long slow breath. *It's just a night with the girls*, I told myself. A couple of fruity drinks sprouting pink umbrellas and wanna-be cowboys in tight jeans two-stepping their way around the Cowboy Corral.

I wondered if one of those fine cowboys would ask me to dance. I couldn't remember the last time I had danced with a guy. Probably the senior prom, and I got pregnant in a motel room afterward and married three months later. Two kids, ten years, and a hundred pounds heavier, I got divorced.

I'd spent the first couple of years after the divorce doting on my kids and gorging myself on chocolate and over-stuffed burritos. I never wanted to subject my kids to the "step-daddy" roulette game so I hid behind them and drowned my man-less world in gallons of sweet tea.

But you have such a pretty face.

Argh! The one thing not to say to a fat woman. Why not just open up a vein and pour salt into it? Why couldn't they just complete the so-called compliment with the truth? *You have such a pretty face. . .too bad it's attached to a pumpkin.* Couldn't they tell that underneath the bulky sweaters and stretch-pants was a siren in waiting?

Pumpkins and size 22 were in my past. I was ready to unleash the vixen.

I did one more fluff of the hair with my fingertips then heard a car horn blow. *This is it, Gina . . . it's showtime!*

I marched headstrong and confident—although a little wobbly in heels—down the hallway. Then I did a mental check of the house—stove and oven off, check; DVR set to record *Lifetime's* Saturday night movie, check; the dog fed, check; kids at Mom and Dad's, check. Belle, our English bulldog, stared at me, head cocked to one side, tongue lolling out the side of her mouth. "But you have such a pretty face," I told her as I bent and scratched the top of her head. She sneezed, spraying me with God-knows-what, then sauntered off into the living room to her blanket. She wasn't used to nights alone and was probably expecting me to follow her and assume my throne, the recliner. "Not tonight, dear Belle. Mommy's joining the real world," I said as I punched the light on over the stove, grabbed my purse, and headed out to my awaiting carriage.

So Angie's Toyota Camry wasn't exactly a carriage, but I did feel like a princess ready for the ball.

Wow—you look fantastic!" Angie said as I got into the car.

"Is this okay? Is it too simple? I've got a silk blouse—and a vest! Maybe I should wear the vest? Cowboys, vests, what do you think?"

She stared at me for a moment then backed out of the driveway. "You look great. It's a country bar, Gina. There is no such thing as 'too simple.' Besides, we're east of the Mississippi. These guys aren't cowboys. They're blue-collar guys in Wrangler jeans who like to dance to country music."

I sighed. "I know. I'm just a little nervous. Do you know how long it's been since I've been *out?*"

"Well, let's see . . . we've both been in accounts receivable, what—eight years?"

We both laughed. Inside, I wanted to cry. I had never really put a timetable on it, but when the truth hit you square in the face, it was hard to ignore. It had been over *eight years* since I had been kissed, other than a peck on the cheek, by a man. Eight plus years since I had been held by a man. And *way* too many years since I'd had sex. I was in my prime—my peak as the magazines say—and I was spending my nights with Belle. Like the pounds I had shed, I was ready to shed the old life for a new one.

"Now if you, you know, get lucky, give me a signal so I'll know not to wait around on you," Angie said. "And if I'm not there when you get ready to leave, well, you'll know I got lucky." She laughed hard and pounded the steering wheel with the palm of her hand.

"It's my first night out in a *long* time—I'm not going to be going home with anyone," I assured her. The thought was there, though. A wild, crazy night of reckless fun. I could always regret it later.

"Tammy and Kim are going to meet us there," Angie said. Both

Tammy and Kim worked in the credit department, and what Angie and I couldn't drag out of Cornado Manufacturing's clients, they collected with threatening letters. "I've got to warn you about Kim—she starts crying when she's had too much to drink. Avoid her at all costs, or she'll have you crying, too. She cries about global warming and about the baby seals and about her dead grandmother's petunias, so unless you want to spend the night sobbing along with her, find someone to dance with as soon as she starts drinking."

Panic surged through my veins. *Find someone to dance with? She meant I'd have to ask?*

The parking lot of the Cowboy Corral looked like a used truck lot. Every make, model, year, and color of pickup truck was well represented. Angie parked beside a massive Ford with a decal of a deer's head on the rear window and an "I'd Rather Be Hunting" bumper sticker. As long as these "cowboys" had all their teeth, they were all right by me. I just hoped they could talk about something other than shooting poor Bambi.

We fell in line at the door behind a group of women who acted like they'd already had one too many. A tall redhead was wearing a skintight skirt that barely covered her butt and a blouse tied just below her massive chest, exposing her bare midriff. Her silver hoop earrings were as big as bracelets. She and the other girls in her group laughed boisterously while tossing their heads and casually eyeing the crowd already inside.

"I hope Tammy and Kim are already here," Angie said. "I told them to save us a table." She laid down her five-dollar cover charge then held out the back of her hand to be stamped.

I did the same, staring at the blue star on the back of my hand as if it were a badge of honor. A tattoo of sorts. I was living wild.

"There they are." Angie waved her arm in the air at Tammy and Kim then grabbed my elbow and herded me toward their table.

The music reverberated through the floor and throbbed in my feet, quickly working its way up my body and relentlessly pounding in my ears. I hadn't heard music this loud since my high school days, and I wasn't looking forward to the headache I knew I'd have later. But I was here to have fun, dance the night away, and maybe even steal a kiss from a good-looking stranger—in all my vixen glory!

"Look at you!" Tammy squealed in her nasally tone. Her eye shadow sparkled with glitter. "You are *hot*." She gave me a quick hug then motioned for the waitress.

Kim was dancing in her seat, sipping a pink-colored drink. She smiled a loopy smile and waved her fingers in my direction.

"Proceed with caution," Angie whispered and laughed.

The waitress, dressed in Daisy Duke shorts and a cut off T-shirt, scurried over and took our drink orders. Angie ordered a margarita and I ordered a strawberry daiquiri. At six dollars a pop, I prayed for some kind gentleman to order the next one.

And it didn't take long for him to appear.

He wasn't Prince Charming, but he wasn't all that bad. He was kind of short, not much taller than me, with a beer belly protruding over the top of his jeans—*but he had a nice face*. I laughed in spite of myself, wondering if men dreaded that compliment as much as women did.

"I'm Kevin," he said, leaning in so his lips all but touched my ear. I didn't know if he was putting the moves on me or making sure I heard him over the music.

"Gina." I offered him my hand and smiled.

"Would you like to dance?"

My heart dropped to my toes. The band was tearing up a fast number with a beat as quick as my pulse. What was I scared of? I now had the body to move to the groove, and there was no better place to prove it than on the dance floor.

"Sure." I allowed him to take my hand and lead me out into the center of the floor.

Two drinks and twelve dollars later, Kevin was still hanging around. His scribbled phone number was on a napkin stuffed in my purse. He was a supervisor at KemTec Chemicals, separated from his wife of thirteen years, and he had an annoying habit of sucking mucus back into his sinuses after every sentence.

I heard something about his wife cheating on him—that was one thing he just couldn't tolerate—and that she was happy. She got the house while he had to rent a single-wide mobile home on his uncle's property and blah blah blah. . .

He lost me when he explained how he had to rip up the carpet because the last tenant had a cocker spaniel that wasn't housebroken. I smiled politely, nodding my head occasionally, while I watched Angie on the dance floor nearly mating with a biker. Tammy was at the bar doing shots with two hunks, while Kim was getting teary-eyed telling the guy who had sauntered up beside her about the plight of the baby seals.

Kevin dragged me back out onto the dance floor for another super fast number and after five drinks, I was getting pretty wobbly and didn't care. Sweat trickled from my brow and ran down my cheeks, and my legs felt like I had run a marathon, but I was one hot momma! When the band went straight into a slow number, Kevin pulled me to him. I wrapped my arms around his drooping shoulders and even though he was far from being a dreamboat, it felt nice being in a man's arms.

I watched over his shoulder at the other couples swaying slowly to the beat, their bodies entwined in perfect harmony. So Kevin and I weren't exactly wrapped around one another and he wasn't the man of my dreams, but I was still out on the dance floor, dancing with a man I had just met. Out with the old life—in with the new.

As Kevin and I moved in tiny circles, I caught the eye of a guy at the bar. Now this guy was a dreamboat! He was tall with dark hair and a five-o'clock shadow, and he was dressed in a plain white button-down shirt and jeans. No goofy cowboy hat or clunky boots or unbuttoned shirt showing sprouting chest hair. He was propped against the bar, a beer in one hand, watching the action on the dance floor.

Now *this* man, I could ask to dance. This man, I could even take home.

As the song faded out, I unwrapped Kevin's arms from around my waist and whispered that I needed to take a bathroom break. He grinned and said he'd be waiting at the table. I smiled and wobbled to the restroom with no intention of ever dancing with Kevin again. My sights were set on the hunk at the bar.

In the restroom, I checked myself in the mirror. My hair was still bouncy, my lips still shined, and my waterproof makeup had held up despite the sweat. Mr. Gorgeous was still at the bar in the same place, his left foot still pulled up behind him and propped on the rail. He was even more gorgeous up close.

I waltzed up beside him and ordered a drink. Not that I needed or even wanted another one, but I wasn't quite brave enough to let him know he was the sole purpose of my trek to the bar. "Hi," I said while I waited on the drink.

"Hi." He smiled the most perfect smile I had ever seen. Light actually bounced off his perfectly white teeth. My breath caught in my throat when he extended his hand. "Matt Sawyer."

I caught my breath while I shook his hand. "Gina Thomas. It's a pleasure to meet you, Matt Sawyer."

"Likewise."

"The band's great tonight, aren't they?" I asked as if I really knew what I was talking about. I had never even heard of the band, let alone listened to them play.

"You really think so?"

Oh no—trapped in my own lie.

Before I could dig myself into a deeper lie, Matt ordered another beer then said, "I own a couple of clubs over in Fairfield and was thinking about booking them."

"Checking out the goods, huh?"

He laughed then glanced over my size-8 body and smiled. "You could say that."

Ooh la la! I fought the urge to pinch myself to see if I had died and gone to heaven. "Well, the only sure way to check out a band is to dance to one of their numbers."

He grinned then took a long swig of his beer. "If I didn't know better, I'd think you were asking me to dance."

"Me? Why I'm a lady—I'd never be so bold."

He slowly nodded, the grin still spread across his beautiful face. "In that case, would you like to dance, Ms. Thomas?"

"I'd love to, Mr. Sawyer."

He sat his beer on the bar and took my hand. His grip was strong and manly, and I swooned in the strength of it. He slipped one arm around my waist and pulled my hand up to his chest with the other, and I melted within this intimacy. Our bodies fit perfectly together with my head easily resting on his shoulder. I imagined being in bed with him—our bodies melded together like pieces of a puzzle, moving like the parts of a fine-tuned machine. Even when the band changed over to a fast tempo song, Matt held me close. We were dancing to our rhythm.

I opened my eyes for a moment and glanced over his shoulder at Angie, who was planted on the biker's lap at the table. She gave me a thumbs up and a wink. Kevin was also at the table, occasionally glancing my way while being victimized by a very drunk and crying Kim. I didn't know if the sadness on his face was my fault or the struggling baby seals'. Or maybe just Kim's drunken ramblings. I felt a little guilty, until it completely evaporated when Matt gently lifted my chin and kissed me.

After the third dance, we went back to the bar and Matt ordered a fresh beer. He asked if I wanted another daiquiri. "I better go with a soft drink," I said and smiled. I wanted to remember everything about this night.

We talked about our jobs—he owned four clubs and two restaurants; about where we grew up—he was originally from Norfolk, a navy brat; and about what we liked and didn't like—he loved old movies, and he hated broccoli and mint-flavored toothpaste. He'd been divorced five years and had no kids, but he and his ex split custody over their dog.

"I have an English Bulldog named Belle," I said. "You know, from *Beauty and the Beast.*"

"And she's supposed to be the beauty?"

I playfully punched his arm. "She's beautiful—for a bulldog."

The lead singer of the band announced last call and introduced their closing number. "Shall we?" he asked.

We headed back out to the dance floor and while we danced in slow, tiny circles, we kissed throughout the entire song. My head was exploding with thoughts of what was to come. He pulled away slightly and smiled. "I was going to offer to take you home but since you're a lady, it probably wouldn't be proper."

I couldn't breathe. No, I wanted to scream. *I'm not a lady!* My heart was racing and telling me to cram my tongue deep in his mouth and tease him with what I had planned for him, but my head argued that he was right. I hadn't been out of the game so long that the rules had changed that much. It never hurt to let them chase you a little.

"You're right," I said, pulling the words up through my raging hormones. "Maybe next time."

"What are you doing tomorrow?"

We both laughed all the way back to the bar. Matt handed me one of his business cards, and then wrote my number on the back of another. "That's my cell number," he said. "Seriously, give me a call tomorrow. I'd like to take you to dinner tomorrow night."

I gnawed on my bottom lip and regrettably shook my head. "I can't tomorrow. My daughter has a dance recital in the afternoon and then we're having a little reception afterward."

"Okay. Maybe next weekend we can meet up here and *then* I'll take you to dinner."

Oh my God, he was sooo gorgeous. I can't believe you didn't leave with him." Angie had always had a flair for the dramatic and today was no different.

It was our lunch break and we were doing our daily three-block power walk, so the fact that she could even talk amazed me.

"I didn't want to rush things," I said breathlessly.

"Honey, we aren't looking for a forever thing. Just a one-night stand to get you out of this rut."

"Why can't it be a forever thing?"

"Because guys like him don't do forever. If you want forever, Kevin's a forever kind of guy. He was heartbroken you left him with Kim."

"He has a sinus problem."

"So? It's allergy season; give the guy a break."

We stopped for a minute to catch our breath and window shop at Talbot's. "Look at that dress. Is that not sexy?" Angie pointed to a red dress hanging in the window. The silky fabric boasted a plunging neckline and a slit rising to the upper thigh. "Come on, you're going to knock Mr. Forever's socks off next weekend."

Before I knew it, I was in the dressing room wiggling my way into a harlot-colored dress I neither needed nor could afford. But a few minutes later, I plunked down the money and carried my seduction dress back to the office.

"You are coming with me next weekend, aren't you?" I asked as we headed to our desks.

"I may be wild, but threesomes aren't my thing, sweetheart." She grinned as she powered up her computer.

"I meant to the bar." Although I knew Matt would be there, I still wasn't quite confident enough to walk into a bar alone.

"Of course I'll be there. Besides, someone has to drive you so you can leave in Prince Charming's carriage."

The next Saturday I spent hours getting ready, taking my time doing my hair so it would be perfect, lazily shaving my legs, and basking in a warm bubble bath. *What are you doing?* I thought. *You can't sleep with this guy—you don't even know him!* Sure, he was gorgeous and had a great sense of humor and geez, he owned many clubs and restaurants, so he obviously had good sense and probably money to boot. But what if he had a disease or something equally horrible? What if he was . . . weird? Like serial killer weird? The last time I had spur-of-the-moment sex was at the prom and I got pregnant.

Oh good grief! You were a love-struck teenager back then. You're a grown adult now. Matt Sawyer is a dream come true and there's no logical reason why you shouldn't sleep with him.

By the time I got dressed, my hormones were pulsing so hard, the softness of the new silk dress sent chills rampaging through my body. I could almost feel Matt's hands caressing my skin, tenderly touching parts of my body that had never been touched, finding secret spots even I wasn't aware of. Serial killer or not, this man was going to have his way with me whether he wanted to or not.

When Angie picked me up, I was so nervous I could feel my heart beating in my ears.

"Take a deep breath and calm down," she said, ever the confident one. "He's just a man, Gina. He puts his pants on one leg at a time like all the others."

"I'm not worried about how he puts his pants on," I said and laughed through the nerves.

The parking lot was just as full as it had been the week before. I looked around at the different cars, wondering which was his. He didn't seem like a truck guy.

Inside, the place was packed but it didn't take me long to spot him. He was in his regular position at the bar, foot propped behind him on the rail, leaning back on one arm, a beer in the other hand. Oh, did he look good! I didn't think it was possible for him to look better than he had looked last weekend, but he was pin-up perfect. He was wearing a lightweight V-neck sweater with the sleeves pushed to below his elbows and dark jeans. A new five-o'clock shadow outlined his strong jawline.

I stopped within a few feet of him and basked in the glory of his admiration of what he saw. "Wow," he said in a deep, soft voice. "You look fantastic."

We barely made it through one song on the dance floor before our hands started roaming over one another's bodies, exploring what we could without being arrested for indecency. His tongue was white-hot as it pushed its way into my mouth, doing a slow tango with my own. My entire body ached for this man. I wanted to feel his hands on my bare body, feel him inside of me.

It had been a while since I had been with a man, but with his body pressed against mine, his desire was unmistakable. "What do you say we get out of here?" He said, his breath coming in shallow gasps.

I couldn't speak. I nodded instead and followed him off the dance floor. We wove our way through the crowd and within minutes were in the backseat of his car.

He lifted my dress and kissed my legs, teasing me with soft kisses to my inner thighs. I moaned and pressed against him, encouraging him to continue on his northward journey. I ran my hands through his hair, lightly grabbing at the roots, digging my fingers deeper into his shiny locks. *Oh, the pleasure! Oh, the . . . ridges? What?*

I was certain I felt ridges on his scalp. Deep-cut ridges. While he was planting sensuous kisses on body parts only my doctor had seen, I was running my fingers along these strange ridges rising from his head. I moaned for good measure while trying to figure out what the heck was in his hair. They were perfectly lined around his hairline, rope-like.

He lifted his head but I pushed it back down then moaned again for dramatic purposes. "Like that, huh?" he whispered.

I dug my fingers back into his hair. The rope-like ridges completely circled his head. *Oh my God—what has happened to this man!*

Is he wearing a high-priced toupee? My heart was about to explode and it had nothing to do with what he was doing down there. What is wrong with me? Why on earth would this bother me? Am I really so shallow that a toupee would turn me off an otherwise perfect man?

"I can't do this," I said as I pushed him away. "I'm sorry, I just can't do it." I scrambled to sit up and fixed my dress.

"What? What happened?" He stared at me with his big, beautiful eyes.

"I've got to go. I'm sorry. Really, I am." I lunged for the door and all but fell out into the parking lot. I hopped on alternate feet while trying to put my heels back on as I hurried back inside.

Angie was at a table with her biker from last week and stared hard at me as I plopped into a chair.

"You look . . . shocked," she said. "You're not supposed to look shocked." Her biker nibbled her ear.

"I can't talk about it right now." I ordered a straight scotch.

"He didn't hurt you, did he?" She pushed her biker away and leaned forward, a more serious look on her face.

I shook my head. "No. Nothing like that. I was just . . . surprised by something."

I downed the scotch. I didn't want to do this anymore. I wasn't cut out for heated sex in backseats with men I barely knew. Maybe taking the time to get to know someone really does make sense after all.

I ordered another drink and willed my nerves to settle down. I took several deep breaths, letting each one out slowly. After a few moments, my reasoning gradually returned. I finally started to realize that a man using an expensive hairpiece was not that different from a woman who worked hard to lose a lot of weight and was wearing a to-die-for hot red dress to look attractive to the opposite sex. How dare I of all people judge him for trying his best to look good.

I had finished off my second drink when I felt a slight tap on my shoulder. *Oh, please let it be him. Please, God—I'll behave from now on if he is willing to forgive me for my craziness.*

I glanced over my shoulder and to my surprise—and relief—to see that my forever man was standing behind my chair.

"Hi," I said. "I am so sorry! I don't know what got into me, but for a moment I was afraid to believe that this could be real. I'm glad you came back to find me."

I sat there for a moment smiling tentatively at him.

At last he said to me, "So am I." THE END